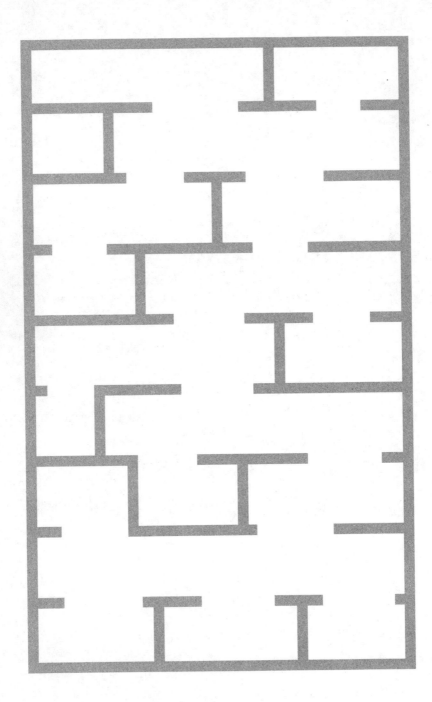

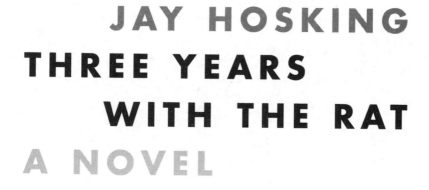

JAY HOSKING
THREE YEARS
WITH THE RAT
A NOVEL

HAMISH HAMILTON

an imprint of Penguin Canada Books Inc., a division of Penguin Random House Canada Limited

Published by the Penguin Group

Penguin Canada Books Inc., 320 Front Street West, Suite 1400, Toronto, Ontario M5V 3B6, Canada

Penguin Group (USA) LLC, 375 Hudson Street, New York, New York 10014, U.S.A.

Penguin Books Ltd, 80 Strand, London WC2R 0RL, England

Penguin Ireland, 25 St Stephen's Green, Dublin 2, Ireland (a division of Penguin Books Ltd)

Penguin Group (Australia), 707 Collins Street, Melbourne, Victoria 3008, Australia

Penguin Books India Pvt Ltd, 11 Community Centre, Panchsheel Park, New Delhi – 110 017, India

Penguin Group (NZ), 67 Apollo Drive, Rosedale, Auckland 0632, New Zealand

Penguin Books (South Africa) (Pty) Ltd, 24 Sturdee Avenue, Rosebank, Johannesburg 2196, South Africa

Penguin Books Ltd, Registered Offices: 80 Strand, London WC2R 0RL, England

First published 2016

1 2 3 4 5 6 7 8 9 10 (RRD)

Copyright © Jay Hosking, 2016

Manufactured in the U.S.A.

Book design: CS Richardson

LIBRARY AND ARCHIVES CANADA CATALOGUING IN PUBLICATION

Hosking, Jay, author
Three years with the rat / Jay Hosking.

ISBN 978-0-670-06937-8 (bound)
eBook ISBN 978-0-14-319363-0

I. Title.

PS8615.O823T47 2015   C813'.6   C2015-906641-7

www.penguinrandomhouse.ca

NOW ONE COULD SAY, *at the risk of some superficiality, that there exist principally two types of scientists. The ones, and they are rare, wish to* understand *the world, to know nature; the others, much more frequent, wish to* explain *it. The first are searching for truth, often with the knowledge that they will not attain it; the second strive for plausibility, for the achievement of an intellectually consistent, and hence successful, view of the world. To the first nature reveals itself in lyrical intensity; to the others in logical clarity,* and they *are the masters of the world. . . . It is almost an intrinsic part of our concept of science that we never know enough. At all times one could almost say that we can explain it all, but understand only very little.*

. . . That the end sanctifies the means has for more than a hundred years been the credo of the sciences; in actual fact, it is the means that have diabolized the end.

—Erwin Chargaff, "A Grammar of Biology,"
Voices in the Labyrinth

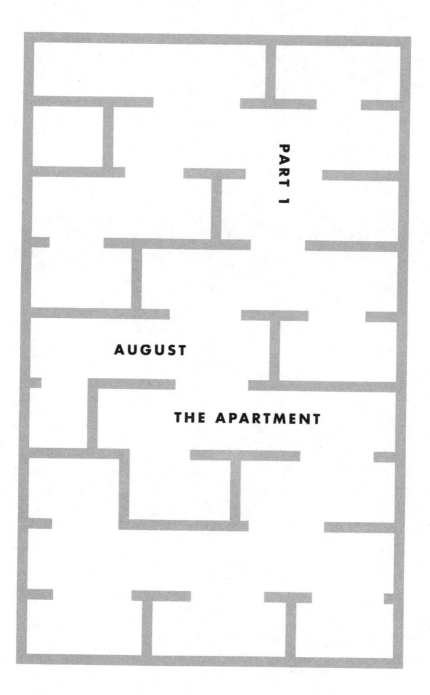

PART 1

AUGUST

THE APARTMENT

2008

THE PHONE RATTLES its way off the little square table and stings the hardwood floor. I shrug an arm from the sheets and bring the phone toward my face. The little panel across the back of it flashes between the time, just before noon, and a number with no associated name. I consider turning it off. Instead I roll onto one side, flip open the phone with my thumb, and graze my ear with the receiver.

My pillow smells like the grease from my hair.

"Hello?" My voice struggles.

"Eh, where is John and Grace?" It's a man's voice, accented, and there is something both distant and familiar about it. I can hear traffic in the background.

"I don't know where they are," I say. I clear my throat. "Who is this?"

The blinds on the window cut the sunlight into shards, bright fragments scattered across the dirty clothes covering my floor. The light causes a stab of pain along the back of my head. I squeeze my eyes closed.

The man's accent is probably European. "He gave me this number."

"What?" Suddenly my body is lurching awake. "John gave you my number? When? Who the hell is this?"

"The cheque bounced," he says. "I call them all week and nothing."

John and Grace's landlord. I don't say anything and he continues.

"I bang on their door and nothing. Another day and still nothing. I don't like nothing. I think maybe there's a problem and look inside. There's a note from John and it doesn't say 'Here's the rent' or 'I'm sorry.' It says call you and remove their things. So now I call you."

I writhe under the sheets, my guts turning over and over. How long would it have taken for John's bank account to run out of money, for his post-dated cheques to bounce? How long has he been gone? I count backward until I reach last December. Eight months, more or less. A year and eight months for Grace.

I clench my stomach and pull up my knees. The sheets scrape my skin. My jaw aches as if I've been grinding my teeth in my sleep.

"Hello?" he shouts.

"I'm here."

"What's wrong with you?"

"Hung over." It's an excuse but also strictly true.

His voice gets deep and sharp. "Eh, I don't give a fuck if you're dying. Get over here and clean out the apartment."

I can taste bile but I don't say anything, only hang up.

—

I stall. Kick the clothes into one large mound in the corner of the room. Pull the blinds and crack open my tiny windows. Stand in the shower until the water runs cold. Select the least dirty clothes and put them on slowly, slowly. Sit on the edge of the bed, breathe, try not to be sick. My stalls run out and I leave. I have to duck a little to get through the door of my basement apartment.

Outside it is almost a proper early August day in Toronto. These last few months have been uncharacteristically cold and grey, but today the sun is out and the breeze carries warm air. The neighbours' kids look like apes as they shake the hell out of my landlord's persimmon tree. They stop and stare when they see me shuffle up the concrete steps to ground level. I grin and stare back, another dumb ape.

My car sits on the street in front of the house. It is unwashed, matte from years of abuse, and rusted around the wheel wells. A flood of hot air hits me when I open the driver's side door, and I'm glad to sink into its murky heat and shut the door behind me. I sit for a few minutes, thinking, then throw all the passenger-seat garbage into the back. The engine turns over disappointingly quickly, as if the car is urging me forward.

At least there is no good way to drive from my house to the apartment. My street is a one-way and forces me into traffic. In this city, drivers are eager to complain about public transit but always polite enough to yield. I turn left onto Dundas Street, eastbound through the Portuguese and Vietnamese neighbourhood, and left again onto Bathurst, northbound past the neuropsychiatric ward of the hospital.

On the other side of the passenger window, people walk around in shorts and skirts, much of their skin bare and tanned. I am overdressed, jeans and a hoodie, and there is no air conditioner in my car, but still I am not hot.

Thoughts of John and Grace keep crashing in, unwanted. I turn on the stereo and Grace's mix CD starts playing. I turn it off again.

My car grinds its way past College Street and Shifty's, and at the gaudy, bulbed storefront of Honest Ed's I turn right. Traffic is just as slow on Bloor as I pass the dingy entrance to the Fortress. Just past the club are the two sushi restaurants and above them, one window still covered with cardboard, is John and Grace's apartment. My destination.

I find parking on the next side street, but on the way back, I stop at Features and order coffee and mashed potatoes. The potatoes come in the shape of a volcano, gravy pooled in the crater. I sit at a bench along the front window and feel my hangover ease. A stream of people moves along Bloor Street, couples smile and touch, friends carry bags of books or records and shout their opinions at one another. Everyone is so goddamned vital and happy in this neighbourhood. I finish my coffee and eat away one side of the potatoes, gravy spilling out onto the plate.

Only then, when I can't possibly delay any longer, I make my way to the apartment.

—

"You get in touch with them?" the landlord asks.

He is paunchy, stained, and graceless. He meets me at the apartment door, between the two sushi restaurants. He does not recognize me, likely on account of my beard.

"I don't know where they are," I say. "Haven't seen them in a long time."

"Why he asked for you in the note, then?" The landlord's finger extends, pokes toward me. He wants to press it against my chest but he is shorter than me and he isn't angry enough yet.

"I don't know," I say.

"I have an idea. I think they don't want to pay rent. I think maybe they found another place."

"Maybe," I say.

He smiles, unfriendly. "And I think they send you to clean up. Because they know me. They know I don't take the bullshit."

I say, "Look. I'm tired. I'd like to get into the apartment. I'd like to help you."

His mouth hangs a little and his finger curls in. He pulls a ring with two keys from his shirt pocket and hands it to me.

"End of today," he grunts. "That's it. I'm gonna paint after that."

"Sure. Sure."

He scuttles up the stairs and I follow him. The only light in the stairwell comes from a window above the front entrance. At the top of the narrow steps is the door. I unlock the door, enter, and lock it behind me, leaving the landlord in the hallway. And for the first time in eight months, I am inside the apartment.

—

The drapes are closed and only a little pale light filters in around their edges. I can see down the front hallway into part of the kitchen and living room. A blanket is neatly folded over the edge of the couch. Everything is tidy and unused, but it smells stale and musty and dead.

I take a few more steps. Grace's Bachelor of Science degree, framed on the wall. The standing coat rack, still buried under Grace's jackets and shawls and scarves. The homemade shelf lined with their indecipherable textbooks. The only photograph John kept, its kitschy frame taken off the wall and now resting on the coffee table. And a flashlight sitting next to the photo.

It quickly becomes clear that the apartment hasn't been occupied in months. The refrigerator is a dank shock of rotten, twisted shapes and jars greening with mould. The garbage can is still full of John's bloodied bandages. Though the apartment has been tidied one last time, the front closet remains jammed with newspapers. Bedding for the rats.

It takes me a couple of minutes before I realize what's wrong with the space. My attention is narrowed, grasping for strangeness in the tiny details, and the obviousness of it only comes to me when I sit on the arm of the couch for a moment. I breathe in sharply.

The door to the second bedroom is open by a few inches.

I stand and walk to the door, press my fingertips against the wood. The oversized key is in the deadbolt. John installed the lock and I strongly doubt he would have provided the landlord with a key. Why am I still holding my breath, trying not to make a sound? I push my arm out and the door swings open, bumping into something soft before the knob hits the wall. The toes of my shoes are on the threshold of the doorway. There is a faint division in the carpet, with the pile in the living room lighter than the bedroom. I step inside.

The room is very dark and the light switch next to the door doesn't do anything, so I flip open my cell phone for light. My eyes can't understand the shapes inside. Some large piece of furniture dominates the centre of the room, all right angles and hardwood. I make my way around it to the covered window, peel the duct tape from the wall, and pull away the cardboard. Daylight floods in and for a moment I cannot see.

In the centre of the room is a wooden box that is large enough to house a person, perhaps five feet in every direction. I circle it. The box is made from six identical, sanded pieces that seem to fit together without nails or hinges. The only noticeable feature is a handle at the bottom of the panel that faces me. Otherwise it is a perfect, symmetrical cube without any knots or imperfections in the wood. I have seen the materials of this box but never imagined what it might be when put together. It is a marvel.

The rest of the room is no more comprehensible. A smaller version of the box, another perfectly sanded cube of wood, sits atop a TV-dinner table in one corner of the room. Instead of a handle, one of its sides has a hole lined with black rubber, and an additional slat leans against the table. Piled on the floor are little cloth pouches, their openings drawn tight with strings. They look like bags of marbles. Between the door and the wall is a large burlap sack with something dark spilled on the carpet around it, and next to it are some discarded tools.

And last, I see the small table near the door. On it is a hardbound, sky-blue notebook, and resting on the book is a handwritten note. It is John's writing.

I'm sorry to put this on you. It was my fault, all of it, and it was supposed to be mine to deal with. Don't stay in there too long. Take the photo, the light, and one of those pouches with you. If you don't see anything right away, it can always be taken apart and put together somewhere else. This is the only way back for us. Thank you.

Some vague story begins to thread its way through the last two years of my life.

I put down the note and look at the large wooden box next to me. I reach down for its handle, first pulling outward without luck, then upward. The side of the box slides up a little and creates a crack of darkness at the bottom. I look down into that space, see movement, and jump back. A moment later I realize that it's reflected light. The floor inside the box is a mirror. I tug on the handle again and the slat slides up by a few feet. The interior of the box is empty but completely covered in mirror, without frames or borders, the edges of the glass connecting seamlessly with one another. The entire inside of the box is reflective surface.

I leave the second bedroom, pace the living room, open and close the fridge, sit down, stand up. I look into the master bedroom, then the washroom, but my thoughts are only of the box and John's written request. I curse at myself and wring my hands. On the coffee table is the framed photo, John and Grace on the day they moved into the apartment. They are smiling without re-serve and I can see myself among the friends in the background of the picture. I grab the photo and flashlight and walk back into the second bedroom.

I work swiftly. The picture frame comes apart without difficulty and I pocket the photograph in my hoodie. I pick up one of the small pouches and it is full of some malleable material. A quick inspection of the large sack on the floor reveals that it's full of soft dirt. The pouch goes in my other pocket. I glance into the box, and after brief consideration I go back to the pile of tools. There I find the hammer, silver and shiny, and feel calm with its weight in my hand. I take one last breath, a pause to consider whether I am doing the right thing.

Then I crouch and step inside the box, using my fingertips to gen-tly lower the open face until I am enveloped by an overwhelming, total darkness.

—

It takes only a click of the flashlight to see the care and precision that have gone into designing this space. I have stood between two mirrors before, in an elevator, and seen reflections of myself curv-ing off into the distance, the mirrors not being exactly parallel. This is not what the box is like. By the pale beam of the flashlight, I can see that copies of my reflection are not turning but rather absolute-ly, perfectly straight in every direction. No matter where I look I see myself, hammer in one hand and light in the other. In the distance are some abstract and indeterminate forms that are probably still composed of parts of me. There is no background to reflect, only reflection that dilates space itself. It is geometric and infinite.

And something is changing. The temperature seems to be drop-ping and I feel the ache of wet, damp air. The sound of my small, shuffling movements enlarges within the box, just like my reflection. I have no free hands so I clear my throat to make noise, and it sounds as though I'm standing in a field instead of sealed in a tiny mirrored box.

Fear seeps into me. In this space is movement and breathing, so much that it could not possibly be mine alone. I am being watched. I turn around and around but see the same thing in every direction, my mirror image threatening and tight. It isn't clear what I should do next.

I jam the hammer under my arm and pull the photograph out of my pocket. My toes are becoming numb. I am sure some *thing* is drawing close to me but I can see nothing but myself in the mirrors. John and Grace look at me from the picture and they have nothing to offer. I fumble and drop the photo, but instead of retrieving it I pull the hammer from under my arm, test its weight again in my hand.

Here it comes.

And then I feel it, as though someone is drawing a rough, curved line down my back. I shout, I twist around, but there is nothing behind me. I can feel the sensation where the arc has been made across me, and soon that touch on my back becomes an itch. The itch becomes burning. The burning becomes vivid pain. My shirt begins to stick to my back. I turn and scour the mirrors but again there is only my own image, my face calmer than I would expect. My legs become uncoordinated, weak. The pain is now torture and something wet is pooling in the small of my back. Worse, I can feel that thing approaching. *Here it comes again.* I do the first and only thing that comes to my mind.

I swing the hammer at a wall.

—

In an instant, the temperature jumps up and the space in the remaining mirrors compresses to reflections of wood and shattered glass.

I try each wall until I find the one that slides up, toss the hammer and flashlight onto the floor in front of me, and crawl out of the box. When I reach my arm around to feel between my shoulder blades, I bring back a hand covered in blood. My body tries to vomit but only a little coffee and gravy come up. I wipe my mouth with my clean hand, bite my lip, and try to stop shaking. A sound catches my attention and I turn.

A black and white rat is standing on the floor of the box, docile, peering out, his pink nose sniffing up at me. I know this rat. Buddy.

This is the only way back for us, the note had said.

I find the rat cages stacked in the closet of the master bedroom, below some of John's clothes. I remove my torn hoodie and replace it with his black jacket. The blood is already sticky along the wound, painful to the touch, but at least it only comes in waves. I return to the second bedroom with a cage and pick Buddy up as John taught me: thumb and middle finger pinched just behind his front legs, index finger lightly on the back of his neck. Buddy seems calm, happy to be back in his cage.

Next I remove the handled slat of the box and the piece opposite to it, the one with the shattered mirror. I use the hammer to clear the half-broken fragments from the wood and lean the two walls of the box against the couch in the living room. With the broom from the kitchen, I sweep the bits of broken glass into a corner. Then, piece by piece, I disassemble the rest of the box. John used grooves and notches rather than nails, so the whole thing comes apart neatly.

I move the walls of the box, the blue notebook, the smaller box with the rubber hole, the sack full of earth, the pouches, the hammer, and Buddy's cage down the stairs and to my car. The wooden pieces are far too big to fit in the interior so I strap them to the roof using bungee cords from the trunk. I stack the six pieces of wood carefully but still worry that the mirrors will break. When I'm finished, the little car is nearly as tall and wide as it is long.

Last of all, I pluck the photograph of John and Grace from the bits of glass and put it in my back pocket, careful not to spoil it with my blood.

The landlord comes up the stairs as I'm preparing to leave the apartment for good. My head is foggy and the line down my back screams to be mended.

"Done," I say.

The landlord looks inside the apartment, looks at me, then back and forth again. "What do you mean, 'done'? It's still full of their shit."

"I've taken everything I can," I tell him.

His lips pinch and his head lowers. "You clean the place, now."

"I need to go to the hospital."

"I don't care if you're dying—"

"Go fuck yourself," I cut him off. "I've heard this story already. See you later."

I begin to stumble down to the front entrance.

"I shoulda never rented to them," he shouts. "I knew she was damaged goods as soon as I met her."

I stop halfway down the stairs. The carpet is filthy with old bits of gum, flattened and black with time. I turn around to face him. My back sings with pain.

"What did you say?" I ask through my teeth. My hands are tight little balls of bone, one still coated in my own blood. "What did you say about my sister?"

His grin becomes nervous, hesitant.

I take a step up the stairs. Another.

"You go," he says, crossing his arms. "You fucken get out. You think I want their trouble? You think this is no problem for me?"

"What did you say about my sister?"

He moves his mouth a little but all I can hear is my pulse in my ears.

By the time I reach the top step, the landlord has slid into the apartment. He closes the door and locks the deadbolt. I stand for a few seconds, spit on the floor, and make my way down to the car.

2007

JOHN STARTED BUILDING on the day I picked him up from the hospital.

It was too early for anyone reasonable to be calling, and besides that, I didn't want to wake Nicole, so I ignored my phone when it hummed. The beginnings of daylight were just starting to filter into the basement. When the phone buzzed again, buried in my jeans on the floor, I crawled out of bed and fished through my pockets. By then the call had gone to my voice mail but I could see that both calls were from John.

On the message he said, "Hey, stranger. I'm checking out today, somewhere around ten-thirty. It would be good to see you. Take care."

Nicole didn't move when I got up, didn't open her eyes or stretch or smile. She just lay there, curled up and motionless. Her orange bangs rested on her forehead and her skin looked oily. The sheets were skewed and a lovely length of her leg was exposed. Her hands were bunched toward her chin, like a boxer, but there was no tension in her face. I thought that this would be the most peaceful she'd be all day. I thought that I enjoyed her company more when she was asleep. I didn't like these thoughts and so I put on my clothes and left the apartment without saying goodbye.

The summer had been one of extremes, classic Toronto heat on some days and torrential storms on others. As I trudged up the steps to ground level, I could see that the mid-August sky was mostly grey, dark in the east, promising rain. The leaves had come late to the persimmon tree that year but now it looked lush in its little square of exposed earth. The tree would be thankful for the coming weather even if I wasn't.

The neuropsychiatric hospital was only three or four streets from my house, at Bathurst, a distance that people in Toronto some-times call *a block*. John had been tossed between there and a centre for addiction and mental health over the past couple of months. Some days I'd visit and we would take a day trip across the street to the coffee shop, sip horrible, ashen swill, laugh hesitantly, and occasionally take long silences to grieve in our personal ways.

The neighbourhood was alive at ten in the morning. The Vietnamese grocery store already had its boxes of bok choy and pep-pers stacked atop milk crates. The Euro nightclub, now doubling as a punk and indie venue, had its storefront opened to air out the smell of beer and rotten limes. I could see through the fancy diner's windows that it was full of people having their weekend brunch. The manager had offered Nicole the head cook position there, but she said she didn't want to work so close to home.

Hospitals always made me think of that year Grace shaved her head, nights I would wake up, ten or eleven years old, and find that I was alone in the house, that everyone else was once again in the emergency room.

The hospital's atrium was just as busy as the street outside. I had no idea how to find John, and so I stood at a hygiene station and spurted sanitizer on my hands. That's how he found me, creating friction between my palms, trying to speed up evaporation, foolish and awkward.

He hugged me and said, "You smell like rubbing alcohol."

———

John's mother and father were born in South Korea. They had married and left for Canada in the 1970s, removing themselves from the politics of their home country at that time. They settled into a suburb about an hour east of the city, called Oshawa, and took over ownership of a local convenience store. They toiled for years, expanding into a few small businesses before even considering children. In the end, they had only one child, a quiet, hesitant boy who in no way resembled my future friend.

As John described it, his teenage life was split between working part time at his parents' gas station and reading comics in the basement. He had a few friends during his high school years, other spindly kids who shared his interest in noisy music or video games, boys who didn't seem to care or notice that he was one of the only "non-white" kids at the school. Most of these friends disappeared when he went to university.

His choice of the University of Waterloo was a message to his parents. By then his father had already suffered one mild heart attack, his mother was micromanaging the three businesses they owned, and John had no interest in following in his family's entrepreneurial footsteps. Waterloo was an hour and a half away from his hometown by car, just far enough that he couldn't come home regularly to work at the stores. He was outside the range of parental pressure, a space where he could exert his independence. His mother and father were disappointed he didn't go somewhere more prestigious, somewhere closer to home, somewhere like Toronto, but they were glad his degree was in practical subjects like computer encryption and mathematics. He excelled in his courses and this kept his family relatively quiet.

The way he told it, John took this new setting as an opportunity to reinvent himself. He exchanged comics for swimming, social invisibility for live shows and dancing. Compared to his peers, John was charming and confident. He found a practicum placement in Toronto and spent half of each year in the city, contributing to a photo-editing application that was to be internet accessible. Newly groomed and living downtown, unable to visit Oshawa often because of his work, he began to make friends. When Grace first met him, she described him to me as "nice clothes, nice shoulders, nice guy."

—

I broke off the hug and said, "O.K. O.K."

He stepped back a little and smiled. His frame had lost a little of its muscle and there was a distinct crease under each eye, but he looked calmer than I had expected. His hair was neat and pushed to one side, and he was wearing his black spring jacket.

"So what's the plan?" I asked.

"I was wondering if you could take me to the hardware store near your place," he said.

"Hardware store?"

He nodded and his smile remained.

I shrugged. "Do you need a lot of things? I mean, will we need my car?"

"If you don't mind," he said.

The walk felt longer than it had on my way to the hospital. He started to approach the house when we turned onto my street, but I pointed him toward the car instead.

"How's Nicole?" he asked.

"Fine. She's fine."

We got in the car and I started the engine. All the while he looked at me, his usual strategy to make me talk.

"You know it's shit with Nicole and me," I said.

He nodded. "Beginning of the end or end of the beginning?"

"Who knows?" I laughed. "Jesus, you're the one who just got out of the fucking hospital. How are *you*? I have no idea how I'm supposed to handle this stuff."

"You're doing just fine," he said.

The inside of the hardware store was visual noise, a collage of textures, colours, and shapes. John pulled a wire shopping basket from the stack and indicated that I should do the same. He didn't rush but seemed to know exactly what he was looking for: wood glue, long steel nails, a chisel with a chunky blade, bits of sandpaper. I couldn't name some of the other tools he picked out. My favourite of his supplies was a heavy silver hammer with a black rubber grip. He put it in my basket but I picked it out and bounced it in my right hand while we shopped.

He discussed wood with the cashier and finally requested some balsa, for practice, and decided to pick up some mahogany later, for the real thing. What the "real thing" was going to be, he didn't say. There was some discussion about mirrors, whether the clerk had more than what was on the shelves, but John went disappointed. I didn't say a word in the store, only watched and waited for any sort of clue as to what John was planning. None came. His face remained friendly as ever, his calmness immutable.

When the supplies were loaded into the car and we were heading north, I finally spoke up. "What was all that about?"

"What do you mean?" He wore that same smile.

"I bet the last time you handled a hammer, you were in high school shop class."

"I didn't take shop. I took home economics instead." He chuckled. "New hobby. I spent some time on the internet while on mental vacation."

I gritted, swallowed. *Vacation*. The word disagreed with me, in light of everything. In light of Grace.

Streetcars. Traffic. College Street. We passed Shifty's and I wished we were inside, eating, drinking, John and Grace making fun of me for not knowing the music, just one more gang of grown-ass adults in this neighbourhood pretending to be kids. We never really got to have our *good old days*.

"I thought some physical work would do me good," he continued. "Keep me from thinking about Grace. Keep the noose and the pills and razor blades out of my hands."

He chuckled. I could feel my jaw rolling under the skin.

"For fuck's sake, is this some kind of joke to you?" I felt un-equipped for all of this. Grace was the psychologist, not me. And moreover, I hated that he made me feel like the agitated one, the unstable one.

John said, "We should just talk about it. Out loud. What do you think?"

I scratched at my week's stubble, spat out the window. "Look. You first, then. Have you heard from Grace?"

"No. Of course not."

There was an open parking space close to the apartment, right in the middle of busy Bloor Street. We pulled the supplies out of the backseat from the passenger side. John just stood on the side-walk, pedestrians moving around him.

He said, "She's gone. And I think that's something you need to understand."

I left him near the car, made my way to the apartment entrance, waited. His smile diminished from kindness to pity. He opened the door for me and I started up the steps, stomping.

"Gone," I said. "What the hell is 'gone'? Who just leaves and doesn't bring their cell phone or ID or credit cards or even a penny of cash? Who doesn't pack or even bother to warn their parents? Who leaves their brother to clean up their mess of a boyfriend?"

I put the shopping bags on the top step and sat with my feet hanging down the stairs, tired. John took the wood from under his arms and placed it on the steps, shifting his strong frame to sit beside me.

"I don't want to go inside," I said.

He put his hand on the back of my neck. The hallway smelled like cigarettes.

"I can hear that you're angry," he said. "You don't understand. You feel betrayed by Grace's actions, by my selfishness."

"Yes. Exactly. I feel like you're both selfish assholes."

"I imagine you're sad. You're pissed off. You're worried."

"Stop with the psych-speak," I said. "Stop shrinking me."

He laughed quietly. "Sorry. It's been my lingua franca for months. But I'm being honest."

We could hear life continuing on Bloor, its idling engines, the excited chirping voices in the sushi restaurants below.

"Let's call it by a different name, then," he said. "Suicide. Grace committed suicide. She said as much to both of us."

What an ugly word, the ugliest. *Suicide.*

His face failed to register any emotion, kept its matter-of-factness. "And I couldn't handle it, couldn't cope. I felt like it was my fault. I did some serious self-harm, and in retrospect I can say that I was trying to kill myself, too."

He took his hand off my neck. I had forgotten it was there. Then he stood and opened the door to his apartment.

"Come on," he said. "This won't be easy for me, either."

—

Grace was everywhere. A standing coat rack full of dark and coarse outer wear. Piles upon piles of her clothes in their bedroom. Her shampoo and toiletries littering all the free space in the washroom. An open bag of her pot on the table. Five or six different types of instant coffee all strewn across the kitchen counters and buried in the cupboards. She loved instant coffee.

But her legacy was most present in the second bedroom. The ruined framed mirror filled most of the wall, cracks circling out from the central point of impact. A small bookshelf was full of Grace's books, most with flaking spines from her rough handling.

I returned to the living room and John was sitting on the old upholstered couch. He was looking through the bag of hardware supplies.

I said, "My mother keeps thinking she's going to walk in the door. It's destroying her, you know, despite their relationship. Without any evidence, I don't know, without her body. She has no idea why Grace would kill herself. If that's what it was. And you know what? I'm not sure, either."

It was an invitation for him to speak, to soothe. But instead his face tightened and he said, "I wish I had something to tell you. I wish I knew anything that would help you."

He met my gaze, briefly, and then looked down.

I cleared my throat. "O.K., so what now for you?"

"There's school in a few weeks."

"You're going back?" I asked.

He got off the couch and put the bags and the wood in the second bedroom.

"Of course," he said from the other room. "I want to finish what I started. A couple more years and you'll have to call me 'doctor.'"

"Fuck that." I laughed and immediately it felt wrong. "Listen. Are you safe? Are you going to hurt yourself again, or whatever?"

"I'm fine." He went to the kitchen and poured water into an electric kettle. "I can handle this."

"People don't just suddenly get better."

He returned to the living room. "What's your sample size?"

I laughed again, and this time it felt a little better. "Don't start that *sample size* shit again."

"I've got good reasons to live," he said. "Who else is going to take care of the rats? And then there's honouring the dead, hence all the wood and tools. I'd like to build her something. Coffee? I'd rather use it up than throw it away."

I moved toward the apartment door. "No. I hate that shit. Anyway, I'm going to go."

His words lingered in the air. *Honouring the dead.*

"Take care, all right?" he said.

"Sure. Look, *you* take care."

As I made my way down the stairs to the front entrance of the building, hiking up my sagging jeans and pulling down my T-shirt, he shouted to me. "You're starting to look very Torontonian, by the way."

I opened the entrance door, looked back, patted my stubble. "Yeah, yeah. Temporary lapse in good judgement."

—

The rain had started but it was light. My phone was sitting on the dashboard of my car, three missed calls, all from Nicole. I would catch hell. I didn't call her back, just flipped the phone closed and set it on the dash again.

On the ride home, watching my wipers streak the windshield, something began to unsettle me. I replayed my conversation with John, dug at the corners of it, looking for what wasn't right.

I kept going back to when he said, about Grace, *I wish I had something to tell you. I wish I knew anything that would help you.*

There was something in it, not a lie exactly but not the truth. He had faltered. He knew something about Grace but he didn't think it would help me. I felt my cheeks getting hot, a nagging itch along my spine. Was he keeping something from me, his idiot friend? Why had I never thought of this before? Was I imagining things? Why didn't I ever press people harder? I pushed my teeth together and ran my dry tongue along the roof of my mouth.

I missed another call while driving but caught the last one just after I'd parked.

"What the hell is your problem?" Nicole said over the line.

I found the basement apartment empty, the bed unmade. I crawled under the sheets and breathed deeply. The pillows smelled of oranges. I slept late into the day and made peace with Nicole when I saw her later.

2006

I'D GOTTEN UP early and left from just west of Winnipeg, the middle of my trip. I'd already covered about two thousand kilometres from Vancouver but had another two thousand before I reached the city. No matter how old I was, no matter where I was living, there was only one place I thought of as "the city." Crossing from Manitoba into Ontario, from endless existential flatlands into the stubborn little hills and gnarled trees of my home province, I felt something turn over in me. I drove all through the day, adding to the pile of plastic wrappers in the backseat. The scenery was tight ditches, blasted rock walls, tiny twists of water and two vast lakes, evergreens and birch shimmering with colour, power lines that went on forever. That night I ordered french fries from a Chinese restaurant near the highway, dipping them in sweet and sour sauce squeezed from a plastic packet onto a beige napkin.

I got on the road again and drove all through the night, shouting along with the stereo. Grace knew that my old car had no auxiliary input for mp3 players so she'd mailed me a few CDs for my trip. I became familiar with each song without knowing any of the bands. One song in particular got a lot of repetition, and I sang along with its hoarse male vocals:

There's no fine future waiting
In the depths of the freshwater seas.
I'll find my oblivion
In the place where the water meets the trees.

I drove until the sky went deep green and watched as the sun and the stars shared the horizon for half an hour. I drove knowing every cliché of driving across the country, every wicked word I would hear from Grace, but I drove anyway. I stopped only for coffee, tortilla chips, gasoline, and to take a piss. I drove until my skin was covered by a layer of grime, until my eyes were rotten and untrustworthy, until finally I was passing signs with names of cities where I had visited before. I weaved between Georgian Bay and Lake Simcoe, past Barrie, and into endless urban sprawl. Other than the road signs, there was no way to tell where the suburbs ended and the municipality began. I took the Don Valley Parkway into the heart of the city and fought my way onto Bloor.

By then I had been awake for more than a day, driving for almost all of it. I was twenty-four years old when I moved to Toronto.

—

"Hello?"
    "Grace."
    "Are you driving and talking on the phone at the same time?"
    "Yes."
    "You're an idiot. You're going to kill somebody."
    "Grace, where am I going?"
    "Bloor and Bathurst. Where are you?"

"Bloor Street. And . . . Dufferin?"

"You missed it. Turn around and park when you see Bathurst. And for Christ's sake, don't drive and talk on y—"

"Bye bye, now."

Click.

—

Grace was the success story of our family, and also the storm that hung over my parents' heads. She had a three-year head start on me in both regards.

When she was seven and I was four, Grace was a natural swimmer, a promising piano student, knew her multiplication tables up to thirteen, and would battle with my parents over every detail of her life. I, on the other hand, would occasionally use the side of a crayon to hash crude circles onto a piece of construction paper, and was generally referred to as a "sunny" kid.

When she was ten and I was seven, Grace won first prize in the provincial speaking competition for a persuasive piece on greenhouse gases, in which she made a joke of my mother always calling it "global *warning*." Tremendous academic success for her was always paired with tremendous family conflict. I quit swimming after a year, piano after a week, and I still can't multiply by thirteen, but my parents were too wrapped up in their own arguing, and in Grace's defiance, to worry about it. My only academic aptitude was, and continues to be, reading, although Grace's love of biology was enough to pique my interest for a brief time.

When she was thirteen and I was ten, Grace's fighting with our parents came to a head. She turned her back on them, on the status quo, and even on her love of science. Bandages started to appear on her arms and thighs, and trips to the hospital became normal for her and my parents. I was kept insulated from the trouble, as if her self-harm was contagious, but from my room I could often hear my parents shouting, demanding to know why Grace was doing this to herself, to them. Grace gave up gender norms, shaved her head, and wore sports bras instead of wired cups. And after the screaming period was over, she didn't speak to any of us, although most afternoons she still sat with me, quietly correcting my homework before my parents came home and broke us up. Some nights I would wake and find her sleeping beside me, on top of the blankets.

When she was sixteen and I was thirteen, Grace had bounced back. She re-grew her hair, started wearing dresses, intellectually dominated her classes, and showed nothing but amused disinterest in boys her age. She was considered the most attractive, unattainable girl in her high school. There were still occasional blow-ups, but Grace and my parents now mostly ignored each other. My only accomplishment for that year was discovering our dad's *Playboy* collection, stashed in a box under the couch where my father now slept most nights. For my birthday that year, Grace bought me a 1950s edition of *Catcher in the Rye* and lovingly threw out my sweatpants.

When she was nineteen and I was sixteen, Grace told me our parents' divorce had been coming for a long time. My father moved to the suburbs west of Toronto and I stayed with my mother in the suburbs to the east. I got my first A in high school that year, in English. Not one to be outdone, Grace accepted a full scholarship for the University of Toronto. And adding insult to injury, I had to live with guys in grade eleven and twelve telling me "your sister is hot." Before she left that year, she surprised me by asking me to stop fighting with our parents.

Grace may have overshadowed my every accomplishment but she was my role model, proof that our family was capable of greatness, even if it was troubled. Her departure from my day-to-day life was painful but it never lessened my loyalty to her, never diminished the memory of being her teammate throughout the progressively more difficult years of our childhood.

After she left for university, I got only snatches of information from her. *Dean's list. Double major. Invited speaker. Contributing author.* I hadn't even known she was an academic writer. And then my mother rejoicing *Grace is dating a boy*, which carried undertones of *Grace isn't a lesbian* with it. Then *Grace is dating an Oriental boy*, which had its own undertones, overtones. By then I had bounced to my dad's new house in hopes of completing high school and getting away from my mom.

Although I was only an hour away from Grace by car, the psychological distance from Toronto to its suburbs is so enormous that it might as well have been the other side of the continent. In 2002 I moved to Vancouver, and then it really was the other side of the continent. It wasn't until 2006, eight years after she went to university, that we found ourselves in the same city again.

—

The sky was white-hot and I started sweating the moment I got out of my car. Even on the quieter side street and in the shade of old trees, the air was thick, oppressive, and sticky, and the simple act of stretching sent beads of perspiration gliding down my ribs. I was damp when I approached the white moving van, its contents mostly emptied by that time, and it seemed as though John and Grace's friends were no better off in the heat.

To my eyes, the three friends looked like misfits, each one a different variety of circus geek. One was a gaunt giant boy in stripes and slacks, not jeans, his face a little fishy but still handsome enough. The girl was of no discernible ethnocultural background, dark-brown hair and eyes and skin, and tightly bound in denim from top to bottom. And half-bent in the trailer of the moving van was the last guy, his eyes hidden by aviator sunglasses, the sleeves of his shirt cut off, his jeans hanging low and exposing the crack of his ass.

He was the one who noticed me. He stood, stared, and when he finally spoke, his voice rattled like a stone in a can. "Fuck me, you look just like Grace."

All three turned their attention my way, parsing me into heritable little bits.

"It's just his eyes," the girl said. "You ever seen Grace smiling all goofy like that? This kid's the sweet one in his family."

She singlehandedly hauled a sofa chair out of the van and walked away. I wondered how she could bend in jeans that tight.

The guy in the sleeveless shirt jumped out of the van, brushed some dirt off his bare shoulder, and extended a hand.

"You're the deadbeat brother, then?" he asked, smiling.

"The one and only," I told him. I put my hand into his and shook.

"I'm the deadbeat friend. Brian." His handshake was strong, welcoming. He turned to the tall guy. "C'mere, Steve, you mopey motherfucker."

Steve walked like a gazelle and his enormous hand was soft and timid. "Oh, hey. Sorry, I'm just kind of awkward with this stuff."

The girl had already taken the sofa around the corner to the apartment and come back. She put her hand gently on Steve's chest, a gesture of affection, and pushed him out of the way. She turned to me. "Nice to finally meet the little brother. You just as much a pain in the ass as big sister?"

"Just as much," I deadpanned, "but in different ways. And you are?"

"Lee. Not at all a pain in the ass." She smiled, nodded, and grabbed a box from the van. Steve grabbed a basket and followed her like a love-struck puppy.

I turned to Brian and asked jokingly, "Where's *your* special someone?"

"Hah! Why the hell would I want that?" He looked over the tops of his mirrored sunglasses at me. Then he laughed again and patted my chest with the back of his hand. "It's hot as balls out here, eh?"

Neither of the boys was clean-shaven and Lee wore no make-up. They weren't sporty or professional, they weren't overly polite or phony, they had no pretense about their adulthood. I was beginning to feel like I was in Toronto.

Brian led me onto Bloor Street, where I took in its noise and bustle and general sense of excitement for the first time, bumper-to-bumper traffic with jaywalkers threading between, the thrum of the record store across the street, pedestrians crowding the sidewalks. The doorway to the apartment was between two packed sushi restaurants, and I followed him up the narrow steps and into the apartment for the first time. My eyes were bleary and tired and they struggled to adjust to the indoor light. I rubbed them with my knuckles, the orbits making a dry clicking sound with every rotation, until I could see again. In comparison to my student dormitory in Vancouver, Grace's place was spacious and old. The walls bulged a little and the paint was textured with layers of history underneath.

I found Grace and John in the master bedroom, leaning on each other and looking out the open window onto the street below. Grace was chewing on her thumb, working at the nail.

"Getting your slaves to do all the work for you?" I asked.

John turned and immediately smiled. I tried to bump shoulders with him, a man hug, but instead he embraced me. I patted his back and it was one big knot of muscle, not overly large but taut and inflexible. The man was all meat and it made me feel puny.

"It's good to see you again," he said. We had met once before.

"You too, John." I wasn't comfortable with such a long, unabashed hug from a man. I was definitely feeling like I was in Toronto.

Grace was clearly amused with my awkwardness.

"I'll let you two catch up," John said. He released me from the vise of his arms and kissed the top of Grace's head before he left the room.

There was a quiet moment. My sister and I hadn't shared a completely private conversation since we were teenagers. She eyed me cautiously from a few feet away, as though she was trying to make a decision. Her hair was long and messy and pinned with a peacock feather, and she wore dark mascara that accentuated the green of her eyes. Layers were her style these days: scarf, tank top, cardigan, necklaces upon necklaces, rolled-up jeans, small black shoes.

"Aren't you hot?" I asked.

"Aren't you ashamed?" Her nervous grin started to emerge.

"Of what?"

"Dropping out. Again."

"Oh," I said. "No. I'm getting used to it."

"Three strikes and you're out."

"Or third time's a charm. I was done with Vancouver, anyway."

Her eyes got bigger. "So does that mean the vagabond is going to stick around?"

I shrugged. "Thought I might find a place here, work, think about what the fuck I'm doing with my life."

Her grin was wide now. She stepped forward as if she was going to hug me. Then she hammered my shoulder with her fist. She stung the bone and I winced.

"That's great!" she said. "I'm glad your little bullshit Kerouac phase is over."

"Don't give me too much credit," I told her. "You at least need aspirations to have a phase."

She showed me around the apartment, described her plans for the space, how she would paint, where the furniture would go. John and the friends steadily came up and down the building's stairs and stacked boxes in the living room. Waves of tiredness came over me and passed. Grace looked a little older but happy enough.

"What are you going to do with the second bedroom?" I asked her. After my dorm life, it was hard to imagine what people would do with so much room.

"We've got some ideas," she said.

Before she could say more, there was a crash on the stairs. Grace flinched and ran to the front door.

"Jesus Christ, be careful with that!" she shouted down the stairs.

I came up behind her and looked over her shoulder. Steve and Lee had been carrying an enormous mirror with a comforter wrapped around it. Steve was at the top of the steps and fumbling to get a grip on the blanket. He looked confused and apologetic. And while Lee's face was half-hidden behind the mirror, she was clearly irritated with my sister's outburst.

"Just lost my grip on it," Steve said. "Sorry."

"Don't apologize," Grace backpedaled. "You were only helping."

"What the hell's the hold-up?" Brian cackled from the bottom of the stairs.

They took the mirror into the second bedroom and set it in the corner. Grace removed the blanket and searched around the frame for damage. There was a small crack along the bottom edge of the frame but the glass was intact.

"I didn't mean to snap at you, Steve," she said. She bit at her thumb again.

Lee gave a small nod.

Brian popped his head into the door frame and poked a thumb in the direction of the living room. "Trouble's here."

A woman's voice, unfamiliar and deep, said, "Shut up, Brian. Sorry I'm late, Grace."

Everyone else went to greet the new friend. I was tired so I stayed where I was, crouched near the mirror. In its reflection my eyes were ringed with red and my clean shave was almost gone. I yawned, scratched the back of my head, slapped my cheeks. I was fading.

"I hear you're the deadbeat brother," the new voice said.

And that was how I met Nicole: curled up near the mirror while she stood in the doorway. She was long, slender, and nearly as tall as me. Her hair was naturally bright orange, a colour I would never call *red*, and it framed the smooth skin of her cheekbones. She wore a high-necked sleeveless navy dress that stopped above her lovely knees and hugged her hips and waist. The belt of her dress and her shoes were bright white and she wore a white kerchief around her neck. Her eyes, hazel-coloured and almond-shaped, were narrowed and amused. She wore red lipstick and only a hint of a smile.

Brian poked his head into the door frame and said, "Trouble, meet Danger."

—

I don't remember much of unpacking the rest of the van, only that it was uninteresting work.

I vaguely remember dinner at one of the sushi restaurants below, seven of us piled into a space meant for four. My cheeks burned from the hot sake and from Nicole's bare leg pressed against mine. There was laughter and enthusiastic discussion about bands I'd never heard of. There was Nicole's hushed voice in my ear and my best attempt at charming replies. There was John's calm face and Grace's careful scrutiny as she watched Nicole and me. At some point, I learned that Grace and Lee and Nicole had all been roommates until a year or so ago, when Nicole moved out. Lee was the last one left in the old place now that Grace lived with John.

I have a memory of sitting on boxes in the new apartment. The stereo was the first thing they set up. Lee was in charge of song selection, and Steve sang along in harmony with the music she chose. It was strange to watch this giant, awkward man-boy suddenly look confident and unselfconscious. Brian played the photographer and the lush at the same time. For a while Grace sat on John's lap and wrapped her frame inside his brawny arms. Somehow the beer was already in the refrigerator and cold, and then it was in my hands. Somehow Nicole was never very far from me but never looking directly at me.

I remember cornering Grace. My eyes were glassy and my words were wet.

"So, science," I shouted at her over the stereo.

"What about it?" She was hanging halfway out the window and smoking a joint.

"What was wrong with philosophy and . . . the other subject?"

She took a deep drag and leaned toward me. "The truth is, I had a vision."

I grinned. "Drug-induced religious awakening. I expected more from you."

I thought we were having fun but her loose smile was gone and she looked serious, even a little unhinged, as in her bad years.

"Listen," she said. "I saw an opportunity to do something big, something I couldn't do if I kept fucking around in the humanities. And so I changed my field. John was part of it, too, so I convinced him to come with me. We're in the same lab, now."

"Doing what, though?"

Grace said something but I didn't hear it because Nicole caught my eye. Her hands were folded neatly in her lap and her smooth legs were crossed. A long white shoe dangled from her toes.

I turned back to my sister. "What? What do you do?"

"Play with rats," John said.

I laughed. "Sounds like world-changing shit."

Lee had chosen a noisy song, a hoarse voice shouting over the clanging guitars, and she was nodding along with the beat. *I'll find my oblivion in the place where the water meets the trees.*

"I know this one!" I told Lee, and again to Grace. "You put this song on the CD for me."

"At least you've learned something this year," she said and smiled.

—

The alcohol and tiredness were a muscular mix. I don't remember when I started holding Nicole's hand, only that it was discreet at first and then open.

"Your sister has been a good friend," she said. She ran her fingers over the contours of my knuckles and it felt incredible. "She really stuck up for me when it counted. We're not so close anymore but I still worry. Please keep an eye on her, for you and for me."

"You don't mean right now, though." I slid toward her, close enough that I could feel the heat radiating from her body, and failed to hold in my smile. "I mean, I'm a little busy at the moment."

Her eyes were stunning, amused but vaguely disinterested, like a cat's. "And don't tell her I said this."

Lee noticed Nicole and me, laughed, and choked on her beer. "If what Grace told me is true, I'm not sure who I should be worried for."

I think Brian was in worse shape than me. I remember his lips and teeth were stained darkly from the wine he drank, and he had a spatter of red drops on his shirt. His smile was ghastly and hilarious.

I don't know when people started to leave, or whether I said goodbye to them. I'd been running my thumb along the ridges of Nicole's slim hands and when I looked up, the room was empty. I offered to walk Nicole home and she didn't refuse.

I imagine John gave me another hug and Grace gave me a sisterly warning about her old roommate. I have no memory of either, though.

The walk home was fragmented: night air that was almost as hot as the day; walking arm in arm with Nicole, a solution to my staggering; pulling her close, inhaling her scent, blurting, "You smell like oranges"; Nicole hushing me, her wet red lips brushing against my ear; the firm skin and sweet taste of her neck.

I slept until the afternoon of the next day, long after Nicole had left for work. Her basement apartment, later *our* apartment and now just *my* apartment, had hardwood floors, seven-foot ceilings, and small windows high in the walls. The bed was firm and the room was cool. She left me a key on the night table, the same key I still use. Her cell phone number was written on a slip of paper curled through the key ring. I folded the pillow over my face and breathed in oranges, all the while thinking that the world was good and anything was possible.

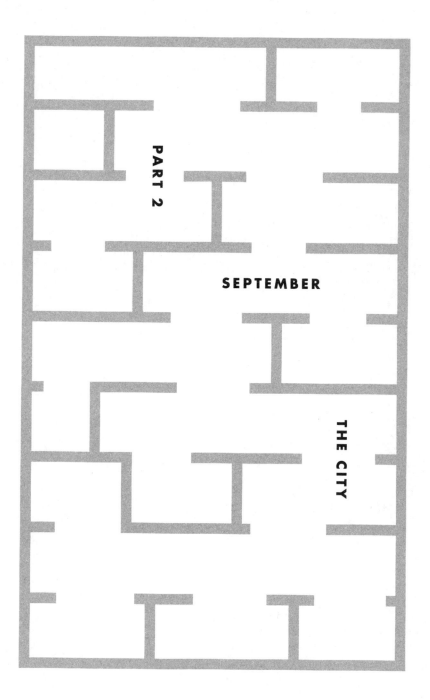

PART 2

SEPTEMBER

THE CITY

2008

IT'S NIGHT WHEN I get back from the hospital, my back full of stitches, and everything is waiting for me in the basement apartment, just as I'd left it: the six wooden panels leaning against the ragged old couch, the large burlap sack and dozen or so tiny pouches of dirt sitting at the edge of the kitchen. Buddy the rat's transparent cage is on the kitchen counter and his pink nose is poking out of a white plastic tube inside of it. Next to the cage is the miniature wooden box with its odd rubberized hole on one side. And on the kitchen tiles, where I threw them upon returning from John's apartment, are the blue notebook and John's note.

I don't know where to start. There's no beer in the fridge, only a few jars and plastic containers of condiments. In the cupboard I find half a bottle of a scotch-whisky blend. I rinse out a small glass and check the freezer for ice cubes but both trays are empty. I close my eyes and listen to the uncorking of the bottle, the way it resonates like my chest when I have the wind knocked out of me. I pour two fingers, add some water, and pick the notebook off the black and white tiles.

I sit on the couch, careful not to lean against my stitches, and look at the notebook. It is blue and hardbound and about one hundred pages thick, the cover adorned with a generic pre-printed white label that says *LAB NOTES*. I open it and find dense, nearly inscrutable algebra that fills every page to which I turn. I compare the handwriting to John's note: from the long ascenders and descenders, from the teardrop bow of the small *g*, I am sure it is his. The scotch won't mix well with the painkillers from the hospital but I take a mouthful anyway.

I told the nurses and the doctors that I'd fallen from a ladder and got sliced by metal siding on the way down. I doubt they believed me but at least they didn't phone the police.

I continue to flip through the book and find that it's all the same algebra, long strings of equations. I'm unsure whether the letters in the formulae are variables or constants but the equations don't ever seem to get solved or even substantially shortened. In the margins are hurriedly written notes with more cryptic initialisms, like "LJx," or just "B." The inside of the front cover has a familiar number written in various motifs:

Key fob then
4-2510- then
2510#- then
2510

The notebook poses more questions than it answers. I am about to give up on it when I flip back to the very first page and notice a single line of text.

The street where I grew up led to a dead end, it says.

I put the book down, John's note slipped inside it, and finish the scotch. In the kitchen I pour myself another large glass and tap Buddy's cage. He comes out of the plastic tube, rears up on his hind legs, and puts his nose up to the wire lid to sniff me. He is black from his shoulder blades to his nose as well as along his spine, and the rest of his fur is white. His front paws are tiny and pink and look like human hands with long thin nails.

"Hey, man," I say to him. He looks at me.

I pry the lid off the cage, gently pick him up, and scratch his ears with my fingertip. He stands on my forearm without complaint and watches as I pick up my scotch. I swirl the drink along the lip of the glass, take a sip, and swish it in my mouth. I hold it in front of Buddy as an offering but he only sniffs it and turns around on my arm.

There is no food in the crook of the cage's wire lid but I have filled the water bottle and slotted the drinking nozzle through the bars. I remember John feeding hard little cylinders to the rats but I have no idea what the pellets actually were. I consider my current options, pasta or toast, and put a slice of bread in the toaster oven. The sight of food reminds me that I haven't eaten since the mashed potatoes so I drop in another slice for myself. I raise my arms to stretch and I can feel the medical tape pull at my skin.

While the bread is toasting, I put Buddy on the top of the miniature box. He would fit comfortably inside. I'm overtaken by a powerful yawn, but when I check my phone it isn't even ten o'clock yet. My legs ache as if I've been up for days. By now the liquor is warming my head and making a film over my eyes.

And then I hear a scrabbling sound and look to the box in time to see Buddy's tail disappear into the rubber hole. My heart begins to race.

"You little shit," I whisper. "You didn't."

I'm not putting my hand into the box to retrieve him. The toaster oven pings. I butter my slice, decide to butter Buddy's, too. I break his piece up and drop it onto the bedding inside the cage. Then I check the refrigerator, find half a head of iceberg lettuce, tear a leaf off, and put it in the cage. I know very little about what rats eat but I doubt toast and lettuce will kill him.

But the box might. I am absolutely not putting my hand into it to retrieve him. I push at the slat with the rubber hole, hoping it will slide, but nothing happens. Then I wipe off the butter knife and use it to pry along one of the edges of the box. I hear a snap and the panel with the rubberized hole detaches. As expected, the inside of the box is lined with mirrors. But Buddy isn't inside. I check the counter, the floor, the corners of the room, the box again. Buddy is gone.

A laugh comes out of me, mean and hard, and I push the box away from me in disgust. I curse their disappearances, Buddy's a few minutes ago, John's last year, Grace's almost two years, now. I can see my reflection inside the box: bearded, worn, unkempt. It would feel satisfying to smash the box to pieces with the hammer. I seriously consider it for a moment.

Instead I empty the scotch bottle into my glass, turn out the lights, and grab the blue lab notebook on my way to the bedroom. I carry the toast in my mouth. I use my toes to pull off my socks and I slip out of my jeans. In bed, I swallow down my meal in a few bites and wipe the crumbs off the comforter. I lie on my side to avoid the stitches and rub at my eyes to clear away the glaze.

Skimming through the lab notebook doesn't help my anger. It could be some code, but none of John's "phrases" in the formulae seem to repeat, as I'd expect to see for words like *the* or *it*.

The street where I grew up led to a dead end.
MOIJX+NEW-T*HHVXI/NRRX+NYUWIFMWVH-
HIDQBQW*ZMXRWLDIYG/RRP+HLRL-KS*XESR/
UCO=QRZE+UACRJBGATWJ=QG-CACYGD*LK/
MVSM+SKFH-VDCJWQZV*HYX/TUKPQPHHD
+FA-JRIL*PHS/YSMFVFUSF[2] . . .

—

I first met John over the holidays, a year and a half before I moved to the city. By then I was on my way to flunking out for the second time at the same university (ultimately the same university where I flunked out a third time). Coming home from Vancouver on a cheap flight was a great excuse to miss exams I didn't care about.

Grace rejected the idea of family dinner at first, but not as fiercely as usual. It was hardly a struggle to convince her, actually. And when I answered the door at my mother's house and found her standing next to John, I understood why: she was happy.

The two of them must have been dating for a year by then, but standing near them as they took off their coats, I could feel the air thrumming with energy. Grace caught his glance and laughed spontaneously, *hah*. She reached out to lean on him as she took off her boots. Meanwhile John was this giant, smiling, calm presence, and best of all to me, he didn't turn to greet me until his interaction with Grace was complete. Then he shook my hand firmly, radiated a gentle authority, and made me feel that anything I had to say was welcome.

That Christmas dinner had the least conflict I'd observed in my family for ten years. Once or twice it got shaky, Grace's patience was tested, but John managed to absorb all the tension in the room. He just sat in my father's old chair at the table and nodded, listened, invited my mother and me to open up. My mother ate up his attention, and if I'm being honest, so did I. And when my sister smiled at him, it wasn't with that sad resigned smile, but warm and whole and enthusiastic about the future. Things weren't perfect for Grace, but they were better than they'd been in a long time, and I couldn't help giving John some of the credit.

—

And then it's morning in my bedroom. Grey-white light is coming in through the window and I know it will be a shitty day outside. I don't know what day it is, though, so I crawl off the bed and dig my phone from the pocket of my jeans. Monday, nine-thirty a.m. I have slept almost twelve hours and I'm thirty minutes late for work.

"Oh, for fuck's sake," I say aloud.

I throw on the same jeans, different socks, and a light sweater over my T-shirt. The sweater makes it a work outfit. On top of this I put John's black jacket. My mouth is hot and acrid so I quickly brush my teeth but there is no time to look at my hair. I am out the door.

As I prepare to run down to Queen Street, something catches my eye: the landlord or somebody else has removed the persimmon tree from the ground. All that remains is a dark, grassless bump in the soil. I will miss the tree. It makes me think of Buddy's disappearance but I've already locked the door and I need to go. I run.

I'm sweating when I get to work. I can feel one of my bosses watching me through the many plates of glass in our office, and soon I hear the heels of his shoes clacking along the hardwood. He corners me while I'm hanging John's jacket in the closet and his cheery voice makes it clear that his wife, my other boss, has sent him to talk to me.

"Do you have anything pressing this morning?" he asks.

I shake my head. "Just those emails to Ottawa, but they can wait."

"Why don't we grab a coffee?" His upbeat tone indicates something heavy is coming.

I look over his shoulder. His wife is in her office and wearing a pinched expression on her face. We make eye contact for a moment. Then she looks down her long nose and through her glasses to the computer screen. I turn to her husband and nod. The sweat on my back irritates the skin around my stitches and my guts are screaming from last night's scotch.

We leave the office and walk in silence past the makeshift art galleries and nonprofits that fill the rest of the building. I will miss this workplace, its wide hallways and head-to-toe wood. The coffee shop is at the front of the building and is mostly empty this time of day. My boss points me to a table and orders for us. I sit. There is a plant on the other side of the glass, something hardy and flowerless, and its pot is full of bent cigarette butts. People hustle through the intersection, their outfits split evenly between semi-formal office wear and very tight denim and plaid.

My boss sets a porcelain cup of café Americano in front of me, a little milk drizzled in it, and a latte next to himself. He is the type to remember what kind of coffee other people drink.

"So." He's speaking in that voice he uses when his wife isn't around, like a frank father. "You're not making it easy for me here."

"I know," I tell him. "I'm sorry for that. I'm sorry it reflects badly on you. She shouldn't punish you for it."

"We know you're good at your job. She gives you a hard time because she knows you're capable. We also know you're going through something, something that started just a few months after you joined the team. But I can only guess, because you haven't said anything."

He pauses. I'm supposed to start speaking, here. I don't. He continues.

"It's hard to be empathic when you don't tell us what's going on. Are you all right?"

"I'm all right," I say. He meant *empathetic*, not *empathic*.

"Is it drugs?"

I look at his sincere face and I can't help but smile a little. "It's not drugs."

"What is it, then?"

I pause, hesitate. "It's a long story."

"Fine." He shrugs angrily. "Well, you know you could have always come to us. We would have listened. Since you didn't, we're going to have to assume that you're fine. You've been around for a while and you know how it is in the nonprofit sector. We have a limited budget and we need to use it wisely."

"O.K."

"You may be good at your job, but quite frankly there are other people who would be just as good *and* more consistent."

"O.K."

"So what I need to hear from you, right now and for the last time, is whether you can be consistent. Can we rely on you or do we need to find someone else?"

We make eye contact and I don't answer right away. I'm not sure how old my boss is, maybe forty or forty-five. He always seems freshly showered and well dressed, always punctual and socially engaging. But the effort he's put into their company is noticeable in the deep, dry lines around his eyes, and in the few extra pounds he carries in his face and around his belly. He is a good man who has worked very hard and it is diminishing him. I can tell by his words that this is tough love, that he's trying to help me.

I say, "I'm sorry, but I don't think you can rely on me."

He puts down his latte and stares at me, puzzled. I speak before he can respond.

"I know you want me to step up, and in some way, it would be nice to be the reliable worker you need. But I'm not going to be, especially not right now. I just don't give a shit about this job. I think you should find someone else."

We sit in our wood and iron chairs for a minute, sipping at our drinks and not saying anything.

I say, "I'm happy to stick around for a couple of weeks and help somebody new learn the ropes, but I'm done."

He nods. "To be honest, this isn't how I expected this talk to go. But I was your age once, working in an office doing admin crap I didn't like."

I want to correct him, tell him that the work is fine, but I keep my mouth shut. We put our empty mugs on the counter, walk back upstairs, and the only sound between us is his soles on the wood. While I'm booting up the computer, I can hear him debriefing with his wife. Her voice is deep and then shrill.

—

A few weeks later my back is free of stitches and I have no job. The toast in Buddy's cage moulds, the leaf of lettuce browns, and Buddy remains absent. The large box is still disassembled and leaning against my couch. John's notebook is under the bed, thrown there in a fit of drunken frustration and never retrieved. My phone shows six missed calls, one from Officer 2510, one from Lee, and the rest from our mother. There are new empty whisky bottles next to the couch and beside the bed. Each day my stomach hurts for the first few hours after I wake up. My beard is just long enough to make the skin underneath itchy and red.

I spend a week walking at night and sleeping during the day. I flip aimlessly through some of the books Nicole left behind, Camus and Kafka and Dostoyevsky. The days shorten and sap the city of any last heat. Autumn comes early this year.

Brian calls one afternoon. I'm lying on the couch with my arm hanging off the side and my fingers grazing the smooth exterior of the disassembled wooden box. The phone vibrates along the floor and I let it go to voice mail. A minute later I flip open the phone and listen to the message.

"Dude. Nobody's heard from you in fucken forever. Lee says you quit, too? Come to the Fortress on Friday. Steve and me are playing. You and I are gonna get shittered. Hah. Seriously, though, enough's enough. Gimme a call, bud."

I don't call him but after the sun goes down on Friday, I make the walk to the concert on Bloor. The sky in the west is fading from pink skin to deep bruise and the air is perfectly cool. Smokers idle around the graffitied entrance to the Fortress and a white van with a small cargo trailer is parked out front. I recognize a few friends of Nicole but they don't know my face anymore.

I make my way past the venue, down the street, until I'm standing in front of the two sushi restaurants. I look up into John and Grace's old apartment, where the windows are open and the lights are on in the second bedroom. The landlord has repainted the walls and there are cardboard boxes stacked in one corner. I'm unsure if someone new is already moving in or if those boxes hold the possessions John and Grace left behind.

I walk back to the Fortress and Brian is now outside having a smoke, staring at his phone. He doesn't bother with cigarettes when he's sober.

"You started without me," I say to get his attention.

He turns and smiles. "I fucken started at dinner, man."

"Sorry, do you want to finish that text message?"

"Dude, this is my new fancy phone. I'm just half-cocked and on the internet, begging people to be my 'friend.' Lee just added me."

"That sounds pretty stupid," I say.

Brian laughs. "You're goddamned right it is. You should get on it."

I take cash out of the bank machine on the way inside. The machine tells me I have just a little more than two months of rent left. I pay the girl working the door and get my wrist stamped in smudged black ink. Then we fold back the dirty curtain and go inside.

The inside of the Fortress is a dark cube of noise. The ceiling is extremely high, all the walls and furniture are painted black, and the only lights are on the stage and above the bar at the back. The sound reverberates off the walls and turns the background music into a din. People appear as silhouetted heads unless they are a foot or two from my face. It smells like an empty, rinsed out aluminum can.

Brian and I squint through the dark and shout over the music, all the way to the bar.

"What are you drinking?" he asks.

"Lately? Scotch, whisky, that sort of thing."

"Fuck me." He laughs. He orders us two shots of whisky from the well and two cheap bottles of beer. "Nothing but the best, eh?"

We tip the shots down our throats and clack the necks of our beer bottles together. My body doesn't even react to the heat of the liquor anymore. The thought is alarming but my first sip of the beer washes it away.

Brian belches into his sleeve. "Remember when you looked all young and wide-eyed and shit?"

"Funny, you look just as rough as you used to," I say.

He laughs again. "Man, this city ruined us."

"Not just the city," I say.

He nods, becomes sombre. "You've had a bad run. I'm sorry, dude."

Brian leads me to the right of the stage where Lee is dressed snugly and standing with a couple of young women I don't recognize. I smile and raise my bottle as a greeting.

"We heard this is where the girlfriends of the band hang out," Brian shouts into Lee's ear, leaning his weight on one foot and then the other. His voice cuts through the sludge of sound. "Can we be band girlfriends, too?"

Lee pushes him away with her elbow and mutters something undoubtedly rude. Her elbow rests against him for a moment longer than necessary, rubbing his chest. It's odd and it makes me wonder about her boyfriend Steve. I look up to the stage and the first band is setting up, plugging in guitars and keyboards in the near dark.

Lee is staring at me when I turn back to my friends. She says something I can't hear and so I lean in with my head turned. She holds her dark curls away from her face so we can speak to each other closely.

"How you holding up, Scruffy?" she asks.

"O.K.," I tell her. Even I can smell the whisky on my breath. "Brian tells me you're his digital friend now."

She pauses and I can see her face flex a bit from the corner of my eye. "You know you can talk to us if you need to, right?"

"I've been hearing that a lot lately," I say, "but yeah, I know. Thank you."

I straighten up and smile to end the conversation. Lee looks upset but there is nothing I want to say, so I put a hand on the shoulder of her jean jacket and nod as if to thank her again.

We drink. I make small talk and listen to news from the last few months: Lee has gone back to college; Steve and Brian are halfway through recording an album; Brian tried to quit his job and got a raise out of it; and Lee tells me she visited my bosses' office this week for a meeting.

"Who's this first band?" I shout. I have no interest in talking about my old job. The lights have dimmed and the musicians are about to start. There is a thin crowd at the front of the stage.

"Don't you know these guys?" Lee asks. "I saw a couple of them talking with Nicole outside."

The look on her face is part consolation and part mischief.

"Oh, great," I say, and we both laugh. "Is she here?"

But I can't hear her reply. The drums and keyboard have started something slow and shuffling built around a single-note riff. Every hit on the snare hangs and echoes off the walls of the Fortress. The kick drum is more of a feeling than a sound. When the rest of the band starts playing, the lights come up a bit and I can see the musicians.

Standing in the centre of the stage is an attractive young woman somewhere near Grace's age, perhaps thirty years old. I typically reserve the expression *tomboy* for girls under fifteen but it is a perfect descriptor for her: short, messy auburn hair with a noticeable wave around the hairline; charcoal jeans that hug her legs but are a little loose around her small waist; plain black T-shirt; a clean face with a smattering of freckles around the nose; and intense eyes that look like concrete from this distance. She has a guitar slung low over her shoulders and only casually scratches at it. She is completely unadorned and should be unremarkable but everyone's attention is on her. She has my attention, too, but especially because she seems familiar. She is singing something low and rhythmic that sounds like a chant. Her voice is honey, thick and amorphous.

The floor in front of the stage fills up and everyone in the Fortress is enrapt. The song keeps building, the guitars get grimy and loud, but the band never rushes the beat. The tomboy looks confident and only dimly aware of everyone's eyes on her. Her voice is strong but not showy. She takes the song to its climax and then the whole thing drops on a single note. There is a beat of dead air in the room, just the whir of electricity and the hum of amplifiers and everyone holding their breath. Then the audience emits a furious cheer. Brian appears obviously impressed. Lee has her arms crossed.

"Wow." Brian nudges me with his shoulder.

"Yeah, not terrible," Lee shouts with too much emphasis. "But Steve tells me their other stuff isn't as good."

"He does, eh?" Brian says sourly. Again the moment hangs just a little too long between them.

I watch the tomboy as she tunes her guitar, a crooked grin on her face, and I say, "I think I know her."

The rest of their set doesn't disappoint, although Lee was right: the first song is their best. Their music is delivered with precise, terse vocals that suggest more emotion than is actually expressed. The guitars are dirty and wild but the vocals never lose their cool. It is a great juxtaposition and the crowd voices their enthusiasm. They play for thirty minutes and the tomboy speaks only once between songs to thank the other bands. Throughout their set I try to grasp where I've seen her before. Nothing specific comes to mind, only an opaque recollection of her sly and unimpressed manner.

—

I signal to Brian that I'll buy the next round. On the way to the bar I stop at the men's room and it is almost as dark as the rest of the club. While I wash my hands, I look into the mirror and see the faint profile of someone standing behind me. I throw an apologetic glance for monopolizing the sink and rinse the suds off my hands. When I turn, though, there is no one waiting. I pause. The men's room door is next to me and it's impossible that someone could have left without my noticing. I'm starting to get worried but then I notice that one of the two stalls is closed. I shake my head and leave.

And on the other side of the door is Nicole, standing in line just outside the women's washroom. Her eyes are on the floor but she looks up when she feels me staring at her. She doesn't smile, of course, but she says, "Here's trouble."

Instinctively I say, "You're Trouble. I'm Danger."

"Not anymore," she reminds me.

There are two very opposite feelings mixing in me and I'm unsure what to say next. She looks at the six or seven women in line in front of her, looks at the men's room door.

"Is it empty in there?"

"One guy in a stall," I tell her.

She makes a little wave of her hand, a shining bracelet sliding along her bare arm, and she says, "Come on. You're on point."

I follow her back into the men's room. She bends at the waist to look under the stall doors. She wears a thick belt over her dress, just above the hips. Then she straightens up and focuses her cat eyes on me. It has been a long time.

"I thought you said someone was in here," she says.

I shrug. She looks bored. Her eyes linger on me for a moment and then she goes into one of the stalls. I'm not sure what to do so I run the cold water and splash a bit on my face.

Her voice flutters over the half-door. "Tell me it's good to see me."

"It's good to see you," I say.

I can see her red Mary Janes under the stall door. Soon she emerges. "Tell me I look good."

"You always look good," I tell her.

"And you look like shit," she says. She uses her shoulder to gently push me and puts her hands under the already running tap. "You look tired. Defeated."

I laugh but it is not funny. "And how would you look, exactly?"

She turns off the tap and doesn't meet my gaze. "I would look like I'm doing something."

She turns to leave the washroom but I block the exit. Her eyes get fierce and her nostrils flare. I don't move. This is how we communicate.

"You don't know about it," I tell her. "This constant grief."

"And why exactly don't I know about it?" she asks. She is focused, framed, crystalline. "I know you don't think they're dead. You said as much without ever saying it."

I open my mouth. I want to say, *There is nothing I can do.* No words come out.

"*I never saw a wild thing sorry for itself,*" she quotes, from whom I don't know. She puts out a hand and touches my arm. I remember this feeling. "Man up or suck it up, Danger. Commit to something or stop your maudlin pity party. You can make your choice or you can have it taken away from you again."

She sidles past me and out the men's room door, leaving only a trail of citrus in the air.

I stand there for a minute doing nothing. There is nothing *to* do. Why couldn't I say it aloud? A sweaty man enters and starts to piss in the back urinal. I leave.

I wade back into the Fortress's sea of silhouettes. I can do nothing. Or I can reconstruct. I know where Buddy the rat comes from. The bag of earth and the lab notebook are less clear but I have a few ideas. And the large wooden box is missing only one panel of mirror.

I pick up one bottle of beer and deliver it to Brian at the stage, where he's setting up his drums. Then I explain to Lee that I have to leave. She's not impressed and not surprised.

As I move to the door I search for Nicole, then for the tomboy, but it's impossible to see faces in such a dark space unless they're right next to me.

—

Back at the house, just before bed, I go to the kitchen. The small wooden box is still on the counter, pushed to the back corner, the slat with the rubberized hole still removed. I try to slide the panel back into place but it won't form a tight seal. When I look closely I can see I broke the grooves when I pried it off with the butter knife. I dig through the apartment until I find the miniature box's extra wall, no hole, no rubber. I slide it into place and complete the wooden cube.

I wake in the night to the sound of broken glass. I turn on every light, move from the bedroom to the living room, hands balled into fists. In the kitchen is the source of the sound: the small box has fallen from the counter to the tiles, coming apart, flattening, and breaking some of the mirrors. And in the wreckage is Buddy, staring up at me as if nothing is out of the ordinary.

This is the only way back for us, the note said.

I want to be surprised and so I stand and wait. When no shock registers I pick up Buddy under his stomach, not at all the way John taught me to handle the rats. As I'm about to put him into his cage, I feel a lump in one side of Buddy's stomach. I lift him upright and gently probe his belly with my fingertips. There is something hard and square inside the rat. The telemetry device, implanted two years ago by Grace and John.

2007

STEVE AND BRIAN ended their set at the Fortress with a long, droning note, Brian hammering the kick drum and cymbals every four beats for what felt like two minutes. It was supposed to be a crescendo but instead it felt like a dull wash of sound. I felt my phone vibrate in my pocket but I didn't take it out. John and Lee and I made our way to the edge of the stage and shouted our support to Steve and Brian, who were kneeling to greet friends. John reached up to shake both of their hands and clasp them on their shoulders. I simply smiled and raised my beer bottle in tribute.

Over at the bar Brian laughed and told us, "Couldn't keep my fucken sticks in one piece for the second half of the set. Flubbed the intro to my favourite song. Fuck, I forgot whole verses of lyrics."

"It was incredible from where we were standing," Lee told him, one arm around Steve's waist but facing our direction. Steve tried to smile but only the muscles around his mouth moved. I remembered what Grace had called that fake smile: *non-Duchenne*.

"Don't mind that gloomy prick," Brian leaned into me and said. "He's just fighting with the bassist again."

Fighting. I put my hand on the pocket of my jeans where I kept my phone.

"That reminds me," I said, and excused myself to the outside air.

—

"Why the hell do you even bother with a cell phone if you never pick up?"

"I was watching a set, Trouble. Our friends' show. You know, that you should be at."

"They're more like your friends than mine, now."

"Don't be like that, Nicole."

"Like what, precisely?"

"Nothing. Nothing."

"So how were Steve and Brian?"

"Well, it wasn't incredible from where I was standing."

"God, can't you ever be supportive? You're so judgemental. What do you know about music?"

"Why did you ask if you didn't want to know? At least I came to the goddamned show. Where are *you?*"

"Out with my friends."

"The Cuckoo, then? Great. Awesome. So we're not going to see you?"

"You don't sound like you want to see me, Danger."

"Look. Why would I be asking if I didn't want to see you? For Christ's sake, Nicole."

"I'm not being talked to like this."

Click.

—

We didn't stick around for the last band. Brian asked if they could store the gear at John's apartment for the night, since their jam space locked up at midnight. John didn't immediately say yes, which surprised me. Once he'd agreed, though, he hoisted a blocky amplifier cabinet and walked straight to his front door, two streets away, without complaint. I have no idea how he got it up the stairs by himself.

I was last into the apartment and it was strangely quiet. The gear was stacked in the living room and John could be heard in the kitchen, getting drinks.

Lee came out of the washroom and said, "Was somebody arguing?"

"I tried to put the gear in the second bedroom," Steve whispered. "There's a lock on the door."

"What? Why?" Lee didn't try to speak quietly.

"Who cares?" Brian said. "It's probably nothing."

Lee looked to me. "What's going on in there, Scruffy?"

Before I could answer she got up from the arm of the sofa chair and went to the second bedroom door. She put her hand out and cranked the knob, which turned but didn't open the door. She fingered the keyhole for the deadbolt with her other hand.

"Lee?" John now stood at the edge of the living room, drinks in each hand. His face was unreadable, a mask.

"What is this?" Lee said.

John slowly put down the glasses. "It's a locked door, Lee. I would ask that you respect it."

Lee flinched. Steve, Brian, and I didn't move.

"You would ask that we be fine with it," Lee said.

"Yes," John told her.

"With a locked door."

"Yes."

"A locked door in the home where our friend was last seen before she disappeared. After you just got out of the mental hospital."

"A month ago," John said.

He took a step toward Lee. His back was to me, then, and he was obscuring my view of all but Lee's elbows that jutted out as she crossed her arms over her chest.

"John. A locked door. You were the last to see her," she said.

Only his head moved, a shallow little wobble of thoughts. I was breathing through my mouth and the air was dry and hot. Then his posture relaxed a little.

"Maybe you're right," John said to Lee. "Maybe it's unreasonable to ask that you be fine with it. But I would ask you to trust me."

He faced all of us, carefully inspecting our eyes one at a time.

"Or I would ask you to leave," John said.

He and Lee took a good look at each other, both of them sad but in different ways. Lee leaned over and picked up her jean jacket, folded it into her arms.

"We're worried about you," she said. "We all are."

The three friends filed out together. Brian said nothing but ran his hands through Grace's coats piled on the rack. Steve held Lee's hand and mumbled a goodbye to me and a thank you to John. Soon I was the last visitor in the apartment and John still stood proud, staring into his empty living room.

Without looking at me, he asked, "Drink?"

I put on my shoes and told him I would see him soon. He closed the door behind me with the tiniest click, then the heavy crank of a deadbolt.

—

I was twenty-five minutes late for work the next day but there were prospective clients in the office all morning and my boss was in such a good mood that she didn't give me her usual grief.

Only once did she leave her glass-encased cubicle and it was to say, "Thank you. That's enough."

At first I had no idea what she was talking about, but then she pointed to my foot. I hadn't realized I'd been humming and tapping one of Steve and Brian's songs.

Nicole made me lunch at her restaurant before her own shift started, couscous, steamed spinach and other vegetables, a rich sauce with garlic, Parmesan on top. She had been dead asleep when I left for work, with her fists curled in and her face slack but pretty. At lunch she worked her hand across the table until I was running my fingertips from her knuckles to her wrist. We didn't say much, only put our pieces together for another day. Every bite tasted meticulous and rich and complex. I ate with my eyes closed. When I was finished, she asked me to help finish her plate. While she washed up for her shift, I smelled traces of her sticky, sweet scent on the back of my hand.

I kissed Nicole goodbye and deliberately held it for too long, until she was laughing and her tongue curled up and our teeth clacked together. She hated this, she loved this, she put her palms on my shoulders and pushed me away. I told her I would make dinner that night and she didn't say anything, only walked backward into the kitchen with a long, genuine smile on her face. *Duchenne.*

Work ended late so I drove to Bloor to buy kimchi, Nicole's current favourite. Even after a year of living in the city, I still found it amazing that the street was so divided at Bathurst, with bookstores and record shops and the Fortress to the east and the vibrant Korean neighbourhood, its restaurants and Asian produce and beauty salons, to the west. Night was already casting its deep pinks and blues over everything. I called Steve on the walk back to my car and told him I'd been humming his song. There wasn't a chance to gauge his reaction, though, because I ended the call when I saw John coming toward me on the other side of the street.

Though the daylight had faded, I could see that John was struggling. Eight or ten planks of wood and a heavy, arrowhead shovel were balanced over his arms. With every step the wood slid and jutted at bad angles. To compensate, he shifted his frame and walked with an increasing lope. But it was no use. Eventually he stumbled under his own gait and dropped the supplies. Other pedestrians circled around him while he fought to collect the wood. As he lifted the pile, the shovel fell out of his hands. As he knelt to grasp the tool, the wood slipped away from him again.

Hands empty, he shouted, "Fuck!"

Passersby scattered and fretted.

By this time, I had jaywalked across the street and was shouting to get John's attention. He startled like an animal when I touched his sleeve but regained some composure when he finally recognized me.

"There's a reason it's evolutionarily conserved, you know." He wouldn't look at me as he spoke. "Anger. Aggression. They're useful. My hands are shaking now, over some inanimate objects, but it's a fair trade-off. Violence is the logical extreme of communication, the only language that people will not ignore, the only language that everyone understands."

While he rambled I separated the wood into two piles on the gritty sidewalk. I helped him up and together we carried the supplies back to his apartment. My hands ached from the chilly air.

John avoided using the overhead bulbs of the apartment and switched on the table lamps instead, a bath of warm light. He left the wood piled at the door and lowered himself onto the couch like an old man. He jammed his fists into his armpits and rocked a little. His shoulders stretched the shirt but his chest had started to look deflated.

On the coffee table was a piece of paper, printed on which was a grid, the alphabet running across the rows and columns.

"It's called a *tabula recta*," John said absently.

"What's it for?" I asked.

"Officer 2510 asked me the same thing when she came by to see me today."

"2510? What did she want?"

"Only to ask me the same questions, as per her usual." He untucked his hands and began to massage his face. "Have I heard from Grace. Do I have any new information. Why am I so convinced she's gone for good. Why am I keeping things from the police."

John pulled his mouth tight at the corners and rubbed his eyes with his knuckles. I sat down on the other end of the couch. He removed his hands from his face and his eyes flitted without focus.

"And what did you tell her?" I asked.

"Nothing she wanted to hear." He coughed, closed his eyes, kept them closed. "I'm starting to treat her like my therapist. Told her I'm swallowing anxiolytics by the handful. Told her I wake up in the middle of the night thinking Grace is in the bed, beside me, whispering in my ear. Told her I'm doing a good job of alienating friends and isolating myself."

I'd had my own conversation with Officer 2510 and could imagine her nonplussed reaction to all of this. Her thick monotone was more memorable to me than her appearance.

I asked, "Did you tell her whether you're alienating friends on purpose or by accident?"

"I didn't, no. Scotch?"

He stood and went to the kitchen. I heard the lovely uncorking sound of the bottle, rocks of ice rolling in glasses, a gentle pour. John returned to the living room and sat at the end of the couch, handing me a small, wide glass of golden liquor. We tapped glasses and drank. The scotch was fairly mellow and as long as I kept my mouth shut, I wasn't revolted by the aftertaste.

"So which is it?" I asked.

John looked at me, unsure.

"Are you alienating us on purpose or by accident?"

"Ah." He raised his chin a little. "Does it matter?"

"Jesus, would I be asking if it didn't?"

"I suppose it's a little of both," he said.

I surveyed the living room. Grace's things were still hanging on the walls, still poking out from under the couch, still taking up every bit of psychological space in the room. I felt closed in, trapped.

I asked, "Look, you want me to trust you, right?"

He nodded.

"Then I need you to trust me. At least a little."

He was about to interrupt but I raised my hand and continued.

"You just told me you're struggling. And O.K., I know that shows trust. And I appreciate it. But you'll have to excuse me if I'm not doing this again. I'm not going to do nothing, this time, while somebody close to me falls apart."

With my right hand I poured the scotch into my mouth, and with my left I waved in a circle, indicating the entire room.

"Look at all this," I said. "You're living in a museum. A shrine."

"Yes," he said.

"I bet that no matter where you turn, you're reminded of her absence."

"Exactly."

"Of our failure to help her."

"No. Of *my* failure."

Each sip was more tolerable than the last. I finished the scotch, took an ice cube in my mouth and crunched it. My back teeth stung with the cold.

"Oh, fuck you," I said. "We all failed her. You don't get ownership on guilt."

John straightened his posture and cleared his throat. "That isn't what I meant."

I waved my hand again, more violently this time. I could feel my belly slosh with heat.

"So what are you going to do about it?" I asked. "About your shrine. Look. Choose to live or choose to remember. But it seems like you can't do both right now."

John didn't respond. He finished his drink and held the empty glass in his hand, staring at the photos on the wall and Grace's coat rack near the front door. Then he got up and poured us two more drinks, this time without ice. We stood and drank. By now I couldn't taste anything.

We made a game plan. First we made piles of Grace's old things according to vague categories. Next we stuffed them into garbage bags and old boxes John kept under the sink.

"What about in there?" I asked, pointing to the locked door.

He hesitated. Then he unlocked the second bedroom and slipped inside. A moment later he came out with a few small things. He'd entered and exited quickly, didn't turn on a light, so I couldn't see what was on the other side of the door. I stared at him and made it clear I was annoyed.

"I'll show you what I'm working on," he said, "when it's finished."

We moved on to the master bedroom. We pulled all her clothes from the closet and crammed all her shawls and scarves and shoes into a laundry basket. We carried the bags and boxes down the stairs into the chilly night air. We filled the trunk and backseat of my car with Grace's possessions, all of it bound for my mother's house.

At the time, I thought he was choosing to live.

John invited me back upstairs for another scotch. I looked at my phone and realized how very, very late I was for dinner with Nicole. I cursed, gave John his customary Toronto man hug, and sprinted home. After the scotches, driving was out of the question.

Nicole wasn't home when I got there but it was clear that she had come and gone. Her work clothes were scattered across the furniture and her fall jacket was on the floor. She'd torn a sheet of paper from her notebook and left it on the kitchen counter. The note said *Thanks for dinner* and she'd cross-hatched a picture of a chubby bird with long tail feathers. I brushed my teeth, put the kimchi on the counter, and considered having another drink.

"Way to go, you dipshit," I said to myself. I left the apartment again and dashed to the Cuckoo.

The night air bit into my skin, strikingly cold for September, a warning of the angry winter to come. I buried my hands in my pockets. Through the front window of the Cuckoo, I could see Nicole talking with a group of people, one or two women but mostly young men. She was smiling and it was clear she was having a good time without me around.

I stood at the window watching them drink and laugh, and then I turned and walked home.

2006

JUST LIKE ANY KIDS, Grace and I sometimes fought, tormented each other, tried out behaviours to see which ones would stick. One summer day, when she was nine and I was six, we went to play in the new subdivision, a construction zone up the hill from our neighbourhood. While we were wandering inside a half-built house, Grace started screaming. I turned around and she had her leg stuck between two planks of wood in the wall, a narrow space that the contractors would one day plaster with drywall. Her plan was obvious, to squeeze through that space and hide on me, only she had gotten stuck on her way through.

I saw my chance, got right in her face and had the last laugh. She cried, no words, only wailing and swatting at me feebly. I wanted her to sweat, so I left her for a satisfying minute and watched with satisfaction.

Once my gloating was over, though, it was clear that something was wrong. She sounded too serious, too hysterical, in too much pain. She was pointing toward the floor. I looked down and was horrified: the problem wasn't that her leg was stuck, but rather that

she'd stepped on a nail. I had no idea how long she had been pointing at her foot.

I remember the nail being huge and rust-coloured, pushed
straight through the sole and poking out the top of her shoe. It was
the ugliest thing I had ever seen. I started crying, too, and ran home
as fast as I could to get help. Our father pulled the station wagon up
to the construction zone, grumbling the whole way, yanked Grace
off the nail without hesitation. We went straight to the hospital,
Grace got shots, and for the rest of the summer she hobbled.

I felt wretched about the incident, an unlovable little brother,
but Grace never held it against me. If anything, it was times like
these that actually bound us together. And after that day, whenever
I saw pain ripple across my sister's face, I recognized it immediately,
viscerally.

—

"You really want to hear this?" Grace asked me.

We were sitting in the Cuckoo at a small table, about a month
after I'd arrived in the city. In the middle of our table was a tea light
in a glass holder, and on either side of it were two large pint glasses
full of amber beer. The bar was dim and most of the other tables
were unoccupied. The bartender had put on some faint music and
an acoustic guitar flickered around the corners of the empty room.
I wasn't sure what day of the week it was. September was almost
over but autumn hadn't come, yet.

Grace was shawled, eyeshadowed, a little uneasy. It was the first
time I'd noticed long vertical lines around her mouth, the first time
I would have used the word *severe* to describe how my sister looked.
Her eyes were candlelit green saucers that flicked between her fidgety hands and my face.

"I should at least have an inkling of what you're doing at the university," I told her. "Need to have something to tell Mom if she calls."

She cupped her beer and tapped her rings against the glass. There was no rhythm in the sound, only the twitch of anxious energy. "Fuck Mom."

I shrugged, neutral.

"I'll have to dumb it down for you," she said. Then she grinned crookedly, amused by her own insult.

I laughed. "Humour your idiot brother."

The bartender stacked some glasses behind the counter. Grace jumped in her seat. Then she straightened herself and drank some beer using both hands to raise the glass.

"I suppose what we're trying to do is measure and quantify subjective experience," she said. "Ultimately, we'd like to do it in the absence of objectivity."

"That's the dumbed-down version?" I asked.

"Yes."

"Can you make it dumber?"

She was visibly irritated by my use of the word *dumber*. I scored it as a point for myself and gave her a smug look.

She shook her head at me, squinted, and tried again. "Did the universe exist before you were born?"

"What?" I asked. She didn't respond so I thought about her question. "O.K. It existed. So?"

"How can you be sure?" she said.

"Are these trick questions?"

"No. So how can you be sure the universe existed?"

"Well," I said. And thought again. "I mean, there's evidence. Science. Dinosaur bones and such. But I guess I can't say for sure, without any doubt, that the universe existed. Or that it exists right now. I could be some brain in a jar. Is that what you're getting at?"

"Not really." She laughed. "But maybe in a roundabout way. You say that all of this"—she swooped one arm in a wide arc—"could just be a figment of your imagination. You could be a brain in a jar and I could just be a creation of your nonconscious bits. That idea, that the only thing that really exists is pure subjectivity, that we're all just figments of your imagination, they call that solipsism. And yet you seem more convinced by dinosaur bones and science, right?"

"I guess it seems more reasonable than being a brain in a jar," I told her.

"Perfect. Yes. Exactly. 'Reasonable.' We have a reasonable degree of information that an objective reality really exists, outside of our minds. It's reasonable to think that the tree is still in the woods, even when there isn't someone there to observe it."

"Oh god," I said. "You're going to do the tree falling in the woods."

She scowled, stood, and scuttled to the bar. Her skirt was long and made of a heavy fabric and it swished like a curtain. A minute later she returned with two more pints of beer, though I wasn't nearly finished my first.

"Yes, you asshole," she said after she'd sat down again, "I'm going to do the tree falling in the woods. Let's say somebody is present, though. The tree falls and causes ripples in air pressure, which in turn are transduced into an electrical signal by specialized cells in your ear. In the end, we hear a sound. What our lab is interested in is the qualitative and quantitative difference between the objective air pressure and the subjective, perceived sounds."

I tried to envision what she was saying but kept getting stuck on something.

"It's just," I said. "Shouldn't that be easy? I mean, in a way they're the same. The form is different, air pressure and brain signals, but shouldn't they be . . . I don't know, parallel? Like a bigger air pressure change would have a larger electrical signal. Or something."

"In a way, that's true. But there are important differences. For example, Weber's Law: we hear logarithmically rather than linearly."

"What the hell does that mean?" I asked. I finished my first beer except for a ring of froth and pushed the glass to the side.

Grace said, "Jesus, it always surprises me how little you know."

I sat back in my chair and smiled. "Hey, come now. You should know exactly how little I know by this point. Anyway, your problem doesn't seem so hard. It still sounds like an equation, something that's already figured out."

Her second glass was somehow empty already. She reached across the table, took mine, and drank deeply.

"Well," she said, "you're right. Somewhat. From air pressure to perception of sound is a relatively trivial problem, although it's hardly 'figured out.' But here's the thing."

Grace leaned forward and her hair swooped down the sides of her face. The light of the candle cast her eyes yellow-white and made the shadows on her face all upside-down. "We're not interested in how objective things influence subjective experience. We're interested in subjectivity on its own. And we're starting with subjective time."

Her last word reminded me. I looked at my phone and said, "Shit. We have to go."

She got visibly excited. "See? That's exactly what we study."

I stood and put on my jacket. She picked up the empty pint glasses to stack.

"Like any other dimension," she said, "objective time can be quantized, quantified. But when you look at subjective time, it seems to speed up and slow down relative to . . ."

She trailed off. I zipped up my tattered jacket and looked to her. She still held the pint glasses, but her hands were shaking too much to slip the one glass into the other. She had focused all her concentration on the task.

"Hey," I said gently, coming around to her side of the table to take the glasses.

"I've got it," she said. "Just give me a second."

Finally she slotted one glass into the other, though the rattle was loud enough to catch the bartender's attention.

"Easy there on the goods," he shouted over in a friendly voice. He pretended to baby the pint glass he was drying with a grey towel.

She made a straight line to the bar and dropped the two glasses on the counter. She said something low and deep that I couldn't hear, but the bartender's face soured and Grace made for the exit without looking back at me.

I quickly stacked the remaining two glasses on our table and brought them to the bartender.

"Like I don't have enough bullshit to deal with," he said.

"Watch it," I snapped. It came out of me like a reflex. Over my first month in the city, the bartender and I had enjoyed a few good conversations, and so we were both surprised by my reaction. Quieter, I said, "Look. Go easy on her."

I put a few more dollars on the bar and walked away.

The bartender shouted, "Why should she get special treatment?"

I turned, ready to defend Grace, but he was looking at me kindly, without any intention of a fight. Because she's my sister, I thought. Because she's always been this way. Because I don't know.

I didn't say anything. I walked away.

—

We struck east toward Nicole's apartment. It was dark and dry and not cold. Grace smoked the end of a joint. Headlights blinded us and lit the pavement as we walked.

"So, should I start calling you Shaky or Grumpy?" I asked.

Grace dismissed me with a wave of her hand.

"I'm serious," I said. "Well, you know what I mean. What the hell was that?"

"Are you planning on getting an apartment any time soon?" Grace's dismissal of my question was obvious. She aimed the words at my feet. "You've been squatting for a month."

She was asking me to back off the conversation, and like a good brother, I did.

"Not quite a month," I told her. "But Nicole has said I'm fine to stay until I find a good place."

Grace snorted. "And how is our princess?"

"Christ, what's with you? You're the one who introduced us."

"I didn't think she'd start fucking my brother," Grace said.

I stopped walking. Grace continued for a few steps. When I didn't follow she stopped and turned to me. "What?"

"Grace," I said. "Are you all right? What's with all this bullshit?"

Her head was shaking back and forth unhappily, *no, no, no.* The streetlamps blackened out her eyes whenever cars weren't passing us.

"Can we just keep walking?" she said.

I started moving again, all the while keeping my eyes on her. We fell into step and she turned to me, aped my concerned stare and turned her palms upward, *what.* Then she checked her behaviour, face a little ashamed, and looked at the sidewalk again. We were rounding the corner to Nicole's apartment.

"I was just thinking," she said.

"You were thinking."

"Maybe you and I could find a place together," she said.

I stopped in my tracks again.

"Jesus, walk!" she said. "You're the one who's in a rush."

"And what about John?" I asked, catching up to her. "You two just moved in together."

"'What about John?' You're supposed to be on my team. I don't love that you two are becoming such fast friends."

We brought our voices down as we passed the persimmon tree and neared the basement apartment door. The bulb above the door washed out the colour on the siding of the house.

"I'm on your team," I said. "I thought things were fine between you and John."

"It's just—I need space. I need to work."

I unlocked the door with my key. Nicole and I didn't call it the *spare* key anymore.

"He's at home," Grace said. "He's at the lab. Everywhere I go, there he is. I'm being consumed by his attention."

"Hello?" I shouted into the apartment. The lights were on but the living room was vacant. I turned back to Grace. "So you're annoyed that he's being what? Clingy?"

"In here," came Nicole's voice. The bedroom.

"I just need my space to work," Grace said quietly. "I'm getting close."

"Come here for a sec," Nicole shouted.

"I'll be right back, Shaky," I said to Grace. I raised my hands as if to put them on her shoulders and all their layers, but Grace frowned at me and took a small step back. I laughed. "Grumpy."

I walked into the bedroom.

Nicole was looking into the mirror above the dresser, the reflection of her eyes on me at the doorway. From her slender ankles upward she was one smooth line, an *S*. The back zip of her dress was still half-open and the line of her black bra cut across the exposed skin of her back. She was long legs and hips contrapposto and bare arms raised with her hands to her head. She pinned her orange hair up with her face turned and mouth just a little open. I watched it all and she watched me. The make-up was dark around her eyes. Her lips were red.

The amusement was too much for her and she smiled, closed her eyes. "Well. Hello."

I walked up behind her.

"You look good." I spoke into the nape of her neck and its downy hair brushed against my lips. There was the smell of fresh fruit.

She turned to me. We scuffled a little, our faces and bellies pressed together. I tugged her back zip down. Her kiss turned into a laugh and she smacked my hands away. She tugged the zipper up again and turned around so I could finish its ascent.

"Flatter me more," she said. My hands were on her shoulders, her arms.

"You smell like oranges," I said.

"Too factual."

"You are impossibly attractive."

"Mmm. Boy whimsy, but still too factual."

She leaned forward to pick up jewellery from the dresser. I tugged at the belt around the waist of her dress and kept our hips close together. She raised her arms again and fastened pearls around her neck.

"Christ," I said, "I want to bed you right now."

"Then do it," Nicole said.

"Can't. My sister's in the other room."

"Tell her to go. We'll meet her there. She's an adult." She tugged at my belt.

I stepped back. "No. Let's go."

"Oh." Nicole looked startled for a moment, but then composed herself. "All right. Leave it to the princess to spoil the party."

Princess. From surprise I laughed, one sharp sound.

Nicole turned to face me, questioningly. Her posture was perfect.

I coughed. "It's a good expression. Never mind. We should get moving."

She stood still for a moment, a flicker of doubt playing across her face. Then she walked over to the closet. She chose a thin cardigan, hung it over her shoulder, and glanced at me coyly as she left the bedroom.

—

Over the last month I'd passed the Fortress a few times on the way to Grace's apartment, but this was the first time I'd paid it any attention. Its outside was grime and graffiti, the adjacent sidewalk covered in cigarettes and old flattened gum, but it managed to exude an excitement, the hum of potential through its reverberating walls and its chirping line-up. Lee, Steve, and Brian were in the middle of that line when we arrived, all of whom I'd seen multiple times since we'd met in August. I stood between cosmopolitan Nicole and bohemian Grace, less fashionable than either of them.

"Lookit this young 'un," Brian said, pointing at me.

"Quite the harem," Lee said, which was doubly funny to all because one of the women was my sister. "And he can't even grow hair on his face yet."

"Not true," I told her. "I just believe in this thing called *shaving*. I know these other guys haven't heard of it, but it's pretty great."

The women started their greetings. The men swayed together like trees.

"Where's John?" I asked.

"Aw, he's sweet," Brian cooed. "True bros."

Steve joined in. "Dude love."

"I can see up your nose," I told Steve, then looked to Brian. "And you. You're just a dick."

Brian laughed. "Sweet and sensitive little fucker. You're fitting in just fine, so far."

"John knows somebody at the door," Steve said.

Beside the entrance to the Fortress was a set of stairs, painted black and filthy with use, and a line of people shuffling. John was there, talking to the bouncer, who smiled, nodded, clamped his considerable hand on John's shoulder and waved us up into Ramp Art, the Fortress's dance club.

On our way in, John greeted us all warmly, and then gave Grace a squeeze. She was wide-eyed, as usual, but her face was otherwise unreadable in response to the affection.

It was a fifties and sixties pop music night. Nicole, the only one of our gang dressed nearly appropriately, disappeared into the crowd of revival fashion. The rest of us were too contemporary to blend.

We drank. We cheered. We shouted over the music and twisted to the simple rhythms. We drank more. I watched Nicole dance, joined her, couldn't stand the proximity without pawing at her, couldn't be so close to her damp skin in the darkness, and went back for more drinks.

John and Grace stood facing the bar, he leaning in to whisper to her. I came up on John's side and ordered another beer. John and Grace were drinking from small, wide glasses. I got their attention, clowned with my eyes as if to say, *What's that?*

John pushed his glass to me. I took a mouthful, swallowed, hacked, forced my jaw open. It felt as if I'd poured acid down my throat. I pushed the glass back to him.

Grace shook her head, looked away. She was amused but embarrassed for me.

"Not so much, next time," John shouted.

"'Next time'?" I laughed. "Eugh. What is it?"

"Scotch." He took a sip.

"Tastes like fire. I've got the mouth sweats."

We stood together and listened to the thrum of music. I scanned for Nicole but could see only Steve and Lee dancing. It looked like an adult dancing with a child.

"Any idea if you're going to keep staying at Nicole's place?" John asked.

I searched his face for subtext, more meaning, but found only his usual warmth.

I said, "Honestly? I'd like that."

"Things are good, then?"

"Things are great." I drank from my new beer and then said what I was thinking. "Trouble loves Danger."

He nodded once and clinked my bottle with his glass.

Lee came over to me, pulling Steve in tow.

"Haven't forgotten, have you?" she asked.

I turned my head, squinted at her.

"Thursday."

"Oh," I shouted. "Yeah, the job interview. When is Thursday?"

Steve and Lee laughed hard. John had been distracted by a girl talking to him on the side opposite to Grace.

Lee said, "You're telling me you don't know what day of the week it is today."

I shrugged. Steve and Lee laughed again.

"Wednesday," Lee said.

I could still feel the scotch roiling my guts. "Ah, O.K. Well, I won't miss it. Thanks again for arranging it."

There was some commotion near me, near John and Grace, but I was trying to focus on Lee to show appreciation.

"Happy to help!" she shouted. "Grace said you needed a job, you seem bright, and I'm on my way out of there anyway. The husband's a bit of a pushover but the wife is a great boss. And anyway, it's easy work. You spend most of your day begging the government for money, essentially."

I felt someone bump into my back, and when I turned I found John and Grace standing in a triangle with a girl I'd never met. The girl had backed into me, away from Grace.

"Come on," she said. "Relax."

"'Relax'?" Grace repeated.

"I asked him where he was from," the girl said. "Like, originally. That's all. Relax."

"'Where he was from'? Like where he got his slanty eyes and yellow skin?"

"Grace," John said.

"No," Grace shot back at him, and then to the girl again. "You. Piss off. Find somebody else to take advantage of you."

The girl took a breath as if she wanted to say more, but then just looked at John pityingly and walked away.

"All right," John said to Grace. "We're done. I'm taking you home."

"John," I said. "Don't talk to her like that."

There was a flicker across my sister's face, that familiar expression of pain, and she made straight for the door. John was about to follow her but I put up my hand.

"I've got it," I said.

"Everything's fine," John said. "She's just working too hard, bringing the stress home with her. A little aggression is healthy, logical."

"Tell Nicole I'll be back."

—

I was annoyed, partly because of the way things had gotten out of hand, and partly because it wasn't surprising for things with Grace to get out of hand. Then I reached the street and saw her standing on her own, wiping her mouth with the back of her hand, a splash of vomit off the curb and the Fortress line-up all giving her a wide berth. She looked in both directions and no one would look back at her. She was a bundle of clothes too heavy for the weather and abandoned near the road.

I put my hand on her elbow and walked her toward the apartment. "Tell me about time."

"Fucking John," she said, knuckling her damp eyes. "He's supposed to be on my team."

"O.K.," I said. "Look. Tell me about subjective time."

We left the club behind but not the crowd. Bloor Street was bustling right up to the door between the two sushi restaurants, what was quickly becoming in my mind a regular Wednesday in Toronto. Grace stayed quiet all the way, just little wisps of words when she exhaled. She unlocked the door and we took the stairs up to her apartment. I went to the kitchen, made her some instant coffee, and when I got back to the living room she was spread across the couch and under a heavy blanket. She looked very drunk.

I helped her sit up and handed her a cup that wasn't too full. She used both hands to hold it.

"I never understood how you could drink this shit any time of day," I said. "Or at all, really."

"Space and time are the same thing," she replied.

I nodded, not wanting to argue.

She noticed. "No, fuck. They are. That's why it's referred to as the fourth dimension."

I couldn't avoid it. "But it isn't the same, Grace."

"Why not?"

"Well, in space we're . . . free. We can go anywhere, right? But time only moves forward."

She smiled, proud. Her eyelids sagged with fatigue. "See, you and I *are* related, after all."

She handed me her mug. She held out her finger horizontally and pointed at its knuckle with a finger from her other hand.

"Does my finger exist here?"

She then pointed at the tip of her finger.

"Or does my finger exist here?"

I put her mug on the coffee table. "What do you mean? It exists at both points."

"So do I exist now," she said, "or do I exist as the teenaged girl who shaved her head?"

Grace had used an electric razor, and the mound of hair she left in the garbage had looked like a dead animal. I'd watched her leave the bathroom, bald except for some wispy bits around the edges, and was hurt that she didn't even seem to notice me.

"Now," I told her. "You only exist now."

She slid low on the couch and pulled the blanket to her mouth.

"I wish you were right," she said. Her words were loose, slurred. "But objectively, it's both. Subjectively, we can't experience more than one 'now,' one little cross-section of time, as the here and now. We sense time moving forward because we have access to the past, but it's all there."

"This is why you play with lab rats? You think you're going to—what? Rodent time travel? Astral projection?"

She turned away from me and faced the back of the couch. "Fuck. Forget it. I don't need your help, or John's. I can do this myself. Nobody tortures rats but themselves. Nobody mentioned fucking time travel. I'm talking about just plain *travel*, about access."

"I'm sorry. I was just trying to keep up our usual banter." I laid my hand on her shoulder, through the blanket. She shuddered and rolled back to look at me.

"Just imagine you could be the past and the present and the future you, all at the same time," she said. "Imagine you had full access. Imagine you knew everything was going to work out, or even if it wasn't going to work out, at least you'd be ready for what's coming. The things you could tell yourself, the intellectual conversations, how quickly you could learn. Imagine how much of a comfort it could be. It's going to be all right. Be proud of yourself. This doesn't destroy you."

"What doesn't destroy you?" I asked.

She didn't answer. Her eyes lay vacant, and just as I began to suspect she was falling asleep, they lit up again. "I think there's more than one dimension of time."

I waited for her to explain but instead her breathing became slow and regular. After a few minutes I switched off the lights and made my way to the door.

As I pulled on my shoes she roused and shouted, "We're living on a fucking sphere of time."

"Yes, we are. Goodnight, Grace."

Without the key, I couldn't lock the door behind me.

Back on the street it felt a little colder. Nicole was standing alone outside the Fortress, a cigarette glowing between her fingers. She looked indifferent to everything, and I wasn't sure why but it was beautiful.

I wrapped her in my arms, careful of the cigarette's burner, and asked, "Can we go home?"

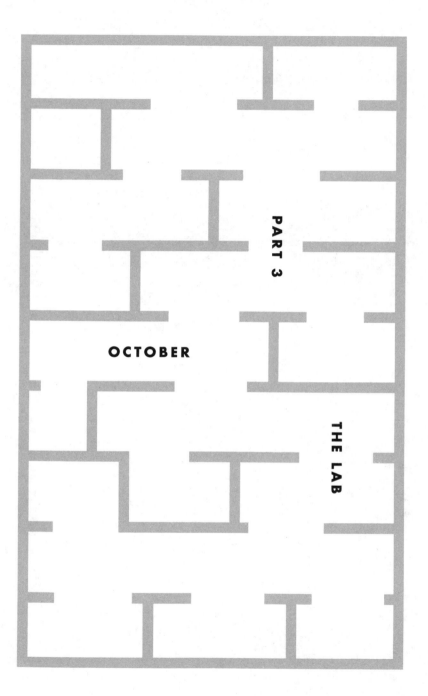

PART 3

OCTOBER

THE LAB

2008

OUTSIDE THE BATHROOM WINDOW it is a crisp, grey, early October morning.

I take a long look at myself in the mirror above the dirty sink. My new clothes were bought specifically for today, a grey hoodie with a pouch and black sweatpants. They are loose and unflattering but they hide the layer of clothes I wear underneath and will blend perfectly with the university undergraduates. My face is concealed by a coarse and wiry beard that has taken months to grow, at first out of indifference but now deliberately. For flair I've added a base-ball cap with a long bill, and the shag of my hair creeps out from underneath it. Altogether it's a nearly perfect disguise.

Except the eyes. I have never considered my eyes to be remark-able but now it feels as if they're a dead giveaway. Not even the new lines in my skin, the subtle crow's feet and sunken-eyed creases of worry, can lessen this. That familial intense green, so similar to Grace's. I scour the bedroom until I find an old, scratched-up pair of sunglasses. I look in the mirror again. With my eyes hidden, the deception is complete.

"O.K.," I say. "You are the detective. You are the spy."

There are only a few preparations left. I remove the keys for my car and the apartment from my keychain and put them into my sweat-pants pocket. I place the other keys on the lip of the sink. I grab my electric razor, give it a quick flip of the switch, its hum reassuring in my hands, and then bury it in the pouch of my hoodie. From the floor next to my bed, I pick up a portable flash drive.

Back in the kitchen, I take the wire lid off Buddy's cage and scoop him up. If he's aware that today is a special day, he makes no sign of it. His body relaxes in my hand and he sniffs idly toward me as I inspect him. His eyes are black and featureless, only the hint of a bluish line around the eyelid.

"O.K., you turd," I say. "No funny business today. I need your help."

I slip him into the pouch of the hoodie, next to the razor and the flash drive. Buddy burrows in.

Next to the cage is John's blue lab notebook. I flip to its front page and run through the instructions one last time:

Key fob then
4-2510- then
2510#- then
2510

At the front door I select my most nondescript shoes from the pile, a pair of slim black runners with dark-grey eyelets, and slide them on. I double-knot the laces so that they won't untie but will still easily slide off and on again.

My landlord is in the garden outside of the apartment when I exit. He is a tiny, soft man and he's worn a white shirt and white trousers to do his gardening. It makes him look filthy to have such pale clothes smeared with dirt.

"Ah, hello," he says as I'm closing the apartment door.

"Good morning," I shout with my back to him. I lock the door and, pretending I'm inspecting my shoes, slide the apartment key under the mat. I turn to greet him and he's standing on the patch of dirt where the persimmon tree used to be. I say, "It was a shame to see it go."

"Eh?" He looks at me strangely.

It was foolish to get into my disguise at the apartment. Now he's seen me dressed this way. I curse myself silently.

"The persimmon tree," I tell him. "I miss the tree."

But still his face is cocked, puzzled. "Eh? What tree?"

There is a quiet moment where neither of us breathes. I look to the earth that used to house the tree, and back to his uncomprehending glare. *What tree?* He wipes the dirt into his white pants and looks at me expectantly.

I consider my options, then give him an apologetic smile and walk away. As I approach the car I bury my hands in the pouch of the hoodie, one hand wrapped around the razor and the other stroking Buddy's soft fur.

———

I park the car just east of Bathurst and College, a busy, anonymous intersection near Shifty's and a city block from my final destination. A credit card bill for parking could later prove I was here, so I pay with coins. The autumn day is too grey for sunglasses and too chilly for only a sweatshirt, but that is my disguise. I keep one hand on Buddy, to warm him and ensure that the little bastard doesn't slip away again.

I walk east. At Spadina Avenue the buildings start to shift from low-rise commercial to ornate university architecture. The only people lingering in this liminal zone are waiting for the soup kitchen to open. I turn north into a shrubbed alleyway and walk slowly, waiting for my opportunity. The animal facility is just up ahead, an unimposing concrete cube with tiny windows and a security door. This is where Buddy came from.

The hardest part will be the beginning. John seemed to have thought things through, and his key fob was probably in plain sight in their apartment, but I didn't see it and now it's too late. Without the key fob, getting through the inner doors will require following someone in. No one is coming down the alley from either end, yet. I slow myself as naturally as I can, turn around, pretend to have forgotten something outside of the alley. Then I pace back to the entrance of the alleyway, walk to the intersection, turn around, and try again.

This time I'm luckier. A young woman is heading toward me and it takes very little work for me to synchronize my arrival at the entrance with hers. She's probably a graduate student or researcher, fair hair in a ponytail, no make-up or jewellery. As we approach each other she smiles at me confidently. I grin but also don't want to attract too much attention. We converge at the glass door to the facility, which I open for her, and she turns to glance at me as we walk inside.

In the alcove I see the wall-mounted security system and a laminated note above it proclaiming

FACILITY PERSONNEL ONLY
UNAUTHORIZED ENTRY PROHIBITED
IT IS EVERY FACILITY MEMBER'S RESPONSIBILITY
TO PROTECT THIS ENTRANCE

The young woman is looking at me, polite but cautious. She digs in her pocket for her key fob but she's also stalling to size me up.

I need to build trust with her and so I take a calculated risk: I remove my sunglasses and look directly at her.

"Good morning," I say in as honest a voice as I can muster, considering I'm trying to break into a restricted university building.

She's cute in a very plain way and has the glistening skin of an athlete. She scrutinizes my eyes and then holds her key fob to the security system. Its little light goes green and the latch clicks as it unlocks. I reach out to pull open the second door for her and follow her inside. I try to swallow down my racing heartbeat but my mouth is dry.

We both nod at the tired security guard across the spacious foyer and make our way to the next barrier. My eyes don't linger on the guard and I can only hope that his don't linger on me. The young woman walks in step with me and has her head turned as if she'd like to make small talk. The only sound is the scuffle of our soft shoes against the tiled floor.

We come to the next door and she pauses. It's clear from her lack of action that I'm expected to open this barrier. My abdomen squirms and I'm not sure whether it's my viscera or Buddy spinning around in the pouch of my hoodie.

I look to the twelve-button number pad next to the door, rehearse John's instructions in my head, and hope the code still works. I don't see a hyphen on the number pad so I make a guess.

With my thumb I press *4 2 5 1 0.*

The light above the security pad goes green and again I hear the click of a lock.

The young woman exhales just loudly enough to be heard. I open the door for her and do my best to withhold my own sigh of relief. Buddy and I are in.

—

The men's changing room reminds me of a public pool, stalls and benches and sinks surrounded by concrete walls and blue laminate wood. Instead of chlorine, it smells of disinfectant. Buddy and I are the only ones in the room. I change into a set of blue hospital scrubs and throw my street clothes, electric razor, and shoes into an empty locker. Buddy wanders back and forth on the bench in the changing stall, casually shits on the wood, one dark wet bolus, and looks up at me.

"You must be feeling awfully proud of yourself," I say to him.

He turns and sniffs at his own shit, his pink nose expanding and contracting.

I grab an extra hospital scrub shirt, stuff Buddy and the flash drive inside, and jam the bundle under my arm. Buddy will be uncomfortable for a minute or two but hopefully he'll be O.K. I slip on a pair of foam shoes near the exit, punch the code *2 5 1 0* and the pound sign on another keypad, and head inside.

The animal facility is a sterile labyrinth. Each hallway seems to stretch and branch endlessly, bland beige and blue tunnels with cold lighting from above. The walls, ceiling, and lights are all segmented and I can't help feeling as if I'm wandering down the inside of a worm. My borrowed shoes are bouncy against the hard floor. The facility is extremely clean and brightly lit but there is a faint trace of something dank in the air. At even intervals are mirrored domes that likely house security cameras, and they make me thankful for my beard and unkempt hair covering my features. I walk past doors with thick panes of glass, turn randomly down hallways, and search for anything that may seem familiar. It has been two years since Grace first showed me this facility.

Eventually I recognize my surroundings. The entire floor may be painted and lit the same way but I have seen this particular configuration of doors and windows, and at the end of the hall is the entrance to Grace and John's supervisor's laboratory. This door has a five-button security lock, with two numbers sharing each button. I punch in the final code, *2 5 1 0*, and watch the green light illuminate. The door opens inward.

The anteroom is small and cluttered with rolling plastic cabinets, boxes of rubber gloves, and hanging lab coats. Opposite the room's entrance is another door, this one with a viewing portal, and through it I see no researchers, only stacked cages. I unwrap Buddy from the blue shirt and set him on my right shoulder. He paces across the back of my neck to my left shoulder, and scurries back again in agitation when I push through the next door into the pitch-black rat colony. My nostrils are flooded with the smell of piss and my ears are filled with the din of hundreds of animals rattling the wire lids of their cages. On the other side of the colony room is the final door, wedged open with a piece of wood, and a little lacquered sign that says *Procedure Room*. It takes a few hard kicks to get the wedge out and the door closed behind me.

In the centre of the procedure room is what I came for: a dark Plexiglas cube that's big enough to house a rat. In the shelving underneath the cube I find extra Plexiglas panels, one with a rubber-lined hole in it, and messy wires that sprout from an electrical box. The wires feed to a desktop computer that sits on a long stainless steel bench. On the shelf above the bench are stacks of papers as well as some other computer supplies, tools, and jagged pieces of plastic and metal.

I have been in this very room once before, but only now does it occur to me: its layout, contents, and purpose are strikingly similar to those of the second bedroom of John and Grace's apartment. It's hard to pin down, but it concerns me that John's wooden box has no wires, no overt mechanisms. In its elegance it seems more sophisticated, more dangerous than this laboratory setup.

"O.K.," I say to Buddy. "Enough wasting time. Let's get moving."

He pays no attention to me. His long whiskers and nose are

twitching furiously and he's dangling off my shoulder to sniff the room. It appears he remembers this place.

I turn on the computer monitor and find an unexpected challenge: the desktop has many log-in names and each is password protected. There are only two names I recognize, John's and Grace's, so I try my sister's log-in first. There is a small "?" icon to the right of the password space and when I press it I'm given a hint that was written by the user.

I realize that if through science I can seize phenomena and enumerate them, I cannot, for all that, ____.

I know this. I remember this. An argument between Grace and Nicole. A talk with John. I've even read this recently: Camus. But I can't remember how the quote ends. I try typing *understand reality* but the system warns me it will lock me out after two more failed attempts.

"Goddamn it," I say to myself, "your head is full of garbage."

I click back to the list of names and try John's log-in instead. His user hint displays as:

The street where I grew up led to a ____.

I type *dead end* and hit the Return key. John's account opens up to me.

I laugh out loud and clench a fist in victory. I am the detective, the spy.

John's desktop background image is a complex geometry of white and grey lines, and the brightness of the monitor makes me squint. There are three program icons along the left side of the screen and many document icons along the right side. I click through the programs, past the spreadsheet and statistics software, and double-click on the icon labelled *Telemetrics 4.0*. A four-windowed program opens with a large *START* button in the top-right corner. Clicking it pops open a message window in the centre of the screen:

Place telemetry device on reader and press OK to continue.

My head doesn't feel so full of garbage after all.

I grab a notebook and pen from the lacquered shelf above my head. The notebook is mostly blank and I tear a sheet from it and write: *I'm coming for you. Hold on.* The shelf and bench are full of supplies but there are no elastic bands, only silver duct tape. I pull a piece of tape from the roll, fold my note into quarters, and adhere the note to the tape. Then I press it against the base of Buddy's neck until it sticks to his fur. Buddy is unhappy with the sensation and spins a few times in discontent. I scoop him up one last time and press my thumb against the hard, manmade nub buried in his belly. *Place telemetry device on reader.*

I walk him over to the black plastic cube and slide open one wall. It's no surprise to find that the inside is covered in mirrors, glinting from the reflection of the artificial lighting above me. Without complaint or hesitation, Buddy scrambles down my arm and into the box. He turns and stares at me, waiting.

I say, "Bring me back something useful, Buddy."

Then I slide the box's wall back into place.

Back at the computer, clicking the *OK* button causes the program to flash *Connection found.* Jagged lines begin to draw themselves across the screen—the telemetry device in Buddy's belly is transmitting its signal and the computer is receiving it. Each line on the screen is labelled: *ECG, EEG, EMG, TMP.* It reminds me of the inscrutable algebra written inside John's lab notebook, how I'd briefly considered that it might be a code, except that none of the "words" repeated and thus substituting letters had revealed nothing.

The jittery lines continue to arc across the computer monitor, presumably some measures of Buddy's well-being, along with a stopwatch measuring the duration of his time in the box.

I minimize the Telemetrics program and look at the many files on the desktop of the computer. Most are named by time and date, and when opened reveal only a spreadsheet of numbers. But one file's name is vaguely familiar, *Tabula Recta*. I open it and immediately remember it from John's apartment:

	A	B	C	D	E	F	G	H	I	J	K	L	M	N	O	P	Q	R	S	T	U	V	W	X	Y	Z
A	A	B	C	D	E	F	G	H	I	J	K	L	M	N	O	P	Q	R	S	T	U	V	W	X	Y	Z
B	B	C	D	E	F	G	H	I	J	K	L	M	N	O	P	Q	R	S	T	U	V	W	X	Y	Z	A
C	C	D	E	F	G	H	I	J	K	L	M	N	O	P	Q	R	S	T	U	V	W	X	Y	Z	A	B
D	D	E	F	G	H	I	J	K	L	M	N	O	P	Q	R	S	T	U	V	W	X	Y	Z	A	B	C
E	E	F	G	H	I	J	K	L	M	N	O	P	Q	R	S	T	U	V	W	X	Y	Z	A	B	C	D
F	F	G	H	I	J	K	L	M	N	O	P	Q	R	S	T	U	V	W	X	Y	Z	A	B	C	D	E
G	G	H	I	J	K	L	M	N	O	P	Q	R	S	T	U	V	W	X	Y	Z	A	B	C	D	E	F
H	H	I	J	K	L	M	N	O	P	Q	R	S	T	U	V	W	X	Y	Z	A	B	C	D	E	F	G
I	I	J	K	L	M	N	O	P	Q	R	S	T	U	V	W	X	Y	Z	A	B	C	D	E	F	G	H
J	J	K	L	M	N	O	P	Q	R	S	T	U	V	W	X	Y	Z	A	B	C	D	E	F	G	H	I
K	K	L	M	N	O	P	Q	R	S	T	U	V	W	X	Y	Z	A	B	C	D	E	F	G	H	I	J
L	L	M	N	O	P	Q	R	S	T	U	V	W	X	Y	Z	A	B	C	D	E	F	G	H	I	J	K
M	M	N	O	P	Q	R	S	T	U	V	W	X	Y	Z	A	B	C	D	E	F	G	H	I	J	K	L
N	N	O	P	Q	R	S	T	U	V	W	X	Y	Z	A	B	C	D	E	F	G	H	I	J	K	L	M
O	O	P	Q	R	S	T	U	V	W	X	Y	Z	A	B	C	D	E	F	G	H	I	J	K	L	M	N
P	P	Q	R	S	T	U	V	W	X	Y	Z	A	B	C	D	E	F	G	H	I	J	K	L	M	N	O
Q	Q	R	S	T	U	V	W	X	Y	Z	A	B	C	D	E	F	G	H	I	J	K	L	M	N	O	P
R	R	S	T	U	V	W	X	Y	Z	A	B	C	D	E	F	G	H	I	J	K	L	M	N	O	P	Q
S	S	T	U	V	W	X	Y	Z	A	B	C	D	E	F	G	H	I	J	K	L	M	N	O	P	Q	R
T	T	U	V	W	X	Y	Z	A	B	C	D	E	F	G	H	I	J	K	L	M	N	O	P	Q	R	S
U	U	V	W	X	Y	Z	A	B	C	D	E	F	G	H	I	J	K	L	M	N	O	P	Q	R	S	T
V	V	W	X	Y	Z	A	B	C	D	E	F	G	H	I	J	K	L	M	N	O	P	Q	R	S	T	U
W	W	X	Y	Z	A	B	C	D	E	F	G	H	I	J	K	L	M	N	O	P	Q	R	S	T	U	V
X	X	Y	Z	A	B	C	D	E	F	G	H	I	J	K	L	M	N	O	P	Q	R	S	T	U	V	W
Y	Y	Z	A	B	C	D	E	F	G	H	I	J	K	L	M	N	O	P	Q	R	S	T	U	V	W	X
Z	Z	A	B	C	D	E	F	G	H	I	J	K	L	M	N	O	P	Q	R	S	T	U	V	W	X	Y

"Fuck me," I say. John's notebook *is* in code. I don't fully understand yet, but somehow the code is moving, shifting, which is why none of the "algebra" seems to repeat.

The computer tower beeps to report an error. Back in the rat-monitoring program's window, the message *Connection lost* is blinking in the bottom-right panel. The jagged lines have all flattened out and become unresponsive. Buddy's signal is gone, and I'm not sure if this is what's supposed to happen.

I approach the cube in the middle of the room. Even leaning with an ear close reveals nothing of what's happening inside the box. I wait one more breath and then slide a wall upward. Sure enough, aside from my reflection, the box is empty.

"Can I help you?" a voice asks from behind me.

—

My body startles without my consent, head pulled down, shoulders up, eyes pinched half-shut. I set my jaw and pivot on one heel.

In front of me is the young woman I met at the entrance. A surgical mask and blue hairnet conceal most of her face but she's still recognizable. She's wearing a yellow gown over her hospital clothes.

"What gave it away?" I ask.

"Your eyes," she says. "I mean, you sort of look like her, but the eyes are exactly the same."

I curse myself silently.

"And we've met once before, haven't we?" she says.

I think back but nothing comes to me. She continues.

"You were holding some party for John. I was with a few colleagues and one of them interrupted your little get-together."

This jolts my memory. "Shifty's, last year."

"She'd been gone awhile, then. I couldn't get over how similar you looked. It was eerie." She takes a step forward, pulls down her surgical mask. "Did you use one of their codes to get in?"

I nod. "John's."

"Then you don't have much time. Security'll notice his number in the system and come take a look."

She takes another step into the procedure room. She looks past me, into the small box where Buddy used to be, and her eyes widen.

"Did you put an animal in there?" She speaks again before I can answer. "*What* animal did you put in there?"

"We always just called him Buddy."

She gets animated now, visibly excited, and paces around the room. Then she asks, "Do you have any idea how long we've been trying to make this thing work again?"

"About a year, I'd say. Since John stopped coming to the lab."

"What are we missing? There must be another component. Why does it only work with John's animals?"

Her eyes betray her busy mind, straying from me for just a moment. Then she collects herself. "Listen to me, now. I can help you escape the facility without any chance of getting caught. I know a way out."

I can guess where this is going, but I ask anyway. "And why would you help me?"

She says slowly, deliberately, "The animal. I want it. We need it."

Her cheeks are smooth and clean and fresh. She's probably a little younger than me.

I gesture to the empty box. "As you can see, I have no rat to give you."

"You know how to get it back," she says.

"I need him, too."

"What could a person like you possibly need him for? His data?"

I laugh once, in part because I'm offended and in part because I'm amused. She sounds like Grace.

I say, "Christ, are all scientists so condescending?"

"I could make you a copy of all the data," she tells me. "John's files. Whatever you need."

Her offer is exactly what I came for but something doesn't feel right. Deep in me is a gnawing sensation. It takes a moment for it to come to the surface.

"What will you do with him?" I ask.

She grunts. "The animal? Look at its data, sacrifice it, see what's possibly different about this particular subject."

Sacrifice it. Kill Buddy. I say, "I can't let you do that."

She coughs. It sounds like she's trying to hold back a laugh. I like her less and less with every passing moment. How can someone so young and fresh be so callous?

She takes a deep breath and composes herself. "It's a lab rat that was bred for one reason. It belongs to this lab. It's stolen property, for god's sake! And you don't want me to have it because of sentimental reasons?"

"Yes. Exactly. He's my last connection."

She stiffens up and sighs. "Fine, then. I'll go get security. We'll figure out how to bring the animal back on our own. And all you'll get out of this is a criminal record."

She says it as a threat, a last chance for me to strike a deal. I don't move or speak or acknowledge what she's said in any way. Her face registers growing surprise, then furrowed annoyance, and finally she clomps out of the room.

I don't have much time. Buddy needs to come back, and quickly.

"Come on, detective, spy," I say to myself. "Think."

And then I realize the ugly reality of what must be done. My mouth goes dry, my heart hammers, and I resist the thought for a moment. Then I take a deep breath and get to work.

I remove one panel from the Plexiglas cube and replace it with the piece that has a rubber-lined hole. The box no longer looks rat-sized, but instead looks wrist-and-hand-sized. The procedure room seems to throb with damp air, and tears of sweat trickle down my ribs. This is an idiotic plan. And before I can back out of it, I rush forward and jam my right fist into the box.

At first there's no difference, but soon the temperature drops inside the cube and my hand stings with coldness. I splay my fingers into the depths of the box but, strangely, nothing is in reach. Judging with my eyes, my fingertips should be able to touch the opposite inside wall of the box. I slide my arm a little farther but still I cannot feel the mirrored wall. There is no doubt now that the inside of the box is bigger than the outside. My stomach turns.

"Oh Christ," I mutter, because of what I'm seeing, and because of what I'm about to do.

I move my arm slowly but steadily forward. The rubber-lined hole in the box envelops my forearm, then elbow, then bicep, but my fingers never reach the inside boundaries of the box, and they never pop out the other side. From my perspective it appears that my arm has been removed and replaced with a small cube of black Plexiglas. The sight of my body without my arm is horrifying. The only comfort is the sensation I'm receiving from my hand, the chilly bite of what seems like outdoor air, the feeble grasps into the unknown abyss. I bend my arm at the elbow, into a ninety-degree angle, and sweep my hand in as wide an arc as I can make.

The computer beeps again. I crane my head around to see the blinking message on the screen: *Connection restored.* Buddy is coming back to me. My arm is now in the box as far as it will reach, and my ribcage is flush with the Plexiglas wall. I reach upward until my hand would be above my head, if it were on this side. I stretch it down low.

My fingers brush against something frayed and wet. It takes closing my eyes to determine what I'm touching: it's grass, dewy with the night air. The blades of grass feel rigid, as if they're close to a frost. Suddenly something small and warm and moist presses against the back of my hand. I feel whiskers brush against my skin.

I turn my hand over and Buddy climbs in, a lump of fur and flesh in my palm. He is wonderfully warm and I can't help shouting with satisfaction. It's a relief when I pull back and watch my bicep and elbow reappear on this side, in the lab.

And then the most bitterly cold fingers I have ever felt wrap themselves around my wrist. They're so icy that my bones ache with the touch. I yank hard, try to escape that grasp, but my arm doesn't budge. The hand has clamped onto me like a vise and I imagine my wrist blackening with frostbite until it freezes solid. Buddy remains cupped in my palm.

Then I feel a cold piece of metal running up and down my forearm while the grip holds me in place. It is only a cold scratch at first but soon it burns as if my skin is splitting and the muscles are falling out. I scream from the pain and the sound dies quickly in the small procedure room. Inch by inch my arm is creeping back out into this world, and it is bloody and ragged. Now only my wrist and hand are inside the box, Buddy included, but the grasp is still draining the warmth out of me and will not let go. The jagged piece of metal continues running along my skin narrowing my attention until I recognize the action I must take.

With my free hand I pry at the edges of the box, desperately, until one wall panel lifts up. The cracks allow light to flood inside and reflect off the mirrors.

Instantly the vise releases my wrist. It slides out of the rubber-lined hole, leaving a ring of blood behind, until my hand and Buddy finally emerge. I switch Buddy to the other hand, hold him in the air, and inspect him. There's a little blood on him but it seems to be mine. And although his whiskers are twitching rapidly, he seems fine otherwise. My right arm, however, is ugly. The metallic thing that cut me was sharp enough to draw blood but coarse enough to scrape the surrounding tissue. The pain is both acute and throbbing. I wrap my arm in the extra scrub shirt I brought with me and the fabric sticks to my skin instantly.

There is still more left to do. The computer screen blinks with some new error, namely that Buddy's telemetry device's transmissions have fallen out of synch with the computer's receiver. I select *Save data* from the menu and record the file on my flash drive.

It occurs to me that the note is no longer taped to Buddy's back.

—

I have more than enough time to get ready for the young researcher's return with the security guard. They make a beeline through the rat colony and into the procedure room, not noticing that I'm slumped behind the stacks of cages in the dark colony. The procedure room door swings closed behind them and I rush out, shoulder first, and pin the door shut with my body weight. Then I slide the wooden wedge in place with my foot, under the crack of the door, and kick it as hard as I can, two, three times. I don't wait to see if it works but instead grab Buddy from the shelf and dash out of the lab. The researcher and the guard thump against the door as I leave, jamming the wedge even farther and locking themselves in place.

I weave down the hall as fast as I can without jogging. In the men's changing room I kick off the hospital scrubs. My makeshift bandage sops with blood. I leave it all on the floor, change back into my disguise, and Buddy happily scuttles back into the pouch of the hoodie. My shoes take a few seconds longer to slip on than I'd like, due to my trembling hands. Blood from my right arm drips and smears everywhere, but thankfully it's difficult to see on the black fabric of my shoes. My disguise is intact.

It takes only a few moments to cross through the security barriers and get to the foyer. No passwords are needed to exit. I walk confidently but without rushing through the lobby. I hear the guard behind me stop talking mid-sentence and stand up, the chair rolling out from under him.

"Excuse me," he says, and his voice cracks a little. He's just a university security guard and has likely never dealt with something like this before.

I walk faster, push through the last two doors and feel the autumn wind nip at my face as I enter the outside world. The security guard shouts at me again, this time more forcefully. I break into a sprint.

No one notices me running past the shoppers and panhandlers and university students. The sweat that covers my body takes little time to chill and soon I'm cold and clammy. My right arm screams as it moves, raw skin brushing against the rough fabric. Buddy and the electric razor bounce against my belly with each step. But all of this only faintly registers. Instead I'm focused on dodging pedestrians, jaywalking, avoiding the bullet-shaped streetcars, and returning to the brown stone building in front of which I parked my car.

I stop running, fold myself in half from all the wretched bodily feedback, and groan with sick apprehension.

My car is gone.

Two possibilities come to mind, *towed or stolen*, but neither is a solution to my current problem. I need to disappear. There doesn't seem to be anyone following me when I look back toward the animal facility, but there's also no reason to wait for them. I straighten myself out and jog west, to the corner of Bathurst.

Shifty's is nearly wall-to-wall windows across the storefront and purposefully layered in graffiti along the exposed bricks that border the windows. Even the glowing sign above and the sandwich board out front carry the same scrawled, hand-painted motif of skull and crossbones. Through the window I can see the appropriately tattooed and dishevelled crowd, my crowd. I enter the restaurant and head straight for the stairs, down to the men's washroom.

I choose one of the dirty stalls and lock the door behind me. From the pouch of the hoodie I take Buddy, the flash drive, and the electric razor, and place them all on the back of the toilet. Then I peel off my top layer of clothes, hoodie and track pants, and put the bundle on the floor. Now I look like a patron of Shifty's, with my black pants and long-sleeved black T-shirt revealed. I should feel relieved without the top layer of clothes but in actuality a thick, viscous grime of perspiration has replaced it. There are pangs where the salt of my sweat seeps into the wounds on my arm, and when I look at it, I can see no pattern. The skin is crudely damaged, as though I was attacked with the sharp end of a rock, and if I don't get stitches my arm will become a network of bubbled scar tissue.

I glance at Buddy, who is sampling the dank basement air, and then at the innumerable messages written on the walls of the bathroom stall. One note, hashed in black permanent marker, catches my eye:

Trouble loves Danger.

It is such a sad reminder. When did I write that?

And suddenly I'm a step removed from myself. I'm Nicole looking at me from a distance. And I see a bloody, sweaty man, no longer a *young man*, in a filthy toilet stall, mangled arm, shaking limbs, winded lungs, hiding from the people he's just robbed. Loveless, friendless, sisterless. My eyes get glassy, my cheeks get tight, and my jaw clenches. It's not fair. My breath whistles through the grimace of my teeth. My nose is running.

This is the thing I have become.

I want to wallow but there's one last step to removing my disguise. Aloud I say, "O.K. Enough."

I lift the seat of the toilet, vision still watery thanks to my brimming eyes, and grab the razor. The electric blade removes the beard without any trouble, and ruddy tufts of me float down into the toilet bowl. Without a mirror, I have to use my fingers to inspect my work. I start making sideburns for myself but then, in a moment of impulse, turn the razor upwards and shave the rest of my head. In a few minutes, my skull feels like a misshapen ball of stubble.

I flush my hair and leave the stall, pausing a moment to inspect my image in the mirror. My face is arresting, thinner, like my idea of a prison inmate. They're the same eyes but my shaved head makes them stand out even more. I toss the hoodie and track pants in the garbage, palm the electric razor in one hand and Buddy in the other. Buddy's long tail dangles against my leg and bobs as we make our way up the stairs. The flash drive is in my back pocket.

A slightly smaller figure almost bumps into me at the top of the stairs. At first I mistake her for a short man but there is something just a little feminine about her hips and stance. The moment throws me into confusion: in front of me, her short hair swept to one side, is certainly the tomboy from the show at the Fortress, but she's wearing heavy boots and a dark uniform with a bulky belt, a holstered pistol, and a metallic badge glinting from her breast. The realization finally comes to me.

"Officer 2510," I say.

She gives me a crooked smile. "Long time no see."

My hands instinctively move behind my back. "You, uh, used to have long hair."

She slowly, firmly shoulders me out of the way and starts down the stairs. She says, "And you used to *have* hair. Things change."

My mind races. She isn't looking for me. She doesn't know.

I cheat my body toward her, hiding Buddy and the razor, but it's ultimately for no good reason. She doesn't even look back at me. "Why do I get the sense I'll be seeing you soon?"

She doesn't wait for an answer, rounding the corner and disappearing into the women's washroom.

—

Back inside my apartment, I look up all the city towing depots. None of them have any record of my missing car. Buddy doesn't protest when I put him back in his cage, and as a reward for a hard day of work, I give him a slice of cheddar off the brick.

With no computer at home, I create my own *tabula recta* from memory, then alternate my attention between it and John's notebook: *The street where I grew up led to a dead end.* *MOIJX+NEW-T*HHVXI/NRRX+NYUWIFMWVH-HIDQBQW** *ZMXRWLDIYG/RRP* . . . There must be a relationship between the table and the code, a way to unlock the one with the other. I try shifting all the letters by a fixed amount, so that *T* equals *A*, *U* equals *B*, *V* equals *C*, and so on. I try letter substitution, with *T* as *M*, the first letter in the code, *H* as *O*, *E* as *I*, and so on. I try nonsensical things, follow hunches about diagonals in the *tabula*, circle letters of the sentence and the code. For an hour or two I get nowhere with it. And then, as I'm on the verge of passing out from exhaustion, the solution reveals itself to me all at once, unravels so completely that at first I doubt it can be so simple and also correct. *MOIJX* becomes *THERE*, *NEW* becomes *WAS*, *T* becomes *A*, and *HHVXI* becomes *LARGE*. I decode thousands of words, hours of effort, but eventually I flip a page and the solution no longer works. For now, the rest of the notebook will remain unsolved. I pick up what I've decoded and read, read it again, again.

SILHOUETTE BREAKS RANK – I

*The street where I grew up led to a dead end. There was
a large, flat, reflective diamond signalling all cars to stop,
but more importantly, it warned us that even crossing the
threshold on foot was forbidden. Beyond the dead-end sign was
undeveloped land, an impossibly large expanse of greens, greys,
and browns all knotted together into something relatively wild
for the suburbs. The plan was always to continue the road once
development had filled that area with unremarkable houses
like our own, but the street was never extended. No one would
remove the sign from the ground.*

*The dead end did have a hint of a footpath, soft and
exposed between the dried leaves and branches. But in all
the secret mornings, sprawling afternoons, and held-breath
evenings I spent wandering those streets alone or with
childhood friends, I never once saw a person using that path
where one world bled into the other.*

*This dead end offered one of many possible ways to enter
what was, to the neighbourhood children at least, a vast forest*

designed to satisfy our imaginations. It bordered the edge of our subdivision to the east. I cannot count the different games we played in those woods, the allegiances that were made and broken, or the secret places and paths designated throughout the forest. What I can count is the number of times we used the dead end to enter or exit the woods, which is precisely zero. We found other ways to the woods, over our fences, through our backyards. The woods may have been bliss for our suburban souls, but the dead-end sign was a border forbidden and completely unrelated to the forest.

Developers finally sank their teeth into our woods, late into my high school years. By then the forest was a place to nervously try our parents' liquor and talk about girls. Construction snuck up and took the trees in what seemed like a single night, and soon there were only dirt piles and machinery that kids would climb on when the contractors had left for the day. Remarkably, the dead end remained and so did its sense of foreboding. Children, teenagers, and construction workers alike avoided crossing that boundary between the undeveloped land and our neighbourhood. It was a brilliantly, collectively, unconsciously unbreakable rule that we didn't even know we knew.

We found a different park for drinking and hanging out, over by the rich neighbourhood, and I would have happily continued to be ignorant of the dead end's hidden rule if we hadn't been busted drinking rye one night. We liked to imagine ourselves as no-good teenagers who were lowering the real estate prices and soiling the lawns we were hired to cut during the summer holidays; in reality, we were the dregs of our peer group, an awkward cadre of comic-book aficionados, "nice boys." Our underage drinking was a way of inflating our self-defined cool, and thus we enjoyed the threat of authority even when we knew none was present. So that moonless evening, when a cop car cornered and pulled close to the park, probably completely at random, we were prepared to bolt.

I swung ninety degrees, legs stiff like a corpse's, and leapt off the slide I'd been sitting atop. My friends dashed in all directions and I pointed myself west, toward home. My comfortable alcoholic haze was now a frustrating fog I had to cut through if I didn't want to get caught. I imagined my father, with his Christian Korean conservative values, would have another heart attack if his only son were brought home in a cop car.

I ran. My legs took care of themselves and my arms flailed for walls and fences. I could swear I heard someone right behind me, their breath hot on the fine hairs of my neck. I hopped four fences and shimmied between a few houses before I made it to the construction zone that used to be our woods.

Everything was suddenly clear and vivid. My shoes, wet from the summer night's grass, were collecting the dust from the construction site. I could smell stale water and damp air. There was perspiration in the webs between my fingers. The saliva in my mouth was acrid from the rye. I skipped and skidded to a halt, just for a moment looking around, long enough to know that I was exposed in an open field and leaving tracks in the loose dirt under my feet. And again I knew someone was just behind me, their cold, dry fingers reaching out to grasp me and never let go. I dashed for home.

And with that looming threat behind me, some monster more menacing than adulthood or authority, I aimed myself at the dead end and crossed the threshold. The effect was transitory, just barely perceptible, but in that instant I could swear I saw light ripple and bend around me, a distortion in the world like looking into a fishbowl or a funhouse mirror.

My shoes transitioned from slippery dirt, almost mud, to the harsh friction of asphalt. I pulled around the first house on the left, our house, and tried to breathe as quietly as possible in the hopes that my pursuer would run past me.

Nighttime makes the suburbs strange. The high street lights have an orangey, vibrating tint to them that makes everything well lit and still somehow very dark. Standing in the small space between our home and our neighbours', I could see my reflection in the big bay window of the house across the street. The street was wide enough for the reflection to be distant but near enough to get a sense of what was mirrored in the glass. There I was, my hands on the bricks of my house, but somehow embedded in that window. I looked thin in that reflection, ghostly, dark holes where my eyes should be. I crouched down, and of course so did my image.

No one ran by the house. No one was chasing me.

I took the opportunity to catch my breath, stare at my filthy shoes, and think about how I would casually walk into my parents' house and pretend I was perfectly sober and not rattled from crossing that threshold. Why did it feel like I had done something wrong? Finally, when I was calm enough, I stood up and prepared myself to enter the house.

And that's when I caught sight of my reflection again in the window of the house across the street. There I was, my mirror image, one hand against the bricks and the other on the back of my neck. There was my house and my neighbours', in opposite arrangement. But in the reflection, between them, was something else. A mass of silhouetted people were in the image, standing, facing me, facing my back. Where there should have been a fence between our houses, there was nothing but the outline of people looking at me. A whole world that wasn't my own was in that window.

I forced myself to turn, slowly. Nothing was behind me but a dark night and our fence. I turned back to the reflection across the street and it was still full of countless people, not so far off in the distance, but clearly restless and shuffling around. Their outline gave nothing away of their faces or bodies. I knew they weren't (but I hoped they were) another trick of the light, a distortion that would shortly vanish. Still, I could feel them right behind me, breathing on my neck and staring at my features. All the hairs on me were on end.

Squinting at the reflection didn't help, so I walked toward the house across the street, intent on getting a closer look. My feet felt gummy and my legs strained with lifting them. I walked carefully and slowly, never taking my eyes off the image in the window. There they were, who knows how many people, milling about in the glass and intent on watching my every move. I realized it wasn't accurate to call them simply a reflection.

Finally, I was right at the window, my hands on the glass. I pushed on the pane with my fingertips and it held. Getting closer hadn't changed the situation; the group of shadowy figures remained back by my mirror house. I could see them no better here, and there seemed no way to get nearer to them. They were beyond close inspection, and I suspected they were happy to stay there.

Well, most were. One silhouette broke from their ranks and stepped onto the reflection of the street. I watched this in the glass and I didn't dare breathe. The figure was a woman, or a girl. I got an impression of her delicate figure and the careful way in which she walked. Then three things happened quickly.

She walked under the reflected street light, and I could see her eyes looking into me.

I looked up to my own reflection, and though the face was mine, I didn't recognize the person.

The curtains on the window swung open and my neighbour inside let out a scream when she saw me.

I'm not sure which of the three things caused me to fall over the neighbours' shrubs and onto my back.

While my neighbours were sure it was me creeping around their house (I was the only non-white kid on the block, after all), they could never convince the police or my parents of any wrongdoing on my part. In a sense, my spotless record with both authorities paid off. Of course, the neighbours never forgave me and were happy to see me leave for Waterloo. By the time university ended and I'd settled in the big city, my parents had sold our suburban house next to the dead end. And despite the occasional sensation of being watched whenever I was near my reflection, I thought my experiences with the unknown, the inexplicable, were past.

Years later I met Grace, and though she didn't recognize me, I knew I had seen her reflection once before.

2007

ON GRACE'S THIRTEENTH BIRTHDAY, the summer before she shaved her head, she invited ten or so girls to the house. My parents, in a drawn-out argument as per usual, kept out of the way, but Grace insisted I be present for the party. I mostly sat in the corner of the living room, using my old toys to recreate crime scenes from the detective book I was reading while I listened to the way the older girls talked to each other. It was a different language, one that matched their tights and make-up, but Grace, in jeans and a boy's button-up shirt, didn't seem to speak it.

Grace left the room for a minute and one of her friends, I think named Laura, came over to my corner.

"What are you playing with?" Her hair was thick and golden and hung to the middle of her back, and she smiled when she looked at me. Something had happened to Grace and her friends recently: they were all beginning to look like women.

I showed her my action figures and she made a little *ooh* sound to appreciate them. I could hear her friends giggling, as if from some great distance, but Laura looked at me so genuinely that I was beaming from the attention.

"You're so sweet," she said. "How old are you again? Eight?"

"I'm ten," I told her, eagerly.

Her smile was so broad I could see her gleaming teeth. She said, "Wow, you're old! Do you have a girlfriend yet?"

My face and my neck got really hot. I could faintly hear one of her friends say, "Oh my god, look at him! He's blushing."

"What are you doing to him?" Grace said. I had no idea she'd returned to the room. My attention finally broke and went to my sister.

"Nothing," Laura said. "He's just such a sweet little kid."

"Leave him alone," my sister told her. "He's not a baby."

"He's ten and he still plays with toys," one of the other girls said, laughing.

Grace spun around and snapped, "The only reason I invited you is because Laura asked me to, as a favour. She felt bad for you."

There was a momentary hush as everyone took in the insult. Then the girls spoke up all at once, high-pitched and pleading. They broke off into plaintive little groups, some moving to the stairway and front hall while others tried to make things right between Grace, Laura, and the other girl. I stayed where I was and my face and neck continued to burn.

The party didn't last much longer, and eventually my mother burst into the room. She said to me, "What the hell happened? What did she do to them?"

Later, Grace came to my room and sat with me on my bed.

"I'm sorry," I told her.

"For what?" Her eyes were puffy.

"For playing with toys. I know I'm too old."

She smiled and sniffled and cried all at the same time, then punched me lightly on the arm. "Don't be an idiot. I like who you are. That's why you're on my team."

—

I awoke to the memory of those words, *That's why you're on my team.* Nicole was already out of bed and from the kitchen came the sound of the kettle and the smell of frying onions. I lay there and played that memory over and over. In bed I could let myself feel the loss of Grace, away from the demands of an increasingly erratic John, away from the need to smile through it all with friends. In bed I could breathe the smell of oranges off the pillows and not worry about whether Nicole and I were getting along or not. In bed I could wallow. I heard Nicole humming to herself, the pads of her feet making a slight sticky sound as she danced along the tiles of the kitchen, and like a miserable piece of shit I pulled the sheets over my head.

Next thing I knew Nicole was lying next to me, her orange hair swept to the side, our noses almost touching. We both smiled in that way that we did after a fight, after extended fighting. Then she kissed my forehead, lips barely pressed against my skin, and pulled me out of the bed.

She sat me at our tiny table and plated me a breakfast: eggs Florentine, her Hollandaise sauce from scratch, potatoes and onions, apple cut into chunks with the skin left on, coffee with cream. These were things I loved, and I felt loved when she served them to me. What had we even been fighting about?

Eventually she took a seat next to me with her own plate and a black tea.

I cut a piece of muffin, egg, spinach, and sauce and forked it into my mouth. I had to chew with my eyes closed. For a moment it was all so perfect.

Then she touched the lip of my mug and said, "It's instant."

I cocked my head. Of course she knew that instant coffee was Grace's favourite. My mouth was full with another bite so I didn't say anything. In fact I chewed slower.

"Please," she said. "This is me asking you to open up. I need more than just snatches from you."

"What are you talking about?" I said. I swallowed some instant coffee and it tasted horrible.

"Please," she said again. "You're going to lose me if you can't tell me what's going on inside your head."

She hadn't touched her food, hadn't even picked up her cutlery. Her face was kindest without make-up, without any sort of defence to it. On mornings like this she could be beautiful without being alluring. She hung there, practically floating above her chair, and waited on what I'd say next. I wanted to open up, but I knew that once I started talking about Grace, I wouldn't be able to stop.

"Look, it's fine," I told her. "I'm fine."

I dug into my food, tore through it with renewed attention, and didn't look away from the plate. When I looked up, she was still staring at me.

"What?" I asked. "I'm just sleepy."

She sat next to me silently for a minute or two more. Then she stood, showered, and left the apartment without another word. I stared at the wall and drank my bitter coffee, twisting everything tight, hands, eyes, guts, and cursing myself for being a fucking idiot. And when she was gone I made my way back to bed, replayed that memory, and fell into a fitful sleep.

Nicole left the city to see her family for an early Thanksgiving dinner, an invitation that had been only half-heartedly extended to me. I avoided the calls from my mother, and instead I got in touch with John. He suggested dinner at his place and mentioned that he had a surprise to show me.

The rats were sitting on the kitchen table in a translucent Plexiglas cage with a wire lid, our dinner displayed on the table around them. There were three of them, each with black fur on their heads and down their spines, and white fur on their bellies and haunches. They had protruding, shiny black eyes, pink paws with sharp clear claws, and awful tails that were as long as their bodies and covered with scales. They were inquisitive, the three of them coming to the front of the cage and twitching their thick whiskers at me when I approached the table, but they were also lanky and repulsive.

Over dinner, John explained that the rats were a present to himself. They were from the lab but no longer needed for research, and so John had snuck them out and brought them home instead of *retiring* them. Though we both actively ignored the topic of Grace and her disappearance, I didn't doubt that these animals were meant to console John in some small way. I imagined that he and Grace had bonded over lab rats early in their relationship. John was still thin, perhaps even thinner, but at least his spirits were higher. I felt hopeful when I left the apartment that night.

I spent much of October at John's place, avoiding arguments with Nicole, keeping an eye on him, and over that time I grew fond of the rats. In a way, they reminded me of dogs: they were furry, curious, established relationships, and seemed to have distinct personalities. Once I got over my initial revulsion, John taught me how to pick them up and how to appease them with a gentle scratch of their bellies or ears. Eventually I even let one crawl up onto my shoulder, its nails like little pinpricks across my skin, its whiskers and nose tickling my neck. I dreamt of that sensation for days.

One evening, while relaxing over scotch and popcorn, I gave one of the rats a kernel. It held it in its forepaws and ate it thoughtfully and I couldn't help thinking it was happy.

"Why rats?" I asked John. "I mean, why are they the lab animal of choice?"

John had the others in his lap, two balls of fur. "Well, plenty of other species get used. Slugs, snails, flies, monkeys, mice. Each is good for a different kind of research."

I held the rat up to my ear and listened to its chewing and light breathing. They were mostly noiseless creatures, despite films and TV portraying them as squeaking all the time. "And what are rats good for that mice aren't?"

"Behaviour," he said. "Mice are morons, really. Put two mice that don't know each other in a cage and one of them will end up dead. With rats, they may scuffle but most of the time they'll get along in the end. Rats are inquisitive, stubborn, resilient. They're successful, evolutionarily speaking, because they find a way to deal with whatever you throw at them."

The door to the second bedroom stayed shut during that period, and John never asked about our group of friends, but in some strange way I felt we were getting back to a normal life, just us and his new pets. Eventually John even named the rats: the largest of them was *Little John* and the fat one with the fewest black markings was *Little Grace*. Although all three were male, we still referred to Little Grace as *her* and *she*. John offered to name the third rat, the runt, after me.

"Not a fucking chance," I told him. "Call him Buddy."

—

The first of the rats to show signs of distress was Little Grace.

It was a particularly bad day. I'd fought with Nicole in the morning, a pointless row that escalated to me shouting, "What the fuck do you want from me?" Between that and skipping breakfast, I was weak and unmotivated at work. My bosses gave me grief, heatedly from the husband and coldly from the wife, over forgetting about a funding deadline. And on top of everything else, John hadn't answered my calls for two days. I was nauseated over the noodle lunch I brought back to my desk, alternately dialling John and Nicole, tumbling between feeling concerned and apologetic. Neither answered my calls.

I skulked out of work early to courier the grant application to Ottawa overnight. The courier service was on Bloor, just a couple of streets east of John's apartment, and so I thought I should check on him before heading home. The light in the second bedroom window was on when I arrived at his doorstep. John's shadow occasionally passed across the wall, as though he was examining something from many angles. I buzzed at the door, hands stuffed in my sleeves from the cold, but he didn't answer. His silhouette continued to flit in the window and after a few minutes I was irritated enough to shout up at the window from the street.

Eventually my yelling caught his attention. He crept up to the windowsill, backlit and ominous, posture rigid. When he finally recognized me, his shoulders relaxed and he disappeared from the window. I stared into the sushi restaurant storefronts. Both were full of happy, smiling, warm people I resented. The entrance to the apartment building opened enough for me to squeeze through, but it seemed as if John was hiding behind the door.

"Sorry, I thought you were someone else," he said.

There was a plaintive sound in the stairwell, and as we ascended it became louder and more urgent. When John opened the door to his apartment, the source became clear: one of the rats was shrieking in their cage. Little Grace was in the corner and raised up onto her back two legs. Her front legs were outstretched like arms and her teeth were bared as if to say, *Stay away from me.* She looked terrified of everything and her fur stuck out in all directions. Buddy crawled into a plastic tube and shuffled the bedding around in nervousness, and Little John kept his distance. I tried to pick up Little Grace but she was too jumpy to grasp.

John claimed to have no idea what was wrong. We watched a little TV but the worried sounds from the cage were too distracting. I saw light filtering out from under the door of the second bedroom. John noticed my glance.

"Still too early," he said. "I'll show you when I'm done."

I left the apartment after thirty minutes.

A few days later, Little Grace was dead. John called me, his tone utterly flat. I assumed that part of his grief was due to losing Grace again, in some symbolic way, and so I rushed over. He had Little Grace laid out on the classified section of a newspaper and the dead rat looked almost camouflaged. There seemed to be nothing wrong with her, only that life had somehow drained out of her and left her rigid and frozen in a snarl. John was inconsolable, his gaze blank, absent. His inky hair had grown shaggy since the summer and he tugged at it with knuckly fists. I told him that it wasn't his fault.

"It's actually looking hopeless," he said, resigned, grim, matter-of-fact, utterly unlike himself. "I can't get anything right these days."

Eventually I convinced him to leave the apartment for a walk. We brought his arrowhead shovel and buried Little Grace in the park just north of his apartment. The earth was hard and dry with the coming frost.

We stood in the dark with our hands behind our backs and had a moment of silence. John's broad shoulders hung heavy and low.

I have no idea what I'm supposed to say, I thought, and from that a memory bubbled to the surface of my consciousness. "John?"

"Hmm?" he said.

"Did Grace tell you about when she and Nicole got into it? Over some quote?"

He made a small, strangled noise.

"What the hell were they so worked up about?" I asked.

He made that sound again, a little louder this time. It was a chuckle. He told me, "Grace's pride. God, she was an obstinate woman."

We shared a small moment, a smile, a sideways glance in the dark.

"They were fighting over a Camus quote," John said. "Nicole was pointing out an epistemological concern to Grace."

"I have no idea what the hell you mean," I said.

He turned to face me. In poor lighting he appeared more like his old self: broadly framed, defined cheekbones, healthy and strong, handsome. He tried again.

"Essentially Nicole was saying, by way of Camus, that you can have all the information about a given system but still not have any understanding. I can describe what the colour red is like to someone who can't see, how it's different from blue and green, how it's the colour of sunsets and blood and love. But that blind person, despite having so much information, will know nothing of what redness really is."

I remained silent. He cleared his throat, dug at the hard soil with the toe of his boot, and continued.

"The same is true about science. I can collect all the data in the universe, but at some point I won't be able to comprehend how all the parts form a whole. My brain, my biology, limits my ability to understand."

We turned and walked away from the little funeral. Somehow it felt as though the air was even colder in the park, away from the illumination of the street lights. We were both silent until we reached the sidewalk heading south, back toward John's apartment.

He said, "There are just some things that are outside of comprehension, even if we can quantify them. At some point, science becomes magic. Do you understand?"

I made a sound in my throat, noncommittal, and asked, "So why was Grace so angry?"

Though his face was heavily shadowed by the street lights, I could see a grim smile.

"Because Nicole was right," he said.

—

It was less than a week before the next death.

In that time, I didn't hear from John once, and instead concerned myself with patching things up with Nicole. I avoided talking to her about the rats, if only because I knew the piercing and accurate words she would use about John. Finally, though, I made my way back to his apartment, this time on a grey weekend afternoon. I tried a combination of buzzing and shouting from the street to get his attention, but I couldn't tell if it was working: he had completely covered up the window of the second bedroom from the inside, effectively making it an impenetrable grey splotch of glass on the side of the building.

I paced back to the curb, considering where I could get lunch before trying again, but then I noticed a little round man unlocking the entrance to the apartment. I ran back and caught the heavy door before it swung closed.

The short man barked from the stairs, "You live here?"

"Friend of John's," I said, smiling blindly. My eyes were adjusting to the dark stairwell and I could hardly see. "Just checking in on him."

He grunted. "You tell those two: take the cardboard outta the front window. Makes the building look bad."

He lumbered up the stairs and disappeared. So he had no idea Grace had been gone since the end of last year.

I knocked on the door, quietly with my knuckles, then loudly with my palm, and finally I spoke up. "John. John, let me in."

There were human sounds in the apartment, then two locks being undone, a chain and a deadbolt, and the door opened for me. He was hiding behind it, out of sight again, and after I entered he closed the door so gently that it hardly made a *click* into place.

The apartment looked no less tidy but it had taken on some harsh odour, somewhere between an animal cage and an unclean man. I was standing near the door and sniffing at the foreign smells when I finally noticed the body of the rat on the living room coffee table. Little John was lashed with bright red, and lay flat and horribly still. As I approached the table, I could see long cuts down his flank and across his face, through his fur and down to the skin. Considerable amounts of blood had been drawn for such a small animal. It looked as though someone had tried to sharpen a knife with Little John, and it looked as though it had been very painful. His snout was curled into a sneer.

I swivelled and faced John. My voice trembled. "What did you do to him?"

"It wasn't me." His voice was hardly more than a whisper.

"What, are you going to tell me Buddy did this to him? That this was some sort of domestic dispute in their fucking cage?"

"Obviously not," he replied, "but it's complicated."

He frowned and furrowed but something was off. His mood was completely the opposite of when Little Grace died. Here, he showed the faintest hint of satisfaction, an upturned mouth, two smooth lines at the edge of each eye.

"Are you fucking smiling?" I was shouting again.

"I didn't hurt him."

"Look at him! Look at yourself! Do you not even remember your breakdown? Can't you see that you need help?"

"Despite what you may think, I'm fine," he said.

"Just like last winter, right? Jesus Christ, John, what would Grace think if she saw this?"

He stood erect and stared at me calmly. "She'd probably understand."

Without thinking I walked away from the conversation, picked up the rat cage, and wedged it under my arm. Buddy stood on his hind feet and sniffed at me through the bars. I turned toward John and looked at him defiantly. He said nothing. I walked past him, still carrying the cage, and left the apartment without closing the door behind me.

—

"Hello?"

"Danger, I'm at the house right now—"

"Nicole, shit, I can explain—"

"—and lo and behold, there's a rat."

"Trouble—"

"It's not my boyfriend, mind you, but a real, actual rat in a cage. In my home. Skulking about. Leaving a terrific smell in my personal space. Without even consulting me, you—where are you?"

"I'm sorry, I needed to—"

"My last question was rhetorical. The answer is: *on my way home.*"

Pause. "I'm on my way home, Nicole."

"To get rid of this rat."

"That's the thing—"

"To get rid of this rat."

Pause. "O.K., Trouble. To get rid of him."

—

In the end, Brian agreed to take care of Buddy. I drove up the alley to his apartment, a residential garage converted into an off-the-books living space far west of my neighbourhood. Brian was wearing cut-off jean shorts and a sleeveless T-shirt on the cusp of winter, and he assured me it would be no problem looking after Buddy.

"Little dude has an awesome existence," he told me. "Eats, shits, sleeps, flies solo. We're rats of a feather, man."

Still, I checked in every day and spent a little time with Brian and Buddy. For his part, the rat didn't show any trouble with the adjustment and enjoyed the cheese puffs that Brian fed him while playing video games.

The rough patch seemed to be passing with Nicole, and I imagined it had something to do with me avoiding John. We went for dinner at Shifty's a couple times, drinks at the Cuckoo even, and had a nice night or two at home. I hadn't told her about what had happened at John's, about Little John and Little Grace, but the window for telling her had come and gone.

And then near Hallowe'en, I got a phone call from John. Nicole and I were spooning on the couch, watching the type of romantic and tragic film that she loved. I fished around the floor for my phone, and we both looked at the display when I picked it up. Nicole stiffened.

"Don't answer it," she said. "Please."

"I have to."

"Why? Why do you have to? Please."

I pressed the *answer* button and brought the phone to my ear. "Hi, John."

Nicole got off the couch and went into the bedroom.

"You were right," John said over the phone, distant. "I'm sorry. I need help. Can you come over?"

Nicole wouldn't look at me when I went into the bedroom for a sweater.

At the apartment that night, John explained what had happened to Little John: how he'd brought the rat back to the lab, how Little John had died there in a hasty experiment. I believed him at the time. He apologized, acknowledged his instability, and stated his need to take care of something, anything, that reminded him of Grace. He swore he would go back to the doctors for more professional help.

I returned Buddy to John the next day.

2006

WE AWOKE TANGLED in the sheets of our bed. We didn't rush to untangle. There were smears of fake blood across our sheets, a smudged imprint of my face on the pillowcase. Nicole's skin was still powdered white and the rouge apples of her cheeks were a mess, but not even day-old clown make-up could diminish her. We kissed.

"All right," she said, meaning *enough*. I moved closer, pressed my lips against her again, and she laughed. "All right! You're going to be late, and you're hideous."

"We've got time." I writhed around Nicole like the vines on the old Annex houses.

"No, we don't. As if your sister needs another reason to dislike me." Nicole pressed her hands into my face, kissed me once firmly, and rose from the bed.

"She likes you just fine," I said.

She stopped at the door of our bedroom, blotches of make-up and artificial gore dappled across her bare back and smooth legs. She turned her head to look at me, narrowed eyes, smile playing across her lips. It was an invitation.

I freed myself from the sheets and followed her into the shower. As she cranked the water Nicole said, "She's always been a bit of a bitch to me. I just wish she'd be a little nicer to you."

Under the water we kissed again.

—

"Sorry I'm late," I said. "Had to wash off the Hallowe'en make-up."

A heavy red streetcar rumbled down College Street, one of my favourite sights in this still-new city. Grace stood in the entrance of an alleyway off the main street and she was not amused. Her hair whipped in the biting wind and she was bundled in layers of dyed wool and heavy fabric. It was almost noon, but the overcast sky would just as easily have fit the morning or later afternoon. Grace didn't say anything, only turned on her heels and headed toward a nondescript glass and metal entrance. Embossed on the front window were the words *The Centre for Animal Modelling*.

"This is your top-secret facility?" I joked. There was nothing top secret about it. "'Animal modelling'? Beauty queen rats, in a scummy alley around the corner from the convenience store?"

"Shut up," she said without turning to me. Her voice nearly died in the wind. "If you didn't really want to see this, you could have just told me."

"What? Of course I want to see it. That's why I asked."

"You're just not in any rush."

"Look," I said, "I'm sorry I was late. I got caught up."

"I bet you did." Grace brought out a small rectangular pass, a key fob, and the door latch clicked as it unlocked for her. In the alcove, she punched some numbers into a pad and the next door opened. She didn't look to me as she muttered, "Nicole has that effect on you. She probably even told you to skip this."

"On the contrary," I said.

We walked into a brightly lit foyer. Grace greeted the security guard with one small, raised hand.

"This is the prospective grad student I was telling you about," she said to the guard. Her words surprised me but I gave an empty smile and played along. He grunted some vague greeting to me and took my driver's licence, but I don't think he noticed that Grace and I shared the same surname or that we looked similar. His eyes were glassy pinpricks surrounded by puffy skin.

He escorted us to the change rooms and pointed out the men's side for me.

Grace said, "Take off your shoes, put your street clothes in an empty locker, and throw on some scrubs. Don't let the scrubs touch the clothes. Then grab some visitor shoes from the rack. I'll meet you on the other side. Got it?"

I nodded.

She turned to the security guard and smiled, an invitation for him to leave, but the thinness of her face made the grin unnecessarily severe.

I did as Grace had told me. She managed to change faster than I did and opened the door from the other side, her hair tied back, the blue scrubs hanging off her bony frame. Standing in the brightly lit corridor, she looked like the recently deceased making her way to heaven.

But most startling were her forearms. They were wrapped with heavy gauze and sealed with some sort of white tape. Along the inside of her arms, the bandage looked sticky or saturated with something discoloured and wet.

"Jesus Christ, Grace, are you"—I leaned in closer and spoke quietly—"are you cutting yourself again?"

"What? Oh." She looked bored by my reaction. "This is just allergies."

"To what? A straight razor?"

She said, "The rats, dipshit. I'm fine. It's been a long, long time since any of that."

We walked down blanched, sterile corridors. Technicians bustled by with racks full of empty cages. Windows along the walls revealed scientists covered in gowns, bonnets, and masks, staring intently at objects too small to make out from the hallway. I could hear the faint hum of air being pushed through fans and pressurized filters. Every turned corner revealed another identical corridor, and I began to feel as if we were walking in circles.

Eventually, though, we reached the end of a hallway and Grace unlocked a door. Inside was a small anteroom.

"Suit up," she said, and in turn she handed me a yellow hospital gown with ribbed cuffs, stretchy blue booties, a translucent blue bonnet, and a pair of blue surgical gloves. All the while she got herself ready, wincing as she slid the gown over her bandaged arms. She taped the wrists of her gloves to the cuffs of her gown, and instructed me to do the same.

"Grace," I said, "if you're always wearing all this, how did your arms get so bad from allergies?"

She fitted a surgical mask to the bridge of her long nose and pulled the straps around her ears. She handed me a mask and said, "Don't be so concerned. Their claws can poke right through the gown. You'll see."

We stepped into the next room and an animal smell hit me. The room had no overhead lights, so as the door swung closed behind us we were enveloped in total darkness. Without my vision, my ears became extremely sensitive and I could hear the soft rustling sound of small animals. Grace was silent. I imagined her standing still a few steps in front of me, smug, letting this moment of pure darkness linger. Soon the animal rustling became scratching and then clanging on metal. The experience was disorienting and I reached out for the cool comfort of a wall. I still couldn't hear Grace or even sense her in the room.

"O.K., enough." My voice sounded feeble, as if it was swallowed up by the overwhelming blackness.

I swear I could hear her smile, mouth open, teeth bared. Finally I heard her booties shuffle a few steps, and with a *click* the room was bathed in a dim red light.

"Just like the darkroom in high school," I said. Though it was still hard to see, I could make out the stacks of cages that filled the room. Inside each cage were two pairs of black, beady eyes that seemed to stare back at me. The sounds of the room made sense now: the rats were pushing against the lids with their forepaws, or chewing on the edge of plastic tubes, or digging through the soft bedding that lined the floor of their homes. The whole room felt alive, boxed but alive.

"Funny," Grace said from behind a stack of cages, "I never thought of that. The red light and photography. We use it because rats can't see red. So we can turn on a light, and not screw up their circadian rhythms."

"Their what?"

"Their sleep and wake cycles." She slid a plastic cage from the rack. Both rats lifted themselves onto their hind legs and tried to sniff through the lid. "They're nocturnal, active mostly at night, so we reverse their light cycles and work with them in the dark."

She carried the cage past me, into the final room of the laboratory. As I followed, I accidentally nudged the door and it started to swing closed.

"For Christ's sake!" Grace shouted, suddenly angry with me. She thrust her shoulder into the door and kicked a wedge out from under it. "The doorstop. It can get really stuck if the techs put it on the other side of the door, which they do way too often. My boss got trapped in here for an hour, once. He shouted the whole time and no one could hear him in the hall. It wasn't until one of us was suiting up that we knew something was wrong."

She set down the cage and flipped on the lights of the procedure room. For a moment I was blinded.

"Then why not get rid of the wedge?" I asked.

"The door is a major pain in the ass when you're running twenty animals."

I scanned the room: a black Plexiglas box in the middle, wires and computer equipment everywhere. I asked, "What is all this?"

"My attempt to measure subjective time," she said.

—

First she plucked one of the rats from the cage, where it had been standing in a pile of its own shit. When she noticed my disgust, she gave me that cruel smile and thrust the rat forward as if she was going to place it on me. I took a step back. She laughed and rested the animal on her forearm, where it seemed to stick like Velcro.

As she booted and prepared the electronics, she explained a little but didn't try to make it easy to understand. Objective time was easy, she told me: humans had been accurately measuring time with clocks for hundreds of years. Subjective time, however, seemed to require some trickery: evidence pointed to things like heart rate and brain activity as good shorthand for an individual's experience of time moving forward. She kept using the word *oscillation*, describing patterns of *delta* and *gamma* without ever really explaining what those were. She had implanted a device in the rats that recorded these measurements and then transmitted them wirelessly to a receiver. Finally, by comparing the external clock to the internal measurements, she could say with some certainty when the objective and subjective significantly veered away from each other. Or at least it seemed like that was what she was saying. All the while the rat clung to her arm, occasionally walking in circles, and I couldn't help thinking it looked a little fat, as though it had too much skin.

"But how do you know?" I asked. "I mean, sure, you can measure these things, but how do you really know what's going on for the rat?"

She was hunched over the computer and setting up some program called Telemetrics when I spoke. A grin came over her face.

"Oh, little brother," she said proudly, "when I'm dead and gone you might end up a good little scientist detective after all."

"Not likely," I said.

She paused for a moment and laughed hard, once. We shared the same laugh. She cackled again and swivelled to me.

"Remember that?" she asked. "'I am the detective! I am the spy!' You used to run around the house screaming that. Ha! You'd look through the bottom of a milk glass as if it were a magnifying glass. Sneaking around the house, detective books under your arm. I could have beaten the shit out of you when I found you under my bed, listening to me talking on the phone."

"I was on the case for a client," I said straight-faced. "Mom."

Grace's grin soured. She stepped away from the computer and placed the rat into the Plexiglas cube in the middle of the room. The inside of the box glinted as if it were made of metal or glass. She replaced one smooth panel of the cube with a wall that had a cylinder and some wires built onto the back.

"So we talked about some of this before," she said. "I can't really know what's going on inside *your* mind, let alone a rat's. But I can make reasonable guesses. I could say to you, 'Clap your hands every time you think five seconds pass.' And, all other things controlled for and considered equal, I would have a good idea of how subjective time passes for you in relation to the objective world."

She gestured for me to look at the cube and the new panel she'd installed. Inside the cylinder were tiny yellow pellets that fed through a rubber tube into the box.

"We can do the same with the rats," she told me. "We train them to raise and lower their paw every five seconds, and the movement registers as muscle activity on our recordings. If they do it too early or too late, they get nothing, but if they're very close to five seconds they get rewarded with a sugar pellet. And just like I guessed, their behaviour correlates extremely well with their electrophysiological activity. Later we take away the time restrictions and let them press whenever they think five seconds has elapsed."

We went back to the computer and she hit the start button on the program. A number of sketchy, sweeping lines began to fill the screen.

"Look," she said, pointing to one of the lines, "he's already started lifting his paw."

And in fact, I could see large, dense squiggles appear every few seconds. We watched the waves draw across the monitor until a thought hit me. It was my turn to laugh.

"So what you're telling me," I said, "is that you've taught these rats to dance in exchange for candy? Grace, what the hell is the point of this?"

She put both her hands on the counter and lowered her head. "Jesus, you really don't understand anything at all, detective. You can't see why this is useful? Think about things for once in your life before you speak."

"Clearly you're the brains of the family, so why don't you just enlighten me and save me from my crippling stupidity."

She bristled at my response. "Once we understand how to measure subjectivity, then we can *manipulate* it. Then we can manage a degree of control over it. Then we can begin to overcome the limitations of the objective world, escape these awful, incontro-vertible facts of reality."

She turned, faced me, and spoke slowly. "Then, little brother, for once in our ignorance-congested, noise-saturated lives, we can be *alone*. We can have time and space to really think."

I didn't hesitate. "What you're saying doesn't make sense. No matter how you manipulate these rats, you can't take out the part where they all live in the real, objective world."

She stopped the Telemetrics program and removed the rat from the cube, throwing it brusquely into its cage. Her every move was harsh and deliberate. She propped open the procedure room door with the wedge and shut out the lights before I had time to leave the room. I could hear her slamming the cage into the rack and making her way back to the anteroom. Why my last statement had made her so angry, I had no idea. By the time I caught up with her she had stripped off most of the extra layers, her gown in a hamper, the rest in the garbage. I followed her example.

—

We wound our way back through the corridors in silence. I phoned Nicole while I changed back into my street clothes and we agreed, in the hushed and excited tones of a young relationship, to meet at Shifty's for a bite and whatever mischief might follow. Grace was waiting impatiently on the other side of the door, shawled again, shifting her weight from foot to foot, arms crossed under innumer-able layers of wool and fabric.

The sun had broken through the clouds by the time we left the animal facility, but it actually felt colder than when we'd entered. We made our way to College Street and headed west.

"Look," I said. "Look. I'm sorry. I wasn't trying to insult your work."

She waved her hand dismissively. "You still don't get it. Every other sense remains *constant* despite changes to the environment. Apples look red regardless of whether you're in the sun or artificial light, even though the reflected wavelengths are totally different. John's voice sounds the same on the telephone, even though all the fundamental frequencies are absent. And that makes sense, right? You want an apple, or John, to remain constant in every situation. You want to be able to trust your senses."

I shrugged and turned my attention to the street. A bicyclist was shouting into the window of a car at the intersection.

Grace said, "So why is time the only exception to the rule? Why does time perception vary so wildly? Why do hours feel like minutes sometimes, or vice versa?"

The light went green and both car and bicycle sped away as if nothing was wrong. We crossed Spadina, continuing west, and I spent a moment thinking about my sister's question before speaking again.

"I don't know, Grace. Maybe time is difficult for our brains to measure."

"Or maybe there's something fundamentally different between the objective and the subjective," she said. Her voice became quiet and I struggled to hear over the noise of traffic. "If objective time is a one-dimensional arrow, maybe subjective time is a two-dimensional wave. Or a three-dimensional spiral. Maybe clocks are only measuring that movement in one dimension, its length, but our brains are sensing our depth and width through time."

"'We're living on a sphere of time,'" I quoted her, only then beginning to dimly understand what she'd been ranting about a month ago.

"Yes," she said. "Or maybe it's four dimensions. Five. We don't know yet."

Grace seemed calmer now, almost at peace.

As we got close to Bathurst I could see Nicole smoking outside of Shifty's. She wore a black-and-white striped dress, dark stockings, and her heavy wool coat. The angle at which she stood made the hair blow away from her face, and she took each drag of the cigarette coolly, without notice of the world bustling around her.

When I turned my attention back to Grace, she was looking at me carefully. Compared to Nicole, she looked dishevelled, wind-whipped, and frightened. I thought about what she was telling me, about multi-dimensional time and subjectivity and the repulsive little rats she played with all day.

"There's still the issue of the real world," I said. "How do you take experience out of reality? How can you use real-world measurements to measure things that aren't in the real world?"

Grace said, "You cheat."

We reached the corner of College and Bathurst but neither of us was ready to cross the intersection.

"It's John," she said. "He hasn't explained it to me yet. Refuses to tell me, in fact. When we implant the telemetry devices, he adds something else he keeps in a pouch. He made me swear not to tell our supervisor. The box, the telemetry recordings, most of it came from his—"

Her gaze caught something behind me, and then her jaw dropped.

"What the hell is *she* doing here?" Grace asked.

I turned and saw Nicole crossing the street toward us.

"You mean my girlfriend? The person I live with?"

"I'm leaving," Grace said.

"For Christ's sake," I grunted under my breath. "Be friendly for two minutes before you run away."

I turned and embraced Nicole. She was warm and soft and smelled great. I put my mouth close to her ear and whispered, "Mmm."

"Good afternoon, Grace," Nicole said when we separated. "Joining us for lunch?"

"No."

"Hey," I said to Nicole, "did you know that Grace is finding a way to separate subjectivity from reality?"

"Oh," Nicole said coolly to Grace. "Why?"

"Isn't it obvious?" my sister said.

"Do you hate the world that much, Grace?"

"Yes." My sister, the shortest of us, kept her gaze on the ground.

"And do you expect that solipsism will suit you better?" Nicole asked. "Or that you would even know what to do with it?"

Grace gritted her teeth, said, "What do you know of knowledge? You prepare people's food for a living."

Nicole didn't hesitate, and in fact smiled. "I know my limitations. 'I realize that if through science I can seize phenomena and enumerate them, I cannot, for all that, apprehend the world.'"

The way that Nicole spoke made it clear that she was quoting, but I didn't recognize the words or even understand what she meant, at the time. Grace kicked at the ground and muttered something too quiet to hear.

"I'm sorry?" Nicole asked. She arched her back and stood tall.

Grace cleared her throat and looked up into my girlfriend's eyes. "I said, fuck you, Nicole. You are intellectual and emotional poison, for all of us."

"Oh, you mean for the friends you haven't bothered to call in months?" Nicole forced a laugh that sounded both cruel and hurt. "Or for the boyfriend you frequently chastise in public?"

Nicole tried to hold it back, glancing at me, but her anger got the better of her. "Or for your own brother, whom you treat like an imbecile? I'm the one poisoning their loyalty to you? You're not doing a good enough job of that on your own?"

There was a long pause in the conversation, Nicole's wrath spent, Grace huddled and defensive, my own jaw slack with shock. Pedestrians veered around us as the lights at the intersection went from red to green to yellow to red again. I should have spoken up, but I had no idea what I was supposed to say.

Finally Grace looked at me, pressed her mouth tightly closed, and shook her head once. Then she turned and walked north.

After watching her for about ten seconds, I turned to Nicole and pulled her close to me. I'd never see her eyes glisten before.

"I love you." I think it was the first time I'd said it to her. "But I have to go."

"I'm trying, you know, to be understanding—" she began but then her voice cracked. She nuzzled my cheek with her nose, squeezed my upper arms once, tightly, and then pushed me away. I ran north after Grace.

When I returned home that night, Nicole and I had our first genuine argument, a shouting match that ended in mutual tears, apologies, and promises never to fight like that again.

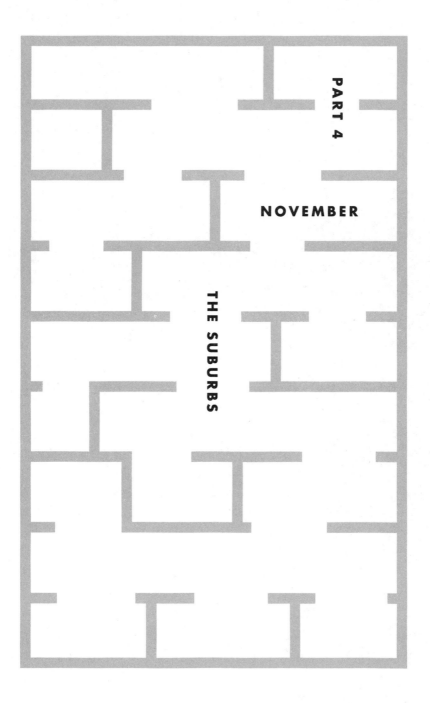

PART 4

NOVEMBER

THE SUBURBS

2008

OFFICER 2510 RAPS her knuckles three decisive times against my door. I can see her through my small window, dressed in civilian clothes again, nothing but her tomboyish stance to suggest she's any sort of authority figure. She looks bored.

I crack the door open but block the entrance with my shoulders. "What kind of a police officer plays club shows with a band?"

"This is the part where you let me in," she says, "for your own good."

I consider the state of my apartment and how I must look to her. I pat some of the sawdust off my jeans and clap my hands together to clean them. Oh well. I go back into my apartment but leave the door open for her.

She takes a moment to look around. The large wooden box is reconstructed and sitting in the middle of my freshly emptied living room. No doubt she saw my corner tables and couch outside, sitting at the curb. One panel of the box is missing and so she takes a slow, deliberate look at its interior. Then her attention shifts to the removed panel, the open plastic bag full of bits of broken mirror, and the fine sandpaper I was just using.

"Arts and crafts?" she asks.

"A machine with no mechanisms, I think. Like meditation, only more pretentious."

She looks to my bandaged arm. "Nobody told me meditation was dangerous."

"I'm supposed to be leaving soon. Mind if I go change?"

I don't wait for a reply. In the bedroom I crawl out of my clothes and wish vainly that I could shower off the grit that sticks to the sweat on my neck and causes my scalp to itch. I peel away the tape on the edge of the bandage to look underneath. It's healing but still ugly. Officer 2510 is likely wandering around my living room and it won't be long before she finds Buddy.

She shouts from the other room. "I looked into your stolen car trouble."

"Oh, great," I say.

"Turns out you never owned a car. At least not with that VIN, and not in this province."

"That's what your colleagues told me. You should tell it to my bank account."

I leave the bedroom, fresh clothes already feeling soiled, and sure enough she's standing in the kitchen. She sticks her fingertips between the bars on the cage lid, and though Buddy noses at her, he's sadly uninterested in taking a bite.

"Considering pursuing a career in science?" she asks.

I look at her, unimpressed. She's wearing a crooked grin that, if the situation were a little different, might be cute.

"I only ask because I got word that somebody broke into your sister's old lab. John's lab." She takes the lid off the cage and scoops up Buddy as if she's had plenty of practice with rats. Buddy, that traitor, snuggles contentedly into the crook of her arm. That grin of hers again. "Bearded guy, from the tapes. Not that you're bearded these days. Thing is, he didn't take anything from the lab, not as far as anyone can tell."

"Do you want to come right out and say it, officer?" I ask. "I'm tired, I feel like shit, and I have a million things to do."

"Oh?" She hands me Buddy and I put him on my shoulder without thinking. "A million things? Your old boss tells me you haven't worked for her in over a month."

"For fuck's sake. Have you interviewed my friends, yet? My ex-girlfriend?"

"Should I?" she asks. "Maybe later. Your mom says she's worried about you. Says she hasn't seen you for months."

"My mother should be used to that."

By now we're two feet from one another, within each other's personal space. She exhales and steps away from me to inspect the room, her eye quickly landing on the sheet of paper on the kitchen counter, the one with the *tabula recta*. She walks to it, picks it up, asks, "You coding or decoding?"

I cross my arms. "Why am I not surprised that you're not surprised?"

"Anyone with an internet connection and a bit of free time could tell you all about it."

I hold my hands out toward the room, palms up, as if to show her there is no internet here.

"Yeah, you don't seem like the smartphone type." She grins again. "What's your cipher?"

I raise an eyebrow.

"The code," she says. "The repeating word or phrase that you use to encrypt or decrypt the text. You know, first letter of the cipher for the first letter of the passage, second for second, third for third, *et cetera ad infinitum* and such."

"It was a sentence," I tell her, "but it only worked for part of the message. I haven't been able to figure out the code for the next section."

But she's already moved on. She nudges the bag of broken mirror with the toe of her boot and runs her finger along the smooth edges of the wooden panel.

"Looks like you're almost finished," she says.

"Just waiting on the hardware store to get me a big enough pane of mirror."

"And then what? Care to tell me what you're going to do with your codes and your rats and your boxes?"

She is almost being polite but it bothers me. Her kindness irritates me. The sight of her in my living room irritates me.

I take Buddy off my shoulder and put him back in his cage. "Is there anything I can do for you, officer?"

She pinches her pretty face as if she's going to spit. "Don't you know what it looks like when someone's trying to help you?"

"Help me with what? Sanding? Gluing the mirror to the wood?"

"*This* I haven't seen before." She nods at the box. Then, as though she's shooting from the hip, she points to me. "*This* I've seen. I saw it last year, in fact. I gather you've seen it twice already, this sudden case of misanthropy and obsession. And look how it ended the last two times."

She steps toward me again, close enough to be considered either intimate or pitying, but I'm not sure which. My spine straightens and my breath catches in my throat.

"You seem decent," she tells me, her mouth near my shoulder. "A bit dopey, I gather, but decent. What I know of your sister is less flattering, and what I know of John is more pathetic. It's a shame what happened to them, whatever happened to them. But it would be foolish if it happened to you, too, after everything you've seen."

"I didn't see enough," I say to the top of her head. "That's the problem: I wasn't paying attention."

"Pay attention to me, now." She looks up at me and her eyes are a cold, hard, bluish grey, like a slab of concrete a few feet under ocean water. "Let them rest. Learn from their mistakes. Nothing good can come of following in their footsteps, not for you, not for anybody. Are you paying attention? If you keep following them, everything else will slip away until all you have are silhouettes in a reflection."

I take a step back. "What?"

"This is the part where I leave," she says, "and you thank me for coming."

"Just a second. What did you just say?"

She smiles a crooked smile, turns, and walks to my door.

"Do you know something?" I ask.

She pulls open the door and leaves me standing in my living room.

———

It takes hardly a moment to put on my boots and John's jacket, and while I'm clearly underdressed for the weather, I don't want to waste any more time. The sky is saturated white with clouds and my ears burn in the air. She's not up the street so I run down to Dundas.

I keep close to the edge of the Portuguese bank on the corner and lean out a little to look. Officer 2510 is about two streets away and walking without hurry. Her confident gait is unmistakable. I follow.

I make up a little of the distance between us, but not too much. She stays on Dundas Street, crossing Bathurst and following the southern edge of the hospital grounds. She slows for a moment to stare north into Kensington Market, toward the fruit shops and cafés, but then continues eastward. I stay behind pedestrians wherever possible, hunched and unassuming, but she never looks back.

She moves quickly through the Chinatown bustle, crosses Spadina and continues east until she reaches the southern parts of the university district, where she disappears down a tiled stairway into the subway. I hold the metal railing as I descend. Daylight fades behind me.

It takes my eyes a moment to adjust to the artificial lighting. St. Patrick station is appropriately green, though it's been dulled by grime and years of use. I dig through my pockets for change and find less than a dollar. The rush-hour gate is still open, despite it not being rush hour, and a tired attendant watches while people drop their money into the glass cube. I stall until a crowd of university students files through, then jam my change in with theirs and cross the gate. The attendant looks at me foully, knows exactly what I'm doing, but says nothing.

I can hear the deep rumble of a train pulling in below. I skip down the stairs as fast as I can and scan the platform. I don't see Officer 2510 at first but then she takes a step backward and practically pops out of the crowd, about fifty feet to my right. The northbound train arrives and she gets on it. I get in, one car behind hers, the doors closing behind me with their characteristic three-note chime.

I weave through the standing passengers until I'm at the doors that separate the two subway cars. Though there are empty seats, Officer 2510 prefers to stand near the exit. She is staring through the doors' windows, out into the black tunnel. Or maybe she's staring at the reflections.

It's only a few minutes, but it feels like forever. We pass a few stations: Queen's Park, Museum, St. George. At Spadina station, she slips out onto the platform. This doesn't make any sense. If she'd wanted Spadina, she could have taken a streetcar north from Chinatown. I've either let myself be seen or she's been toying with me all along. I set my teeth hard and walk briskly to catch up with her.

But I can't. No matter how quickly I move, she keeps ahead. She weaves effortlessly through the crowds while people seem to block my way forward. She glides up the stairs while I fight my way around shoulders and elbows.

I'm blinded by the white sky when I emerge from the underground. It's cold. I look in every direction until finally I catch her rounding the corner onto Bloor Street, now heading west. I cut through traffic and hear car horns, shout some noncommittal apology. I reach the corner where I last saw her and scour the view in all directions. She's gone.

I curse. I continue on, searching for Officer 2510 in the crowds on the sidewalk ahead of me. Something tugs at my unconscious, something unsettled and agitated. The storefronts along Bloor Street become familiar and that feeling tugs at me harder until my shiver turns into a shudder and I'm hugging myself for comfort. As I look down the street at the Fortress, I can't help feeling that something is very wrong.

And then it dawns on me.

John and Grace's apartment is missing.

It's as if a chunk of Bloor Street has been seamlessly removed and the two adjoining pieces fit together perfectly. The building, with its stairwell and sushi restaurants, has been cut out of the city. The fucking apartment building is gone. I reel, lurch, crouch near the pavement. Thick drool drips out of my mouth and I think I'm going to vomit, but it doesn't come.

For a while I stay on one knee with my face near the sidewalk. I can feel pedestrians moving by me, some slowing, concerned but too hesitant or polite to ask if I'm all right. My head throbs until it doesn't. I concentrate, spit a mouthful of saliva on the ground beneath me, and force myself to stand up.

I run my hand along the curve of my skull, through the centimetre of hair I've grown on my scalp over the last month. The wind picks up and bites at my ears a little. My huddled image is in the shop window that used to be just east of the sushi restaurants, and I'm no longer surprised to see my eyes in that gaunt and serious face.

And then I see her. In the reflection, not six feet from my mirror image, Officer 2510 stands and watches me losing my shit. Her eyes are fixed on me and her hands are on her hips.

"Oh, come on," I say and turn around, but she's not on the sidewalk. Instead it's just the mindless bustle of Bloor Street, unaware of the events taking place or the absence of an entire apartment building. I take a breath before I look back to the glass. Officer 2510 is no longer in the reflection, no longer visible anywhere.

Some great tether is unravelling and my body is floating further and further from anything recognizable. I stand stock-still in the flow of human traffic, my eyes now on the pavement at my feet. It feels like someone is breathing on my neck, watching me.

Slowly, carefully, I extend my arm in front of me and curl my hand until it's a fist. Then I extend my middle finger into a nice, rigid line. "Go fuck yourself," I scream.

The pedestrians around me flinch as if they've just heard a gunshot.

A moan slips out of me, some scared and lost sound.

—

"Hello? Scruffy?"

"Shit. Sorry, Lee, I meant to call Brian."

"No, no. You got the right number. He's just out getting us some beer and left his phone here."

"Can you leave him a message to check in on Buddy over the next couple of days?"

"Sorry? 'Buddy'?"

"My rat. He'll understand. Tell him my apartment key is under the mat."

"Sure. You all right, young 'un?"

"Hmm. Yeah. Don't worry about it. Big plans for you three tonight?"

"Two, not three."

"No Steve?"

"That's sort of exactly what I'm trying to say, young 'un. No Steve."

"Do you mean 'no more Steve'? As in forever?"

"As in 'indefinitely,' anyway."

"Jesus, Lee. Are *you* all right?"

"Everything changes, Scruffy. It was a long time coming."

"Listen. Can I ask you a weird question? You know John and Grace's apartment?"

"Whose apartment?"

"Grace. As in my sister."

"I don't think I even knew you had a sister. You sure I've met her?" A pause.

"Scruffy? What's up?"

"Look, Lee, I have to go. Please just give Brian the message."

—

There is only standing room on the subway heading south. I lean myself against one of the filthy chrome handrails and feel every bump as the cars grind over the tracks beneath.

At Union Station we spill out of the subway like a head wound, then flow up the stairs and into daylight. Every face is pointed in the same direction: upward, outward, homeward. I buy my train ticket out of town from the unremarkable lower floor of Union and make my way to the platform. There's a free seat on the middle level of the train, the small section that connects the stairs between upper and lower decks. I sit facing east, shoulder to the window. The train fills but I don't look at the other passengers. Instead I stare out the glass.

The sprawl doesn't end, but instead shifts in form and function. Near to the train tracks are trees that whip past my viewpoint so fast as to make them phantoms. The background is industrial space, old factories that have been appropriated for beer and re-appropriated for yuppie first dates. We reach the edge of the city and the background changes to cramped residential neighbour-hoods, their yards littered with the evidence of childhoods past: bicycle frames, rusted swing sets, swimming pools emptied for the year and covered in a film of dead leaves. Soon the landscape is changing again, this time into three-level townhomes that look like sanatoriums, the last of which bump against another block of industrial buildings. It is all manufactured hideousness.

And then, for a minute or two before we reach my stop, the train veers south and bursts from a layer of scratty trees and the only thing I can see is the blinding, brilliant surface of Lake Ontario, seemingly endless and capped with small diamonds of light. Across the lake, the sun has broken out of the clouds and casts intense beams across the water. There is the faintest froth where the waves rush onto the pebbled shore and the grass just beyond it looks alive and intensely green despite how cold it must be outside. An occasional tree still flickers past my vision, next to the train, but otherwise this image of the shimmeringly perfect and endless lake persists long enough for me to realize that I've been holding my breath all the while. Out there no fate is fixed and nothing is wrong with the world. Out there shows me that peace is a possibility. Then the gnarled and leafless trees swallow up the view and the train turns a little northward, toward the highway, and again the scenery becomes grey cement and empty transport trucks.

The next time the train slows into a station, I stand and exit. The scenery is still sprawl, but everything in the suburbs is wider, more spacious, somehow gaudy in its girth. I transfer onto a bus that takes me north, past the buzzing highway, the bloated mega-stores, the vast parking lots, and finally into the unending residen-tial zone.

The bus leaves me on a corner next to a gas station. Here, the grass is dead and the sky is grey and the lake is far, far from sight. I walk off the main road and breach the heart of the suburbs.

It has taken about two hours to return to my mother's home.

The house is an unremarkable structure, speaking both absolutely and relatively. It is grey brick and blue-grey aluminum siding, with the same blue-grey painted across the garage door. If it didn't have an angled roof, it would be a box. There is a small wedge of lawn on either side of the driveway, too small for anything but a patch of ornamental grass. To the left and right of the property are exactly the same model of house, one in tones of beige, the other a ruddy colour, and their yards are similar in size and shape. My mother's house is in the middle of a street that endlessly repeats and it would be nearly impossible to notice if it disappeared forever.

It was my home for years but still I choose to knock on the door, then ring the bell when my mother doesn't answer. I peer through the thin pane next to the door, and finally I see her come down the stairs into the foyer. She is in a bathrobe, her hair is frazzled, and she's practically screeching when she opens the door. "Jesus Christ, sweetheart, why don't you visit me anymore?"

———

It doesn't take me long to notice the changes.

I take off my shoes and jacket, mutter acknowledgement of my mother's incessant chit-chat, and say, "Where are Grace's things? I need to look through them."

My mother is puzzled. "Whose things?"

I grit my teeth. "This is a three-bedroom house, Mom. Who lived in the third bedroom?"

She tucks in her chin, her eyes wide and surprised like Grace's. "What the hell are you on about, sweetheart?"

I demand an answer with my silence.

"Nobody," she says. "Why would I rent out the third room? This is our home."

So now I don't have a sister. I want to be more surprised than I am.

"Christ, you used to have so much fun here," she tells me. Meanwhile she picks at something stuck to my shirt, loosening it with some saliva on her thumb and forefinger. "I wish you'd come home more. This is *nice*."

She flutters around me and prattles away but I hardly listen. Any information I could have gleaned from this house has disappeared along with Grace's possessions. Still, it may not be a pointless journey. I dig my hands into my jeans pockets and feel the nub of the flash drive demanding my attention.

I interrupt my mother mid-sentence. "Gotta check my email. Back in a sec."

Before she can say anything I've left the foyer. I boot up the computer in my mother's office and plug in the key. The Telemetrics file turns out to be a text file, full of mostly unlabelled numbers. Still, one piece of information is clear and pertinent: the computer's timer shows that Buddy was in the box for a few minutes, whereas the readout of Buddy's timer says he was gone for almost a day. The little rat's data suggest a way to reach my vanishing sister.

I take a walk around the block to get some air. Outside, the sun has disappeared below the horizon and the streets are lit by the yellow glow of the lights above. I pass the park where I played as a child, the houses of old friends, and approach my old school. For a moment I stand in the teachers' parking lot, where I got into my only fight and lost, and with a jolt it comes to me: *Thornton*. His name is a word I haven't tried yet, a potential cipher, an obvious possibility that hadn't occurred to me. I call a taxi.

"What the hell do you mean you're leaving?" my mother says when I get back to the house. "No. You can't leave. You only just got here."

I deflect, feign some excuse, and give her a perfunctory kiss. Then I hop in the cab and head to the train station.

Hours later, back at home in Toronto, John's notebook reveals its next section to me when I use that piece of shit Thornton's name as the key.

SILHOUETTE BREAKS RANK – II

A few minutes down the street from Shifty's is an old church with a park bench in front of it. During the day, the bench is a favourite spot for the homeless of Toronto; at night, though, the area is almost always empty and perfect for quiet summer conversations, despite being just a few feet from College Street and all its bustle.

Grace and I sat there talking on the night I met her. Well, not talking, exactly. She and I just sat there, with me staring at her and her smiling blindly into some memory or idle thought. Of course, her absent gaze was probably because I was looking at her so intensely. I doubt I have ever looked so hard at anyone as I did that night.

It was barely summer, then. The air was getting warmer but it was restless, and it came in bursts that would cause her hair to dance around her face. The Toronto skyline was reflecting off an overcast ceiling, painting the city in bright reds, and I wished I had my camera to preserve something of the night.

Instead, my memory was all I had to capture those first moments. Her cheekbone and lips were caught by the white light of the fire station just across the street. She wore a small summer dress that left her legs bare. This was before her obsession with wearing layers upon layers, before she starting losing what little weight she had; the woman was not yet lost in the clothes. Back then she was light, ethereal, and delicate. Because of the breeze, I had given her my black spring jacket to wear, and she kept the zipper undone. A small, thin necklace cut across her skin and hung just above the line of her dress, and my eyes kept moving back to that meeting of silver and fabric, no matter how hard I tried to be polite and look at the rest of the city.

I shuffled in my seat, my knees wide and my hands clasped between them and pressed on the bench. I could hardly sit still. She leaned back and her beautiful legs slid forward, one dangling over the other. Still she looked away, something a little restless behind her half-smile.

Finally I spoke up and asked her what she was thinking about.

She took a good, long time before saying something like, Imagine this was the last time you'd ever see me. Imagine this was all you got.

I pointed out that the way in which she phrased her words suggested she wasn't going anywhere. Then I panicked: did I sound smug? Or like the nerd I used to be?

In any case, she laughed, one hard Ha. Her family's laugh, I would later learn. She repeated, emphasized: Imagine, John. This is your last chance before I leave. What are you going to do with it?

I told her I'd use the opportunity to convince her to stay.

She said, *If you did, it would be a waste of time for both of us.
I'm not the type that stays.*

She turned to me and said, *Be more creative.*

It was a challenge.

She said, *What are you waiting for?*

Without thinking I stood up, reached out, grabbed her
hand, and pulled her up. Her face rushed to me, her nose near
my collarbone. I could smell the darkness of her hair and feel
her nervous vibration finally dissipate into stillness next to me.
It was a challenge. Then, catching even myself by surprise, I
started running down the quiet Toronto side streets, pulling
her along.

—

Hours before, the three roommates had proven nearly
inseparable at their party. Lee, Nicole, Grace.

Lee had her hair drawn back and was wearing gloves with
cut-off fingertips and tight jeans. She was too interested in
conversation with her friends to notice the attention she was
gathering from the young men around her. The only time she
broke away was to chastise people for pulling her records out of
their sleeves and getting fingerprints all over the vinyl.

Nicole, on the other hand, was acutely aware of the male
gaze and enjoying shooting down their flirtations. She was the
only one at the party wearing a party dress. She could have
acted like the archetypal vixen, pouting her lipsticked kiss or
thrusting her curvy hips, but instead she was demure and coy
in a very authentic way. There was a moment between us, an
instant with her eyebrow raised and me politely declining, and
then there was no attention from her at all.

And there was Grace.

When I think back to that party, I imagine Grace standing stock-still in the middle of a hundred bodies buzzing and flitting like a sped-up film reel. Small, skinny, wide-eyed, clearly beautiful and brilliant Grace, nervously glued to the shoulders of her roommates. I had no doubts as to why men would be attracted to Lee or Nicole, but for the first time in my life, I felt something visceral in response to a woman. Here was the girl I had seen in a vision, no longer a reflection from some hallucination, but real, corporeal, and directly in front of me. What I felt for her was a need.

—

Grace and I ran down that dark street with our hands pressed together and the skirt of her dress flapping gently behind her. Her sandals clopped in rhythm. Three or four times I actually howled, something between a laugh of surprise and a whoop of victory. Her hand was soft and firm with good bones and no intention of letting go. She was smiling with her teeth, perfect and monstrously white under the street lights. Amber-tinted houses passed, then a lonely parking lot, then a street corner. We entered Kensington Market along a path I'd never taken before.

We found ourselves in Bellevue Square, a cluster of small trees, a patch of unremarkable grass, and some sand that could be called a playground only by definition. The park was abandoned and waiting for us. There was a bronze statue of the King of Kensington, gentle and frozen in place, and he stood over two park benches near the entrance. In his sincerity and humble appearance I always felt something like pride and pity mixed together. He was our spectator, silent, hands held out in a gesture of friendship.

We slowed ourselves into a walk and it was clear that we were both enjoying the heavier breathing. She looked at me and smiled hard enough to crease the corners of her eyes. Our hands were still clasped together.

I told her that the King of Kensington welcomed her.

She said, I'm sure he welcomes everyone.

Not true, I said. I had a co-op placement down the street, and I have to tell you, sometimes those arms are pushing people out of Kensington, not drawing them in.

And are they going to push me out of the market or draw me in?

In, but they won't be able to make you stay.

She said, See, now you're getting it.

She pulled me to her, put her palms on my shoulders and pressed her right cheek against my chest. I took a deep breath and told myself, remember this moment. *Wisps of her hair made my nose itchy. The collar of my jacket was bunched up on her downy neck and her hands barely poked out of the sleeves. The new muscles I had built wrapped around her and I felt a pressure in my neck disappear. I would not move until she did.*

Across the street was a row of houses, silent and sleeping. I saw us mirrored in someone's kitchen window, my ridiculously rigid stance, the slender silhouette I held in my arms, the King of Kensington. But there was more.

In the reflection, countless shadowed figures had surrounded us and were witnessing the whole event unfold. Dark shapes stared at us from the glass, intent on ruining this perfect moment. I hadn't seen them since the dead end, years before. But here they were again, shuffling in that unsettled way they

*had before, and I was certain it had something to do with
meeting Grace.*

Do you see that? I asked.

*She looked up at me and I pointed with my chin to the
reflections in the windows.*

Everyone's asleep, she said.

In the reflection. Figures. Do you see?

*She turned back to me, confused. She had seen nothing.
How could she have been on the other side of that threshold
but have no knowledge of it? I pulled her close again and
kept my eyes on the mass of figures shuffling toward us in the
windows. They were encircling us, draining the light from all
around us.*

*I see strange things, I told her. Once before, I saw this. And
again tonight.*

*She recited, Research suggests an association between
creativity and psychological instability.*

*I'm not particularly creative, I said. I'm not sure if they're
real, but twice now I've seen people watching me.*

*The people on the other side of the reflection shuffled
together and swallowed up our image until there was only an
inky blackness.*

*She said, Did you know Nicole and I had a bit of an
argument over you? We always argue, of course. That's what best
friends do. But these days, I find myself irritated with her all
the time. And your arrival in our little social circle didn't help
one bit.*

She pressed her smile against my chest.

I'm trying to tell you something, I said.

*I heard you. Don't worry. Crazy can spot itself from a mile
away.*

I asked, And why are you *crazy?*

She separated her body from mine and I wondered if I had ruined the moment. She frowned and lowered her head and cast her face in shadow. She asked, Can I trust you to keep a secret?

I cleared my throat and said, Yes, you can.

Then ask me again.

It took me a moment, and then, Why are you crazy?

She put her hand on the back of my neck and pulled me close. She kissed my cheek once, lightly, and whispered, Because of the things a man did to me when I was thirteen. Because my mother and father pretended the whole thing didn't happen. Because I have murder in my heart.

And before my mind could catch up with her words, her whole attitude changed. She straightened, she laughed again, Ha, and she hid everything else away.

She said, Now please stop looking at me like what I just told you defines me. Go back to being the handsome boy with the nice shoulders. And kiss me.

I obliged her. It should have been a perfect moment, but it wasn't.

When I opened my eyes again, we were the only ones reflected in the window. Not yet, *I thought.* Tonight, she's mine. *And I chased that perfect moment until I found it in her lips. We stayed in the park until the sun threatened to break the horizon, until the clouds broke to a deep-green sky, and until the need for a long sleep couldn't be ignored any longer.*

2007

GRACE, THIRTEEN YEARS OLD, head freshly shaven with wisps around the hairline, raccoon eyes, nails bitten to the quick. On the washroom counter are a box cutter and a chewed pencil. She looks at me in the mirror and says "It'll be O.K." before she closes the door. I can hear her sucking air, wincing, on the other side. My mother drags me away before my father shoulders and breaks the door frame. Grace shouts, "Don't touch me."

I woke out of the dream in our chilly basement apartment and was surprised to find myself still in my clothes, sleeping on the couch again. I dug through my jeans until I found my cell phone and called in sick to work. My bosses weren't in the office yet so I left a message.

Sometime later that morning, Nicole stood over me and spoke. "You're late for work."

"Mental health day," I said and immediately drifted back to sleep.

The night before she'd been frigid and distant, which was somehow much worse than if she'd been heated and angry with me as per usual.

The next time I awoke, the sun was filtering in through our little window near the front door. My phone was vibrating against a hard surface somewhere in the apartment. I wandered around the basement, wrapped in the blanket, until I found the phone skimming across the kitchen counter.

"Hello," I said.

My eyes were bleary and wouldn't stay open.

"You busy?" John asked.

There was no sign of Nicole.

—

I put on my pea coat and locked up. Outside the apartment, the persimmon tree had lost most of its leaves but the plump, colourful fruit still hung from its branches. There were patches of blue in the sky but the air was bitterly cold in my lungs. Winter was coming too quickly.

I parked my car around the corner from John's apartment and ate some mashed potatoes at Features while I waited for him. He arrived carrying his shovel and a backpack and neither of us said much until we got back to the car. He saw the pile of Grace's belongings in the backseat, the boxes and bags of possessions that had once filled his apartment, and he said, "I hope it wasn't too inconvenient to pack it in the car again."

"Didn't unpack it in the first place," I told him. "It's been in my car for months, since we put it there."

John lightly placed the shovel on top of Grace's things, the handle poking between the two front seats and interrupting our view of each other. I started the car and followed Bathurst Street to Highway 401 out of town, then eastward.

"Where to first?" I asked. "Your parents' place or mine?"

"My parents' house is farther," he said, "so let's start there."

The highway bordered the northern edge of the city and traffic was light. The skeletons of twenty-storey condominiums occasionally lined the sides of the 401, half-constructed promises of more sprawl. The rest of the landscape was concrete boxes, strip malls, and long lines of asphalt. We crossed the Don Valley Parkway and continued into the suburbs of Toronto.

"Is Buddy O.K.?" I asked.

"He's fine," John said. It was hard to gauge where he was looking with the shovel's handle blocking his eyes. "Lots of food, lots of play for him. And how's Nicole?"

"Fine. She's fine."

"And things?"

"Same," I said.

He opened the glove box and started sifting through it. "Can you see a future?"

"I don't know. She's impossible to please."

"Don't be so hard on her," he said, catching me off guard. "She's a good woman, and I imagine you haven't been easy to be around this year."

I grunted, noncommittal.

"I imagine no small part of that is my fault," he said.

I kept both hands on the wheel and checked my mirrors.

"Well," he said, "for what it's worth, I'm sorry. And for what it's worth, I think she's a keeper."

"Thanks," I told him.

Then I heard his breath catch in his throat and he was silent for a moment.

"What is it?" I asked. I looked over and in his hands was the CD Grace had made for my journey back to Ontario. She'd scrawled *Oblivion* across its surface. John had found it in the glove box.

"It's been some time since I've seen her handwriting," he said. Without asking, he slipped the CD into the player and turned up the stereo.

The music filled our silences. We passed through the Green Belt and its temporary respite from the endless development, and at points the trees in the surrounding valley were below the height of the road. As always, I paid special attention to the second song on the CD, and even skipped back to it at one point: *I'll find my oblivion in the place where the water meets the trees.*

"Shouldn't we have seen it coming?" I said, and recited the line to John.

"That isn't fair to Grace," he told me. "If you judged everyone by the sad art and music and film that we consume, we'd all seem suicidal. And oblivion is never what she wanted."

"What do you mean?"

"Oblivion is the annihilation of the self. Grace was looking for the opposite, a way to remove everything *but* the self."

"Didn't that ever offend you? That we were all obstacles in her desire to be alone?"

"Of course," he said. "But I doubt she'd really want it once she got it."

"Then where is she?" I asked.

The exits for my hometown came and went, and the highway narrowed from twelve lanes to six.

Finally John spoke again. "Take the next exit."

We passed the welcome sign for Oshawa, *The City That Moto-vates*, and followed the off-ramp over a gentle hill and into the city. The roads were wide and littered with franchise coffee shops, like where I grew up, but overall the city had an older, unmaintained feeling to it, grubbier storefronts and virtually no pedestrians.

"Are you going to need gas?" John asked.

"Eventually," I said.

John pointed me through the city, turn for turn, and without the regularity of a grid I soon had no idea which direction we were travelling. Eventually he pointed out a gas station that was bright and clean compared to everything around it. We pulled in.

He climbed out of the car and walked toward the station. "Fill it up, then come inside for a moment."

I slouched out of the wind and kicked at my back tires as I pumped. The sun had hidden behind some clouds. My hands were stiff with the cold and my teeth were chattering by the time I finished.

I made my way into the station, a bell chiming above the glass door as I entered. John was leaning on the counter and talking to a middle-aged Asian woman behind the cash register. Her face was puffy with fatigue, but her hair was frosted and her make-up was impeccable. She didn't smile.

She glanced at me and said something in what I imagined was Korean.

"Yes, yes, I will, don't worry," John said to her. Then he turned to me. "This is my mom. Mom, this is Grace's brother."

"Nice to meet you," his mother said, then looked to John and broke into a long string of Korean again. The only word I understood was *Grace*. John responded to her in Korean, and she fired back at him. I wasn't entirely sure if they were arguing.

"Pleased to finally meet you," I said, waved, and walked out.

John returned to the car a minute or two later. He was quiet. I didn't know where we were going so I didn't start the engine.

"Everything all right?" I asked.

"As much as it ever is," he said. "We're just a few minutes down the road from here."

I drove and waited for him to speak. The shovel handle still blocked his eyes, but his mouth was pressed tightly into a thin line. Finally I said, "Care to tell me what that was all about?"

We passed into a newer subdivision, its look more familiar to me.

"My mom just doesn't think highly of someone voluntarily disappearing," he said.

"Neither do I."

He pointed down the street, the end of which had a diamond-shaped sign tiled in yellow and black. "Park near the dead end. My mom would just rather I forgot about anything to do with Grace."

"Including me," I said.

"Of course."

I parked the car and we got out. He dragged the shovel and his backpack through the passenger side door and the pointed blade of the shovel clinked against the asphalt. He said, "I need to dig something up."

"What? Here?"

"Here. Keep watch and tell me if anyone notices what we're doing."

He walked toward the dead end. I could hear the sound of the shovel striking the hard earth, John jumping on the blade's footrest to sink it deep into the ground. I leaned against the back of my car and scanned the houses for activity.

"What are we doing here?" I asked.

"See the beige house? I used to live there."

I examined the house but nothing suggested it was any different from any of the others in the neighbourhood. Behind me there was the unzipping of the backpack and John's breath coming heavily. He shovelled for a few more minutes, interrupted once by a brief, deep thud, and then he made his way back to the car. The backpack looked full and hung heavily from the straps.

"Step one is complete," he said. "Let's get to your mom's house and unload your car."

As we pulled away, I noticed that the diamond-shaped dead-end sign had been toppled and there was a large hole where it had stood. John's face had a glaze of sweat across it and he looked rattled.

—

We unloaded Grace's things into the foyer of my childhood home. My mother cried and cursed and tugged at her hair, saying, "She was always so goddamned difficult."

I hugged her short, squat frame, the older and overweight version of Grace's figure, and avoided her questions about why I'd visited so infrequently over the last year. I wasn't entirely sure myself, but it had something to do with the last family dinner we'd had. John stayed out of the way.

My mother said, "Why would she do this to me?"

After our visit I waved to her as we drove off. John didn't look back and didn't wave, which bothered me, but he spoke up before I could mention it.

"School's almost out," he said.

"What?"

"You and Grace went to the same school until grade eight, right? Would you mind showing it to me?"

I pulled into the next driveway and turned around. We passed my mother's house again but she was no longer on the front porch. We continued down the slow curve of the street. At the corner was the patch of grass we once called a park, and as always it was flooded in parts and the sod was torn down to the mud by kids playing sports. A line of unremarkable children trudged along the sidewalk toward their equally unremarkable houses in the subdivision. At the origin of this line of children was my old elementary school.

I turned left and followed the edge of the park until we reached the parking lot of the school. It was still mostly full of cars but there was a slow trickle of adults coming out the teachers' exit.

"Have you ever thought about why we swing things like sticks and bats?" John asked.

I put the car in park and turned off the ignition. "Jesus Christ, John, what are you on about? Do you want to see this school or not?"

"I do," he said. "I was just thinking about physics. Who is that?"

A pudgy, be-sweatered teacher was huffing his way through the parking lot.

"No idea," I said.

John was staring at his hands, squeezing and releasing them slowly. "I mean, why not just use your fist or hand in baseball? Why use a bat?"

I sighed. "Because it hurts."

He shook his head. "Tennis, then. Tennis balls don't hurt. Why do we use a racket?"

"This is sounding like a conversation with Grace," I told him. He didn't reply, so I thought about it for a moment. "I suppose we use sticks and bats because we can hit the ball farther."

"Exactly," he practically shouted. An older woman made her way to her car. "So why can we hit the ball farther with a stick versus our hands?"

"No idea. Because it's harder? Because it makes our arms sort of longer?"

John smiled, opened his door, and got out of the car. Before he closed the door he reached back inside for the shovel. He said, "Come on."

I climbed out of the car but left the keys in the ignition. The car made a persistent dinging sound while my door was open. Outside it was still brisk but some sun had found a hole in the cloud cover and it felt amazing on my face. Another man left the school and John asked again, "Who is that?"

The man was bundled heavily and his hair was a little greyer but it still didn't take long to recognize him. "Christ, that's Mr. Stanley. I had him for homeroom in grade six. He taught the junior elementary kids science. I can't believe he's still here."

"Speaking of science," John said and grasped the shovel's handle like a bat. He lifted the arrowheaded blade off the ground a little and feigned hitting a ball. "So what's happening in a swing that's so magical?"

"No idea. John, what are we doing here?"

"In a minute," he said. He stuck the blade in the ground and pulled a toque and gloves from his pocket. I couldn't help smiling at his outfit: black pants, black pea coat, black toque, black gloves. He grabbed the shovel again by the end of the handle. "I'm going to swing again and you tell me what you see. Observation! That's half of science."

He stood in front of me waggling the blade of the shovel like an idiot until I said, "John, I have no idea what the hell you're getting at."

"Well, how far is the end of the shovel moving in one swing?" he asked.

"I don't know. A couple of feet?"

"And how far are my hands moving?"

I paused, a glimmer of insight coming to me. "Not very far. A couple of inches each way. Is that it? The end is moving faster than your hands."

"Almost!" he said. "Do you remember Newton's equations from high school?"

"Are you joking?"

John was wired with energy now, practically skipping from one foot to the other in excitement. I'd never seen him so boisterous before, never experienced anything other than calm and control from him. "Acceleration is the key. If you want more force, you need more acceleration. So your hands pull at the handle, which makes the tip speed up much faster than your hands could on their own, which increases the force. Then that force is transferred to the ball. Isn't that great?"

"Riveting," I said. I brought my hands to my face and blew on them. My fingers became warm for a moment and got cold again almost instantly. A few more teachers passed through the exit, one of whom was Ms. White, another of my homeroom teachers. It was amazing to go so unrecognized by these people, to be a couple of oddballs standing outside the parking lot with a shovel. "Is there a point to all of this, John?"

He smiled at me and stepped forward. His voice was quiet but bristling. "I've been reading about this, trying to figure out how to maximize my swing. Turns out the secret is in your hands. Poor swingers pull both of their hands in the same direction, trying to make the bat move forward faster. But professionals know you need to pull your hands in opposite directions."

He took another slow swing, showing me his right hand moving toward his body and his left hand moving away. He said, "When your hands move in opposite directions, it creates torque, and that increases the acceleration at the end of the bat. Therefore, more force. Who are they?"

Two men exited the school together. One was young and burly, and the other was much older but looked like he used to be a physical presence. I recognized the older teacher.

"What's his name?" I said aloud. "He taught Grace for two years in a row. The second year, she practically begged my parents to leave his class—"

"Thornton," John said.

"What? How—"

"Two of them. That's a shame."

It happened fast. John sprang away with the shovel trailing behind him a little. Something about the lightness of his steps reminded me of a deer running full speed. He shouted, "Hey," and both teachers looked up at him. There was one last step, still gripping the shovel at its end, and then he swung. His wide shoulders twisted perfectly and his hands pulled in opposite directions to maximize torque and all the force in the flat end of the shovel transferred into the face of Mr. Thornton.

The sound was like dropping a rock on a pile of meat. The old teacher stumbled and took a knee. At first he looked all right, only stunned. The younger teacher looked at John in utter confusion and before he could gather his senses John cross-checked him with the handle of the shovel as hard as he could. The push caused John's coat to rip along the seam of the shoulder and the younger teacher bounced off the hood of a car and onto the ground. This happened in an instant.

I looked back to Thornton and a black stream of blood began to gush from each nostril. He opened his mouth and it was a red, wet hole. John turned and said something to me but all I could hear was my heartbeat.

A dozen disjointed pieces of my sister's life suddenly fit together, connections that I'd been either too stupid to make or too eager to avoid. On his knees in front of me was the source of so much of Grace's unhappiness, the scar that my parents never truly acknowledged because they were too wrapped up in their own fighting, the secret everyone had kept from me. There was enough of a pause that I could have stopped what was about to happen, enough space and time to shout at John or hold him back. But instead I crossed my arms and let John continue. He took two quick steps toward the old man, like a track and field athlete, and swung again as hard as he could.

This time John's aim wasn't as precise and the shovel made contact where the blade's footrest and the handle connected. There was a terrific snap and I wasn't sure if it was the shovel or Thornton's cheekbone. Thornton twisted and fell and his face made a rough sound as it scraped across the asphalt. He was unconscious but he coughed and bits of teeth and tissue sputtered into a pool in front of him.

I thought for an instant that it would be cathartic, this late revenge for Grace. Instead it felt empty, a mistake, and John's logical extreme was horrific, not heroic. I ran to stop him from doing anything else, grabbed his shoulder, and he turned to me with a fist raised. When he saw it was me, he gave me a grotesque smile. Then he looked over my shoulder and stiffened.

The young, brutish teacher was rushing toward us. I put out my arms to block him and said, "Hold on—"

He grabbed my right arm and pulled it down and toward him. I stumbled forward into his blocky fist. It made contact with my left eye and I heard a crack and my neck snapped back. There were white and pink flashes and something hard slammed against the back of my head. I tried to move and realized I was on the ground, on my back. The world swam when I lifted my head so I put it down as lightly as I could.

There was a scuffling sound and some grunted half-words and another sharp crack. Then there were hands on me, pulling me up by the collar of my coat. I heard John say, "Come on. Come on."

He wrapped one of my arms around his neck and carried me. The toes of my shoes dragged against the ground. He opened a car door and threw me into a seat, and a moment later I heard the interior bell dinging for a few seconds as John got in. The ignition turned, the car went into gear, and we were away. It surprised me that he didn't squeal the tires but rather drove off calmly.

—

Eventually I could open both eyes and found that we were on the highway. The sun was setting and the sky was getting dark. I put my hand up to my bad eye and found that it was swollen and tender from the eyebrow to the cheekbone. The lid was closed.

I turned my head to look at John in the driver's seat. The world was still reeling in my vision and I groaned.

"You're all right," he said, "but you probably have a concussion."

I straightened my body in the seat and immediately felt lightning travel from my abdomen to my throat. I cranked open the window as quickly as I could, my stomach wrung itself out, and I vomited into the open air. A car honked behind us.

"You almost certainly have a concussion," he said.

The air on my skin was too much so I closed the window. The signs on the side of the road made it clear we were travelling west, back into the city. There were a number of things I wanted to say, all cycling through me. I settled on "What the fuck is wrong with you?"

"I'm sorry for dragging you into this," he said. "I keep saying that to myself, and then I keep dragging you in even further."

"Just shut up," I said. "Shut up. I'm done. I don't want to hear it."

He complied. We drove the highway in silence, no radio, and veered south into town. John parked us right in front of my basement apartment. He turned off the car but didn't get out. I wouldn't look at him but I could feel his eyes on me.

He said, "You know that I had a good reason for what just happened."

"Get the fuck out of my car, John," I told him.

"You could have stopped me but you didn't."

"Get out!"

He paused, almost said more, and then he opened the driver's side door and exited. He left the door open and the bell dinging straight into my skull. Eventually I raised myself from the passenger seat, collected the keys, and locked all the doors. My reliable car looked empty and useless without all of Grace's belongings filling the backseat. I looked north and could see the dark outline of John making his way toward home, the heavy backpack on his shoulders. The shovel was nowhere to be seen.

The lights were on in the apartment and it smelled like garlic when I came in the door. Nicole was at the kitchen counter and wearing a spattered apron.

"Hi," she said without turning to me. "I hope you're hungry."

The sight and smell of food, even the hiss of the frying pan, made me nauseated. I kicked off my shoes, made my way to the couch, lay down, and closed my eye. I didn't bother taking off my coat.

Eventually Nicole noticed my face and came over. "Oh god. Are you all right?"

"Fine," I told her.

"Hold on." She went back to the kitchen and brought some ice in a paper towel. "What happened?"

"Nothing," I said. She kept thrusting the ice at my face but it stung to the touch and I didn't like having her arms so close to me. I pushed her hands away and closed my eyes. "Just lay off for a minute. Jesus."

"Did you get mugged? Have you been to the hospital?"

She was breathing all over me, her hands just above my face. I said, "Can you just leave me alone for once? It's nothing."

She held her breath. She was still. Then she stood up.

"What the fuck is wrong with you?" she asked.

She went to the kitchen, then yanked out some drawers in the bedroom, and finally she slammed the front door. I kept my eyes closed and must have fallen asleep. When I awoke, I found a half-cooked dinner, cold and congealed. Nicole didn't come home after that.

2006

IT WAS A SLOW MORNING at work. My bosses sent me out on a coffee run, and when I returned there was a sticky note on the computer monitor at my desk.

Nicole called
P.S. Keep personal calls to minimum

I waited until they were out of the office for lunch.

"Hi, Trouble."

"Danger. Your boss man wasn't pleased to hear from me."

"He's probably in a fight with boss lady. There's nothing else to do around here right now."

"They should let you come home, then. I could find something for you to do."

"Hah. Right."

"*The idea that the poor should have leisure has always been shocking to the rich.* Your bosses should read Russell."

"I'll let them know. Not sure they'll take philosophic advice from my cook girlfriend, though."

"What, I can't have a rich, intellectual life? Do I suddenly have to frame all my metaphors with food?" She was smiling through the phone. "Listen, when do you want to leave tonight? I want to make sure I have enough time to bake something for your mom."

"About that . . . I've been thinking."

"Hey." A pause. "Don't do this."

"I'm sorry, Nicole. It's just that, after the whole fight between you and Grace—"

"This has been planned for over a month."

"I just think it'd be better if you two weren't duking it out at the kitchen table. Grace and my mother already don't get along well."

"I booked the day off work."

"I'm sorry, Trouble."

"I have to go."

Nicole was reading in bed when I got home, her legs tucked under the covers. She put down her book when I came into the room. "So let me get this straight: you, Grace, and John are all going to dinner."

"Yes," I said.

"It's just me who is excluded."

"I know it sounds horrible—"

"It *is* horrible!" she said. "Do you have any idea how that makes a person feel?"

"I really am sorry," I said, crouching in front of her. "If it's any consolation, I think you're the lucky one in all this. I'd rather stay here and read with you."

"*Read?*" The faintest hint of a smile, which was a relief for me. She leaned forward for a kiss and then shoved me away. "Now out of my sight, thank you."

—

Despite the mild weather, Grace was huddled with John's arms draped over her. She climbed into the front passenger seat and John got in the back. I was double-parked and cars honked at me as they got in.

"You're late," Grace told me.

"What the hell do you care?" I said. "You don't even want to go."

"Jesus, you're snippy. What's your problem?"

I looked in the rear-view mirror. John and I exchanged a nod of greeting.

"Anyway, you're right," Grace said. "I have zero interest in going. So let's just cancel."

"We're going," I told her. I put the car in gear and drove off. "Mom harasses me about visiting every week."

"So go visit without me," she said.

"You're a real charmer tonight," I told her. "Mom harasses me about *you* visiting every week."

"If she wants to know about me, she can ask me herself."

"You'd have to pick up your phone," John said from the back.

The car was quiet until we reached the highway. My phone buzzed in my pocket and I knew it was my mother, wondering where we were. Grace and John stared out the window and watched as the storefronts became unfamiliar, then absent. I veered the car onto the 401 and, sick of the silence, I turned on the stereo.

Grace's mix CD started to play. I skipped back to the second song. Some indeterminate squeal, maybe an electric keyboard, droned away until the bass and kick drum dropped in. And as always, just as I felt I was getting the hang of the rhythm, the guitars and cymbals crashed in and reset the beat.

"God, I love these guys," I said.

"What's your sample size?" John asked from the back. He was smiling, trying to be light.

"What?"

Grace was hunched in her seat, bundled in her layers. She chewed at her thumb and didn't turn away from her view out the window.

"You said you love these guys," John said. "How many of their songs do you know?"

"I don't know. Really only this one, I guess."

"So your sample size is one. Not exactly statistically significant."

I laughed. "You're a dick. O.K., I love this song. I've listened to this song hundreds of times. Sample size is hundreds. Totally statistically significant. Dick."

I let the CD play out and we didn't talk much. We watched the landscape make its familiar transformations and took all the usual exits to my mother's house. I pulled into the driveway.

"I should be at work," Grace said.

"It'll wait," John said from the back.

"This was a mistake," Grace muttered.

"Come on," I said. "She's waiting at the door."

"I don't want to do this," Grace said.

"It'll just be a couple of hours," John said. He reached a hand to her shoulder in the front. "We can do this."

"It's not you who has to *do* anything, goddamn it," Grace said, her voice getting high. "Don't act like this is difficult for you."

"It shouldn't be difficult for anybody," I said. "It's *dinner*. Suck it up."

I climbed out of the car and came around to the passenger side. Grace didn't budge when I opened the door for her.

"Out," I said.

Reluctantly she began to move. John followed her, patting me on the arm as he passed me. Our mother made a shrill sound from the front porch. The three of us approached the house, myself in the front.

"Oh," our mother cried. She'd left her work clothes on and tried to tame the frizz of her hair with some water. She passed me without any acknowledgement and put her arms around Grace. "Christ almighty, I wouldn't believe it if I didn't see it."

———

Dinner was surprisingly civil to start, most likely because my sister snuck out beforehand to smoke a joint. Our mother fired questions at Grace, John answered most of them, and I diverted our mother's attention whenever I could. We sat at the dining room table and didn't move. The rest of the house was dim and quiet except for the hum of the television in the living room.

After dinner I collected the plates from the table and told my mother, "Nicole wishes she could be here."

"Nicole, eh?" my mother said. She couldn't have cared less about what was going on in my life, and Nicole's name passed, flickered, and disappeared from her awareness. "Coffee, anybody?"

"Please," John told her.

When the table was clear, I sat down again with John and Grace. My mother scurried around the kitchen. The white noise of an electric kettle rose in the background and made me feel uneasy. Over that anxious sound, my mother shouted, "God, it's nice to have everyone under one roof again."

"Everyone?" Grace said, meaning our father.

My mother unplugged the kettle and brought it to the table, its cord dangling behind her, then shuffled back into the kitchen.

"I miss the good old days," she said.

"When was that, exactly?" Grace asked.

"Oh hell, you know what I mean," my mother said. She brought four mugs to the table. "It was just so nice when you were kids."

Grace was becoming agitated, fidgety. "Are you joking?"

Our mother brought a jar of instant coffee and some milk to the table and sat down.

"Hey, instant coffee," John said to Grace, in a calm voice. "Everybody's favourite."

But whatever soothing effect John had had the last time we four ate dinner together, it had faded. Grace just glared at him.

My mother was spooning the coffee powder into the mugs and not paying attention to the subtleties of the conversation. She smiled at John. "Things were just simpler, you know? She was always so bloody bright. A royal pain in my ass, of course, but she was happy, and so how could I complain?"

"What kind of revisionist bullshit is this?" Grace demanded.

"Grace," I said.

"Honey," our mother said, "I know it was a little tough when your father left—"

Grace interrupted, "I'm not talking about Dad—"

"—and obviously there was going to be some acting out, you said and did some things, you always had a temper, ever since you were a baby. But we got over it, didn't we?" She seemed to suddenly realize how fraught this conversation had become, and smiled at Grace to calm her.

There was a painful silence and then Grace spat, "Are you fucking insane?"

My mother's face pinched a little at the curse. She looked old. "Jesus, honey. Show some respect."

I wanted none of this conversation. I'd witnessed enough variants of it from the time my sister shaved her head at thirteen until she finally moved out for university. "Can we just take a time-out for a second?"

"You stay out of this," Grace said to me, quietly. "Do you have any idea what it was like for me, Mom?"

"Why are you being like this?" my mother said and frowned. "You talk like I was such a bad mother."

"You were," Grace said. "You were the worst."

"Will you give it a rest?" I said.

In one quick motion Grace pushed back her chair and stood. She stomped through the carpeted living room and straight into the foyer. John rose and followed her. There was some muttering between them, then the sound of keys, then the slamming of the front door.

"She was always so difficult," my mother said. "Always convinced that everyone was against her, willing to do or say whatever, just to get revenge. Your father and I would just sit back and wait for the storm to blow over."

Her eyes were brimming and shiny. She bit the dry flakes of skin from her bottom lip. "But I wasn't so bad, was I?"

"No, Mom," I said. I put my hand on hers. Still, something Grace had said was bothering me. I'd heard them fight countless times but I had never heard anything that suggested there was some specific catalyst: *Do you have any idea what it was like for me, Mom?*

John came back to the dining room and sat down. My mother excused herself and went upstairs.

"She took your car," John said.

Before I realized what he was telling me, I heard Grace screech out of the driveway.

—

The three of us sat on the old couch and watched television. My mother held my hand and occasionally squeezed it. I wanted to scream but instead I smiled at her.

Two hours later, I heard Grace lay on my car horn for ten straight seconds. I rushed to the front door and gave her an angry stare through the window. We put on our coats and shoes and I hugged my mother goodbye. She got shrill again and urged me to visit soon. During the goodbyes, Grace lay on the horn another time and I swung open the door and shouted, "For Christ's sake, enough."

My mother stood on the porch and waved at Grace. I couldn't make out the expression on her face.

When I opened the driver's side door, the interior light came on and it was immediately apparent that Grace hadn't just been driving around. She was scattered, wild haired, and dirty. I was too annoyed to care. I shouted at her, "Move."

She slid to the passenger seat, her eyes like saucers. She didn't seem to notice my mother waving at her but instead wore a vacant look. I took the driver's seat and found that the car had an odd, unwashed-human smell. John climbed into the backseat.

I reversed out of the driveway, sped through the suburbs as quickly as I could. The stereo was off and I left it that way. No one spoke for thirty minutes. Cars flickered by but all I saw was their headlights. I drove over the speed limit the entire time.

Finally John spoke up. "Are you all right?"

Grace said nothing. She only stared, the gloss of her eyes catching electric light as it approached and passed.

"What the hell were you thinking," I said, not a question. And then, feeling John's disapproval from the backseat, "Where have you been?"

The question seemed to resonate. Her wide eyes became slits and her slack face became taut.

"Looking into a dead end," she said.

"What the hell does that mean?" I asked. I wanted to demand an answer but she was turned to the backseat, facing John.

"You *lied* to me," she said. "You've watched me fail in the lab, over and over, and all this time—all this time!—you've known how. You've been keeping the truth from me, in your little code book."

John squared his jaw and faced his accuser. He didn't say a word. I glanced in the rear-view mirror and over at the passenger seat but ultimately I had to keep my eyes on the road.

"Is anyone going to let me in on what the hell we're talking about, for once?" I asked.

No one spoke again for the rest of the trip.

I left Grace and John on the sidewalk in front of their apartment door. It was late but the lights were on in the basement when I got home, warming the windows with a yellow glow. I unlocked the door, entered quietly, and found the room full of the smell of baking. Nicole was sprawled out on the couch watching a movie, still wearing her apron. When she saw the look on my face, she immediately stood, walked to the door, and wrapped her arms around me. I hugged her back and felt my muscles loosen.

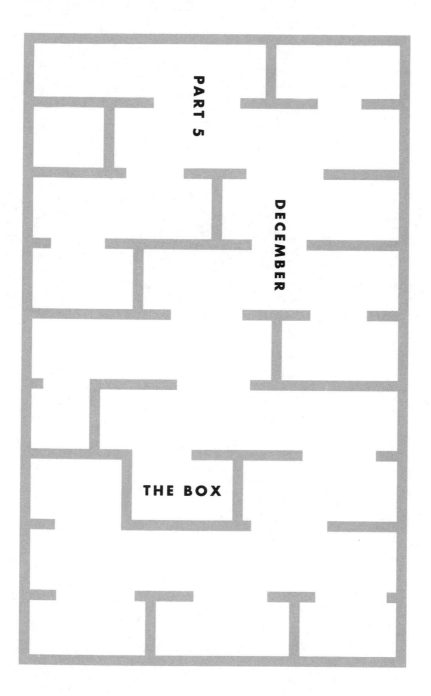

PART 5

DECEMBER

THE BOX

2008

THE NEW RULES are slippery. I phone Brian again and take some comfort in a familiar voice, but, like Lee, he doesn't remember John or Grace. The next time I call him he's unsure of who I am, tries hard to be friendly but ultimately treats me like a stranger. The last time I pick up the phone, I find that my cellular service has been disconnected. It isn't clear whether it's because I haven't paid the bill in months or because I no longer exist in their registry.

Still, at the hardware store down the street, looking for a large pane of mirror, I'm in luck.

"Some guy ordered it but never came back," the clerk says.

"What guy?" I ask.

He looks through his computer but there's no longer any record of my name. He doesn't seem to remember my face, either. I convince him to sell me the mirror as well as a small flashlight and a set of batteries.

I stay indoors mostly, waiting for the landlord to knock on my door and ask for rent money I don't have. It never comes. In fact I don't recognize the people I see using the suite upstairs, and they don't seem to notice me peering through my blinds in the basement window. I leave the apartment only for cheap food, bell peppers and onions and tofu and rice from the Vietnamese grocer on Dundas Street, using the cash I took from the machine while it still worked. My key still fits in the lock whenever I return, and what few belongings I have are always there.

My money dwindles and all but disappears. No one visits.

It takes a week of false starts and careless errors to sand the glue and residue off the broken panel, affix the large mirror to its inner surface, and polish the glass inside the box until the reflection is free of oily fingerprints and dust. I test the alignment of the refurbished panel with the rest of the box and make small corrections, careful to never fully enclose myself inside. Buddy stands on the roof of the box and observes.

Cautious about inexplicable prying eyes, I drape towels over every mirror and reflective surface in the house, and without day–night cycles I soon lose track of time. I read and reread John's decoded pages, and try cipher after cipher on the remaining sections of his lab notebook. Using *whatsyoursamplesize* as the key, I unlock a third section of the notebook, and pore over it for any crucial information. There's no longer a couch to sit on, there wasn't a television to begin with, and the few CDs in the apartment are from my undergraduate days in Vancouver and bring me no comfort. Every sound outside makes me hold my breath and listen. I stop putting Buddy back in his cage, and some nights I wake and see his two glistening eyes looking at me from the end of the bed. If he judges me, he stays silent about it. In exchange, I clean up his shit wherever I find it.

Nearly everything is ready. The box is as complete and perfect as I can make it. One pouch of earth should be enough for my journey, and I have Buddy for a guide. But first I have some unfinished business.

—

Throughout the day I peek out the basement window, waiting for dusk. When it finally comes, I unveil the mirror above the washroom sink. My head looks round and fuzzy, like a tennis ball, so I use the electric razor to trim the hair back. I shower and shave and take a good look. The face is thin, the eyes are sunken, but the line of cheek and jaw isn't displeasing. The short haircut makes me look younger. Altogether my appearance isn't as horrible as it could be. And though I'm the only figure in the reflection, I cover the mirror again to be safe and leave the bathroom.

I put on my best clothes, black pants and a white collared shirt. As I dress, I rehearse lines of dialogue, witticisms, the act of smiling. Blood swishes through my ears and my heart is racing. Buddy watches me muttering to myself.

"I'm nervous," I say to him. "Isn't that absurd?"

He doesn't respond, only twitches his nose and turns away.

After bundling myself in warm layers, I slip on my winter boots and leave the apartment.

Outside it is dark and quiet. The city lights reflect off the cloud cover and so the sky has a little pink and orange mixed in the deep blue. Winter has arrived, and fat flakes of snow fall gently to earth. This first layer quickly melts and chills the surface of Toronto. Snowfall passes through the electric-yellow light of the street lamps in a steady, curved current. It is beautiful. Flakes land on my shoulders and in my grey knitted scarf. They melt on my face like cold kisses.

It's a short walk down the street to the Cuckoo. Through its bay window, I can see her, the life of the party and the centre of her friends' attention. Nicole.

My focus shifts to my reflection, to the glint of a mirrored streetcar rumbling down Dundas. There are no shadowy figures but still

I expect they're watching. There isn't any more time to waste. I take a deep breath and enter the bar.

Moving toward Nicole's table, I recognize Lee and Brian among the group, their elbows and thighs pressed against each other, their smiles private, their presence at the table only cursory. It isn't surprising that Steve is absent. I raise a hand in greeting to them and they stare, puzzled, and look to each other for clarity.

On the other side of the table is the woman with whom I used to live. At first the group continues to chirp, to drink, to chuckle, to gaze in Nicole's direction. Then my looming presence begins to weigh on them until they become quiet and agitated. Attention shifts to me, Nicole's last of all. She looks at me, really looks at me, and I cannot help but smile. She smiles in return, but there is something strange in it. She is sizing me up.

"Hi," I say to her. I can feel all eyes on me.

"Hello," she says. She wears a simple dress and leggings for warmth and less make-up than her usual. She looks perfect.

"Happy birthday," I tell her.

Her smile broadens, her eyes squint a little, and she cocks her head to the side ever so slightly. I have seen this look before.

"Where do I know you from?" she asks. My smile falters.

Someone at the table coughs. I glance at Brian and Lee. Brian turns away, uncomfortable, but Lee stares back with some kind of abstract concern. I am just a sickly-looking stranger standing over a crowd of friends at a birthday party.

"Oh Christ," I say. "O.K. There are a few things I need to say to you, Nicole. Please. I don't think it'll take too long."

It feels as though the group is holding its collective breath. Only Nicole looks relaxed.

"You don't have to trust me," I say. My throat is dry and it makes my voice hoarse. "You just have to be too intrigued to say no."

Her gaze hasn't broken from mine and in it I feel no judgement, only curiosity. She takes a moment before she speaks. "Sure, I'll listen. Provided you stop standing awkwardly over the table."

And while she pokes fun at me, there is only kindness in her manner.

———

The walk is her idea but it is exactly what I wanted. We move south down a side street, into the neighbourhood of her new apartment. At first we are silent. Snow tumbles down and the streets are cold enough now that it sticks to the hoods of cars and the branches of trees. We are two black shapes moving across a pale landscape.

Nicole matches my pace step for step but does not look at me.

"I suppose Lee warned you that this was a bad idea," I say. The two of them had spoken in harsh tones before we left.

"I suppose she did," Nicole says. "You seem to know an awful lot about us."

"Just about you, and a little about her and Brian and Steve." Our footsteps make a soft crunching sound. "You really don't remember anything? There's nothing familiar about me?"

She opens her mouth as if to say something, but then closes it again. Finally she says, "Sorry. I have a lot of suitors."

"Yes, you do." I laugh. And then it's gone and I feel like there is very little to laugh about. "Everything I had to say to you was based on you knowing who I am."

"If that were true, then you wouldn't have left the Cuckoo with me." She's right. We walk a few more paces and suddenly she stops, pivots on the sidewalk, faces me. "So then?"

"So." I turn to her and she looks up at me. Under the street light I can see that her cheeks and nose are pink from the chilly air.

A few wisps of hair poke out of her toque. "I guess I wanted to say happy birthday—"

"Which you've done."

"—and I'm sorry. And that you were right."

She narrows her eyes and examines my face. I'm not sure what she sees. Then she turns and continues walking. I fall into step with her.

I say, "And I told myself that if we got this far then I would ask something small of you."

She is staring at her feet as she walks, thinking. "What's that?"

"I wanted to hear a song."

———

We enter through the front door of the Victorian-style house and make our way up the stairs. Her room is painted in a light coffee colour and has large windows facing the quiet residential street. She has far fewer material possessions than when we lived together, but the overflowing bookshelf looks the same. There is no overhead lighting, only a string of warm Christmas lights tacked to the wall and a table lamp in the corner. It smells like her apartment, like oranges.

"I've never been inside here before," I say.

"Well, that's some small comfort," she replies. She pulls off her outer layers.

I consider what this must be like from her perspective. "Do you often bring suitors into your apartment, the first time you meet them?"

"Only if I like them. Or, as in your case, if I think they're pathetic and harmless. Coat." She hangs my pea coat in the front closet. "To be honest, there's something so familiar about you but I can't place it. Like an itch I can't seem to scratch. Sit."

She motions to the couch and I sit. It's firm but made with a soft material, far nicer than the one we used to own, a grown-up's couch. I run my hand along its arm and watch as she sifts through a pile of burned CDs next to the stereo. She is crouched, a smooth curved figure. Her orange hair is tied up and leaves the nape of her neck exposed.

Without turning away from her task she asks, "Why are you sorry?"

I sit forward and take a moment to consider my answer. "I wasn't good to you. You need someone who tells you what's going on in his head, someone who can communicate how he's feeling, someone who doesn't resent you for stupid reasons. I wasn't that person and it ruined us. And that's why I'm sorry."

She turns to me and asks, "When was this?"

There's something a little sad in her expression. I wonder if she can feel hurt about a breakup that never existed for her. I wonder if she is even the same woman who broke up with me, whether she's been rewritten or perhaps just replaced with another version of herself. Or maybe it's me who never existed. Maybe she's thinking about the relationships that took place in my absence.

When she realizes I'm not going to respond, she goes back to searching the CD collection. "And you said I was right about something?"

"You gave me advice, recently," I say. "Told me I needed to put on my big-boy pants and stop feeling sorry for myself."

"Well, that part sounds like me." She lifts a broken jewel case into the air, takes the CD out, and places it in the player. Then she comes and sits on the arm of the couch, as far from me as she can be while still sharing the same seat. "But you know it couldn't have been me. It isn't possible. Either that or you *don't* know. I suppose you could be sadder and more deranged than you already look."

How would she respond in my position? Then it comes to me. "Does it matter if it's possible? Whether my memories are of real events, whether my feelings come from things that actually happened . . . none of that changes the fact that I have these memories and these feelings."

"The feelings are real," she says, "even if the events aren't."

I nod.

"So you *are* deranged, then," she says.

I smile. "Objectively speaking, yes. Subjectively, I've got my shit together now more than ever."

She frowns at me, wants to be nonplussed, but I know those upturned corners of her mouth. For once she has no retort. To busy herself she tucks her hair behind her ears and then reaches for the remote control to the stereo. Her lips pout just a little. The song starts. I close my eyes.

How many times have I heard this song? Hiss, whirr, organ, bass, kick drum, simmer, explode. The song crescendos once even before the first lyric is sung, then comes down again and leaves room for a single male voice. He is hoarse and urgent.

There's no fine future waiting
In the depths of the freshwater seas.
I'll find my oblivion
In the place where the water meets the trees.
There is no point in asking
The truth of the vision a man sees.
Shine a light on oblivion
In the place where the water meets the trees.

The song moves in waves, trails off, seems as if it's about to fade, and out of nowhere the voice shouts the refrain again, *In the place where the water meets the trees.* The song builds to an unbearable wall of noise and then stops all at once.

I open my eyes and look at Nicole. Hers are still shut. Her fists are bunched together and pressed against her lips, as when she sleeps. Her shoulders rise and fall with her slow breaths. Then she opens her eyes and stops the CD.

"That's clever," she says. "I never noticed the reference before."

"What?" I ask.

"In Iroquois, it's more like *The place where there are trees in the water*, or *where trees stand in the water*, but I suppose that isn't quite as poetic in English." Her eyes are hazel and looking only at me. "It's the meaning of the word *Toronto*."

—

By the time we head back to the Cuckoo, the snow has formed thick white sediment over the city and reflects the artificial light until everything is pink and orange and black. We walk closer together than before and I notice that her mittened hand is within my reach.

"You don't know me," she says quietly.

"You work as a cook in a restaurant in Kensington," I tell her.

"Too factual."

"You spend your weekends volunteering at a soup kitchen."

"Too factual."

"You arc always reading something good. You're a smoker."

"I quit about a year ago." She shakes her head. Snow is piling up on her toque and shoulders. "This is all too factual. It's just content."

"What are you talking about?"

She says, "You're describing my existence, the content, but not my essence. *Existence precedes essence.*"

"You're an insufferable quoter," I tell her. "You can be hard on others but you're a good person. When you're asleep you look like you're dreaming about a boxing match."

She keeps shaking her head and I can feel the space widening between us. "Who am I? What do I really want? What am I afraid of? What do I love? You don't know me at all. At all."

Her mittened hand is still close, but I don't reach for it. She avoids looking at me and huddles herself for warmth.

"And I don't know why that makes me *so sad*," she says. Her voice cracks.

We round the corner onto Dundas. The Cuckoo is just a few steps away, where she'll be lost to me again. Did I ever have her?

"You're right," I say. "I don't know you well enough. But I know you a little. I know that all you really want is to receive what you give. You want someone to think you're always the most interesting person at the party."

She glances my way. She isn't smiling but she doesn't look unhappy. The toque pushes her hair down and it frames her face. We keep eye contact for a moment and it feels like filling my lungs after I've held my breath underwater.

A moment later we reach the bar. Nicole waves to her friends through the front window and indicates she'll be one more minute.

"Come inside," she says kindly, then makes a game of it. "That isn't a promise of anything, just an opportunity."

Following her *is* an opportunity, one that I hadn't considered. It could be a new beginning, free of our past and all its disappointments. This is a chance to get things right with Nicole, to grieve, to heal. We could fall in love again, I could find a meaningful job, and we could be happy. All I have to do is leave Grace and John to their own devices. And Nicole would never know I abandoned them.

"I can't," I tell her. "Some of my loved ones are in trouble, and in part it was my fault. I need to help them if I can."

"Well, that makes about as much sense as everything else you've said." She smiles. "Do you have a plan?"

"I have some ideas, but I've been kind of making it up as I go. To be honest, I've been met with resistance at almost every step of the way."

"Well," she says, "you'll always find what you bring with you."

"Is that Aristotle?" I ask.

She laughs and shakes her head. She grabs onto the lapels of my coat and stands on tiptoes. Then she kisses me on the cheek, once, lightly. She says, "Goodbye, strange boy."

Without another glance she turns and walks inside. Through the bay window I watch her reunite with her friends, them raising their glasses in tribute, her shrugging and smiling unapologetically. My cheek burns. I smell oranges.

—

There's no point locking the apartment door behind me. I don't take off my winter coat or my boots or my toque.

"Buddy!" I shout. "Come on. It's time to do this."

Eventually he crawls out from the folds of the comforter on my bed. I scoop him up and pet him along his snout before placing him on my shoulder.

In the left pocket of my pea coat I place a small pouch full of earth from the dead end near John's childhood home. In my right pocket is my new flashlight, fresh batteries already installed. The photograph of John and Grace is in my back pocket, as is a photograph of Nicole. I consider taking a knife or a hammer or some other violent means, but Nicole's words echo in me: *You'll always find what you bring with you.* In the end I take no weapons.

The wooden box is the only object left in my living room. It is only slightly less impressive and perfect than it looked in John and Grace's apartment. The edges are rounded and smooth to the touch, and the grain of the wood is beautiful. When I reach the side with the handle, I slide open the panel and look at the cube's crystalline interior. It is flawless aside from my image. I crouch and step inside.

On my shoulder, Buddy taps at me with one of his forepaws in a slow, steady rhythm. He learned this behaviour from my sister, or perhaps from John, while living in the sterile laboratory.

"Sorry, Buddy," I say. "I don't have any sugar pellets for you."

He continues to raise and lower his paw. It's a gentle feeling and it calms me as I stand on the glass inside the box. Through the open panel, I take one last look at the basement apartment, the little world I once built.

I think of John and Grace.

I think of Nicole.

I think of all the resistance that preceded this moment.

And then I let go.

—

I close the panel of the mirrored box and lock myself inside.

SILHOUETTE BREAKS RANK – III

*Grace used to boil a kettle just before she sat down to supper.
When she finished eating, she'd put her plate in the sink and
bring the kettle, a mug, and a jar of instant coffee to the
table. I usually stayed to watch her heave one large spoonful
of instant coffee into the mug and pour the water in slowly.
I would say nothing, only breathe deeply and enjoy the rich
smell of her after-dinner ritual.*

*On the table would be a small container of spoons, and
from it she'd carefully consider and draw one for stirring.
While the coffee was still spinning, she would add cream, only
a pale thread at first but eventually undermining the deep
colour in the mug. When it had stopped swirling, Grace would
dip her spoon just under the surface and ladle out a small pool.
This tiny serving of coffee would absorb all her attention until
the steam was nearly gone and she put the spoon to her mouth.
Only then, after her satisfactory first taste of instant coffee,
would she look to me, smile, and acknowledge my presence.
Some days, she would dip that spoon in again and pull out a*

little coffee for me. I hated the bitterness, that liquid ash, but I would never refuse such a moment of sharing.

Of course, I am not at my lover's table and this is not our kitchen. This is the psychiatric wing of Toronto-Bathurst Hospital, walls the blandest shade of green one could imagine, two simple and hard beds, an ancient oak desk that was likely donated by a wealthy benefactor, a single window that does not open. These spoonfuls of coffee, delicate and full, are not in Grace's hand but rather in my own. The mug is not one of her handcrafted discoveries but is instead labelled as property of the hospital. There are no jars full of spoons, and in fact there are no metal utensils or nail clippers or anything with which one could puncture, stab, or in general wound oneself. There is only the thick double door that keeps out the human din, entered and exited only with permission of the front staff, and the beautiful quietude that such a barrier provides. This is a space where I can sleep.

—

About two months after she disappeared, Grace started visiting at night. The first time, she was in the broken mirror of our spare bedroom. She was standing alone, arms wrapped around herself as if she were cold. She lifted her head, illuminating her face, and I had no doubt that it was her. I checked the room, but she wasn't there; only her reflection remained, looking at me, lips moving, saying something. I pressed my ear against the shattered glass, but of course I heard only my pulse.

She looked different each time she visited. Some nights she was filthy, her clothes torn and her face smudged with dirt. Other nights she was clean, dressed in simple, fitted clothes I did not recognize. Seemingly at random her hair grew and shrank, frizzed and flattened, greyed and browned. And for about a month, she haunted me with no obvious purpose or motivation. Her face was always inscrutable.

Then the whispers began, as polarized as her appearance. The first time she woke me to say, I shouldn't have closed myself off from you at the end. Another night she said, You're a fucking pathetic, lying, worthless human being. You were never on my team. She vacillated from love to hate, praise to scorn. The whispers became increasingly frequent, almost nightly occurrences, and the anticipation was as bad as the experience. I found myself waking every few hours even when she wasn't around, terrified that she'd come again, terrified that I might have missed her.

I never responded to her, never replied or spoke. Giving words to it would have made it real, an impossible terror; or worse, it would have shattered the hallucination, taken away any last connection to her, even if it was caused by prolonged wakefulness.

I'd long since stopped going to the lab, so there was nothing to keep me in the city. I stayed in a few motels for a few weeks, visiting tourist towns around the Great Lakes in their off season, and for a short time I thought it had worked. Then one night in Grand Bend I awoke to her shouting. You can't escape me, she said. You can't just run away from your mistakes.

The next morning, I took a few buses back to the city and out to my parents' house in Oshawa. I told them I was taking a spring break. My mother complained about the dark circles under my eyes, but she was enthusiastic about feeding me, and excited to have me as unpaid labour for the gas station. My father was happy to have my mother's attention off himself and, of course, to commiserate with me later over his evening television.

Nights, I would lie in my childhood bed and watch the headlights of an occasional car pass by my window. Inevitably Grace would come, speak to me so quietly that she must have been standing beside the bed, although I could see nothing of her on my side. I took my mother's compact mirror from her bathroom and kept it under my pillow. Some nights, when Grace's voice would come to me, I would flip open the compact and see nothing. Other nights, her lips would be next to my ear, whispering. Only some of it made sense.

I miss you.

I will fucking kill you if you tell my brother anything.

Thank you for what you did to Thornton.

You will always be weak.

How are you doing, my love?

—

I stopped sleeping altogether.

The memories of that period become jumbled, mixed in with each other. My mother became suspicious when my week-long break turned into months, when I made no attempts to leave the house except to work for her. In that time, I must have finally said something about Grace's disappearance; even her name became enough to get my mother upset. Meanwhile, Grace began visiting multiple times a night, her mood alternating more wildly than ever. There was an incident at the gas station involving a small fire, but the details are confused in my memory. My mother sent me home to bed.

It was still light outside when I lay down, still noisy with suburban activity, but the next thing I knew it was a black, silent night. Grace was near me. I could feel her breath on my cheek.

In a hoarse voice she said, You could have been here with me this entire time. You could have been the one to bring me here. You knew where there was an entrance, but you were too chickenshit to do anything about it. That first night in Bellevue Square, you mumbled about being able to see strange things. You had been given such a gift and you were miserable about it!

Then, almost immediately after, she spoke again, only this time in my other ear and her voice seemed smooth, calm. She said, I'm sorry for all of this, John. It isn't simple, here. I miss you.

I was delirious, exhausted. I began to shout: Where are you? What do you want from me? Why did you go to the dead end? Why are you doing this to me? Please come back to me.

I fumbled over my words and I pounded my fists against the floor. I had kept my mouth closed for months and now I couldn't stop screaming. Please come back to me. Please come back to me. My parents came to my room, shouting at each other, What is wrong with him? When I finally quieted, my mother looked at my father and said, I told you that girl was trouble. Before her, he had a good job. Remember?

I calmed myself, told them I'd had a nightmare and sent them back to bed. When I was sure they were asleep, I packed my belongings and walked the five kilometres from my parents' new house to the neighbourhood where I had grown up.

It was dawn when I reached the dead end. The sign still stood where it always had, a defiant diamond just out of range of direct sunlight. A small, dirty patch of land remained undeveloped between our old subdivision and the new one, and it seemed remarkable that no one could acknowledge the absurdity of a dead end between two finished communities. Its secret remained kept even after all these years, except to Grace and me. A few times, I had visited this site to collect tiny samples of earth, to secretly supplement Grace's rat research, and it had felt harmless. This time, the threat of the place was palpable.

I walked across the empty street, stepped from the curb, and approached the threshold of the dead end without hesitation or pomp. Something around me lurched and turned over as I stood next to the sign, caused light to briefly bend and shimmer around me. Something was furious with me, with my desire to cross. And it dawned on me, although I was more tired than I had ever been: if I crossed that threshold, I would be at the mercy of those forces. I might find Grace on the other side but I would be powerless. This was someone else's entrance.

And that was when the plan started to form, a simple variation on the research with the rats. If I built my own entrance, I could cross to the other side on my own terms. I could control this phenomenon. I couldn't use the earth from the dead end anymore; I had to find another solution. I walked away from that threshold and took the next train back to Toronto.

—

It's been a false start, of course. Those first nights back in the city, I stayed up waiting to be terrified and comforted by the ghost of Grace. She didn't come. I took to walking the streets until dawn, trying to tire myself sufficiently to sleep, but no amount of walking could suffice. It was with horror that I realized her absence was worse than any awful thing she could have said to me, any scare she could have delivered. What little grip I had on waking life slipped completely.

*I knew better than to try sleeping pills, knew their
harmful and cumulative effects, but try them I did. I tried
them and tried them and tried them. Then one evening I
awoke. I was so happy to have slept that at first I didn't
realize I had been hospitalized. Someone had found me
in the hallway of our apartment, face down on the stairs.
When the nurse came to my hospital bed, she tried to
comfort me by telling me that no one had stolen my
possessions while I was unconscious.*

 *The emergency team quickly decided I needed the mental
health team, and a few referrals later I found myself here.
Each night I sleep more than the previous one, and it has been
glorious. I spend days looking through the window. Outside
are lovers, wanderers, streetcars, and the first hints of summer.
I tell my psychiatrist about the distance I feel between everyone
and how I don't want to believe it's right or normal. For a
time, Grace was here and that distance was closed, and even
her apparition (or hallucination, as I describe it to the doctor)
was better than no Grace at all. I make instant coffee five times
a day, and I sip it from the plastic spoons the ward provides. I
build my strength each day by degrees. I write these fragments
of my life to remind myself that they were real, not simply some
manifestation of my grief, and I encode them so the doctors can't
read them. I listen, and I wait.*

 *There have been no unusual reflections, no whispers in the
night from Grace. In fact my world has become much more
mundane. Her brother visits me in the hospital from time
to time, and I can't help but pity his need for approval from
those he thinks more intelligent than himself. Like a puppy,
he's loyal and eager to please, but his presence makes me
lonelier than I thought possible. I can't decide which is worse:*

*being absolutely known by the unknown, or being absolutely
unknown by the known.*

*Each day I tell them all I am feeling a little better, and in
a sense it is true.*

*I can't wait to leave this place and start building my
entrance. I can't wait to have control. And I can't wait to see
that other side with Grace.*

2007

THERE WAS NO BLOW-UP, no defining moment, just a few more scattered arguments and then nothing at all. One morning I awoke on the couch again and realized Nicole hadn't come home the previous night. I wasn't sure if she had been home the night before that, either.

Her things began to disappear. I got back to the apartment after work each day and something new had vanished: clothes, shoes, make-up, books. One day the nice pots and pans were gone. Another day it was the bookshelf, then the night table and alarm clock, then the art from the walls. One afternoon she took her pillow. It's amazing how sad a bed looks with only one pillow on it.

We had each other's telephone numbers. We didn't use them.

One day it simply stopped. I found her key in the mailbox. When I entered the basement, many of her things were still there: couch, cutlery, bed, linens, and an assortment of books scattered about the apartment. She had successfully removed me from her life but had left her own removal incomplete. I considered throwing out her belongings, buying new furniture, maybe even a houseplant. Then I started sleeping in the bed again and leafing through the books. I lived with the remnants of her.

—

John called me at work one afternoon. I'd been ignoring him since the attack on Thornton, uninterested in his extremes or his empty promises. It wouldn't have surprised me to see the police show up at my door. So when he called my work, I told him flatly that I was busy and would get in touch when it was convenient. The next day, my bosses left me a note that John had called while I was on lunch. Without Nicole at home, I'd found myself working longer hours and this had proved a boon for my employers. They likely tied this new-found motivation to my "mugging" and the black eye I'd received, and so they were suddenly forgiving about things like personal calls to the office.

I didn't return his calls.

A few days later Lee showed up at the office. She reminisced with my bosses, went for coffee with them downstairs, and when the social call was finished, she came to my desk. She wore no denim, had wrapped her coarse hair tightly into a bun, and looked nothing at all like she did in her free time.

She planted one hand on my desk, previously her desk, leaned in and spoke quietly. "Scruffy, are you ignoring John?"

"Hi, Lee."

"C'mon. Don't you think you're going to hurt his feelings? The big guy loves you."

I leaned back and shrugged.

"Let's try this again," she said. "You're the soft guy, the fixer. He needs you. You're his shoulder to lean on."

"He's been leaning a little too hard," I told her.

She smiled and stood up straight. Her posture was as professional as her outfit. "I get it. He hasn't made it easy to be his friend this year. But when was the last time you saw him happy? Big man's practically manic over some sort of breakthrough at work. Wants to celebrate."

"I don't know, Lee."

"Don't worry. Nicole won't be there." The look on my face must have been obvious because she laughed. "She and I lived together for years. You think I wouldn't know what's up with you two?"

—

That night a blizzard hit, grinding the city to a halt, and over the next day the temperature sank and turned the snow into a sheen of hard, slippery ice. The weekend came and against my better judgement I trudged through the streets to Shifty's. I looked through the window and saw John, Lee, Steve, and Brian sharing a couple of pitchers. John noticed me through the window and rushed between the tables to greet me at the entrance. He hugged me hard, lifted me off my feet.

"Hey, buddy," he said.

It was a nice greeting from everyone at the table, equal parts cheer for John and sympathy for my breakup. John acted like a true master of ceremonies and ensured that everyone was engaged in the conversation. Even Steve put aside his morose attitude and got involved. Of course everyone could see how thin John had become, how his teeth pushed against the skin around his mouth. But it seemed that the gang was eager to find him back to his old self, even if they had to ignore details that suggested otherwise.

The beer went to my head. I caught myself smiling in conversation and felt immediately annoyed at my good spirits.

"So what's this big news?" I asked John. They were the first words I'd spoken to him all night.

He beamed, a skeleton with a sheet of skin pulled over it. "It's complicated."

"Just for once, John, why don't you try? I'm not a fucking idiot."

My tone must have caught the ears of the others, but they didn't speak up.

John's face stiffened. He said, "I got Grace's project up and working again. I just needed to try a technique I had abandoned."

It wasn't a complete surprise. "The rats. Subjective whatever. And Buddy?"

This made him smile again. "He's a star. A hero for science."

"Is he all right, though?"

I didn't get an answer. A large group of people had entered the restaurant and John's attention shifted to them. The server led the group to the same area as us and as they approached our table, they all went silent. They were young men and women, mostly unkempt, not particularly stylish or consistent in their dress.

"Holy shit. John?" One of their group stepped forward. He was spindly and his voice was a little unsteady but he seemed more confident than the rest. "Are you kidding me? Do you have any idea the friggin' trouble you've caused?"

"Hey, just ease down there, eh?" Brian said.

John's face was frozen and unreadable. "I suppose there was a risk of this happening. Hi, Will."

The group's spokesperson, Will, kept weaving forward and back as if he'd been drinking. "Where the hell have you been for three months?"

Suddenly their group made sense to me: they were graduate students.

John said, "It's none of your business, Will. This is why I've been avoiding places like Shifty's."

Some of the grad students frowned and shook their heads, and others muttered to one another.

Will, though, was bold in his disgust. "Do you think this is funny? Trivial? Not only does our supervisor have to deal with you disappearing, but you take the rats out of the lab? Some of them had friggin' telemetry devices in them. She's *still* knee deep in crap! She could lose her job. Have you gone insane?"

John stood up slowly and his body looked wide but hollow. His hands were tucked into fists and I couldn't help remembering what had happened in the school parking lot.

"You better sort this mess out *right now*," Will said quietly. He didn't back away but clearly John's physical presence diminished him a little.

John stepped around the table and toward the students. He looked coiled tight and ready to spring, and they could see it.

"You've been unbelievably selfish," Will said, his voice faltering.

"You're right," John said finally. He sounded calm but not apologetic. He took another step forward. "I *have* acted selfishly. And I'll have to pay for it. Now leave us alone."

Will involuntarily took a half-step back, then looked at the scared group of students around him and mustered his courage. He said, "Grace was a bad influence on you. She was the lab's biggest mistake."

I was on my feet. I resisted the urge to strangle that little bastard and instead looked to one of the others, a young woman with a ponytail.

"Take your friend away," I told her. "Right now."

She pulled on Will's sleeve and it broke his attention from the scene. He backed off and they all made their way to the back of the restaurant instead. For a moment, nothing happened at our table. John and I still stood. Lee, Steve, and Brian watched from their seats.

And then John let out a sigh and said, "Excuse me for a moment. I need to use the washroom."

I sat down again.

"He lied to us about the lab," Lee said.

"Dude's had it rough this year," Brian said.

"I'm not really good with these kinds of situations," Steve told us.

"I should've known better," Lee said. "Just look how skinny he is now. What are we gonna do?"

In the end there was no point in wondering. John never came back to the table. I checked the washroom and the grad students' table at the back but there was no sign of him. He'd left Shifty's without even bothering to take his coat. We went to his apartment but the lights were off upstairs and we couldn't get inside. We tried his phone but he didn't answer. There was no sign of John for a week.

—

Then one evening my cell phone rang.

"I need to see you," he said.

I skipped my prepackaged dinner and went straight to his house. The front door to his building was wedged open with a rock and he was inside the apartment, sitting calmly on the couch.

He looked different. His hair was cropped short and his T-shirt and pants looked new. They were tight on his diminished body. Layers and layers of warm clothes were piled next to him, and he was wearing heavy winter boots. His eyes were so sunken that his brow cast a shadow over them, but there was resolve and focus on his face.

His right forearm was heavily bandaged.

"I wanted to say thank you and goodbye before I go," he said.

He gestured to a seat and I took it but sat on the edge.

"Go where?" I asked. "Where are you going in this state? Where the hell have you been? What happened to your arm?"

"I've been getting things ready," he said.

"Ready for what, goddamn it?"

He took a moment, then said it slowly. "I'm going to find Grace."

I shot out of my seat and paced the room. I wrapped my arms around myself to prevent them from lashing out at the wall or throwing small objects.

"If Grace wanted to be found," I said, "she would have left a fucking address or some way to get in touch. But she didn't. She wanted to leave us behind, like we were pieces of garbage to be discarded. Just like her clothes, her degree, and the rest of her life. Remember?"

"Maybe she didn't have a choice," he said.

"And maybe you're wrong!" The frustration was so powerful that I actually laughed, one hard note. "I can't do this anymore. What do you know? Yeah, yeah, you two were in love. Wow, you lived together for a few months. But she was *my* sister. Mine, not yours. I knew her my whole life. How long did you know her, John? Jesus Christ. You don't get to be the only one who's grieving."

Something hot and angry pressed against the inside of my throat. I could feel a headache coming on.

John stood up and faced me. He put out his thin arms and rested his hands on my shoulders, his manner peaceful. He said, "All right, maybe I need to think about this a little more, figure out a next step. You're right. Would you mind giving me a day or two to consider what you've said?"

I wiped my face with my sleeve. "You're going to leave and not tell me. I'm so tired of people leaving without saying goodbye."

"I won't. I just want some time to evaluate my options."

"I'm going to call you tonight."

"Checking in," he said. "Sure. Now please go."

My body was numb all over when I walked out the door. I took the streetcar to my house. I waited. I called John and he did not pick up. Hours passed, then a day. I made my way back to the apartment but the front door was locked and the lights in his windows were out. I buzzed for the better part of an hour and no one answered. My hands wouldn't work anymore in the cold and so I left. He had lied to me again.

That was the last time I saw him.

2006

THE LIGHTS WERE ON in the basement apartment when I got home, but at first I couldn't see Nicole. I found her in the washroom. She sat on the counter, feet in the sink with the faucet running, hot water splashing from ankles to toes. She was wearing a very small sheer dress and brushing her teeth. Her legs were folded up, bare and smooth, and I could practically see the rest of her through the fabric.

"What are you doing?" I asked.

"I'm cold," she said through a mouth full of toothpaste. She kicked her feet lightly in the sink and splashed water onto the counter.

"You're only wearing a nightgown."

"I prefer *negligee*." She smiled. "'Nightgown' is thoroughly too frumpy a word."

She spun her feet out of the sink and pointed them at me. She made a face that was pleading and joking at the same time. I folded the towel around her feet and rubbed them dry.

"In any case," I said, "it's not exactly a good fit for the season. Why wear it now?"

She rinsed her mouth and gave me another look.

"*Oh*," I said. I lifted her up with one arm under her knees and the other arm around the small of her back. Then I carried her to bed.

She nuzzled into my neck. "You smell like beer."

"And you smell like oranges," I said.

A few hours later Nicole shook me until I awoke. Nothing made any sense at first.

"Don't you hear that?" she whispered into my ear. We held our breaths and listened until finally there was a hard knocking against our bedroom window. "You see? It was coming from the living room first."

I scanned the room for a weapon and some clothes. It was too dark to make anything out.

"Who's there?" I shouted.

"Let me in." The voice was muffled on the other side of the glass but unmistakably Grace.

"Jesus Christ. Go to the front door."

I switched on the night-table light and handed Nicole the first clothes I could find. She was hiding under the blankets and still wired with fear. I found my own clothes and went out into the living room. Grace's outline was on the window of the front door.

I unlocked the deadbolt and hissed, "What are you doing?"

Grace was bundled in her parka and was carrying a small backpack. She stepped inside and took off her hood. Her hair was tangled and oily.

"I need to borrow your car," she said.

"Absolutely not," I told her. "It's the middle of the goddamned night. Couldn't you have called?"

"Why can't I borrow the car?" she asked.

I raised my voice. "Because you took it without asking, at Mom's house. Remember?"

"You're making a mistake. Do you remember the nail?" She looked me in the eyes. Then she walked off into the night as if she hadn't just scared the shit out of us.

I curled up behind Nicole and let my breathing settle again. Just before I drifted off, Nicole roused me. "What's 'the nail'?"

I thought of that day when we were kids, the vivid image of the rusty nail pushing through Grace's shoe, my obliviousness to her suffering, my foolish behaviour, all that shame I had carried, and I told Nicole, "I don't know. Something from when we were kids, I guess."

She pushed her warm, soft body against me and said, "She's getting worse. You should call John."

But I didn't.

—

The next afternoon, Grace called from the Yorkdale shopping mall, the northern edge of town, looking to be picked up. She sounded near the point of exhaustion. She was standing in the parking lot near the highway when I arrived, and her appearance was shocking. Gone were most of her bohemian layers of shawls and fabric, replaced with a thin shirt and trousers. Her hair had been chopped down to a bob with short bangs. There seemed to be strands of grey in her hair. She had no winter coat and wore only canvas shoes.

I brought her back to the basement apartment. There, Nicole greeted us cautiously and helped me get Grace onto the couch, where she fell asleep at once.

"You need to call somebody," Nicole told me.

"I tried John but—"

"No, someone who can actually help."

"Who?" I asked. "Who's the expert in this situation?"

"You can't handle this alone."

In the end I called my father. He listened as I explained the last few months leading up to that day.

"What the hell do you want me to do about it?" he asked.

I said, "Maybe she could come stay with you for a little while."

"Christ, son. She's never listened to me once in her goddamned life and I don't expect her to start now. Take her to somebody who can help. What do you think I am, a shrink?"

No, Dad, I think you're a shitty father. "I have to go."

Nicole stayed with me and made a simple dinner with what was in the house. Grace roused herself from the couch as Nicole was plating our meals.

"You look young," she said to me. Her skin was puffy and pale. "When is it?"

"What? It's seven o'clock."

"What's the date?"

"It's the fifteenth," I said.

"December? 2006?"

Nicole put two plates down on the table. "Grace, are you all right?"

"You stay out of this," Grace snapped.

"Hey," I said. "You can just stop that bullshit right now. Sit down."

She listened, and Nicole brought her a plate. It was hardly out of Nicole's hands before Grace tore into the food. I had never seen her eat with such enthusiasm.

Through a mouthful she said, "You wouldn't believe the things I've seen."

"I've seen the side of the highway before," I told her. "What the hell were you doing out there?"

"Hitchhiking."

"And what happened to your parka? You could have frozen."

She chewed her food and ignored me. Nicole took her own plate to the living room and ate there. I watched my sister clean her plate, fill it again from the pan, and finish her second serving.

"You need to come with me," she said. "For your own good."

"What are you talking about? Come with you where?"

"You have to trust me. You wouldn't believe it unless you saw it for yourself."

I cleared the table and did the dishes. Grace didn't stir from her seat. As I was drying my hands there was a knock at the door. I found John standing on our doorstep.

"Why the hell are you here?" Grace said.

"I can't imagine it's for the pleasant company," Nicole said.

"Mind your own business," Grace told her.

"You're in my house," Nicole said. "That makes it my business."

"Let's go home, Grace," John said.

Grace turned from them and pleaded to me. "Come with me. Show me it isn't inevitable."

"You're unstable," Nicole said. "You need help."

"You don't know a fucking thing!" Grace turned her head and shouted. "God, you're unbelievable. Never have I seen someone give so little and get so much in return. Why do you get to live out the rest of your meaningless, ignorant life in such bliss?"

Then she looked back to me and bared her teeth in a horrid, pleading smile. "Come on, little brother. Prove yourself wrong. Help yourself. You just have to trust me."

I didn't recognize the person standing in front of me, not her smile or her closely cropped hair or her sudden appeals. I said, "Grace, I'm not going anywhere. Nicole's right. You do need help."

She looked devastated, flattened. She moved John out of the way and opened the apartment door. "Fuck you both, then. I should have known you couldn't help but choose her, when it came down to it."

"Please take her to the hospital," Nicole said to John.

I took a few steps toward Grace. She was shivering. "Please just take it easy, O.K.? I'll come see you tomorrow."

"It won't be tomorrow," she said.

John had taken a taxi to the apartment. He walked Grace to the cab and they drove off. Nicole came up behind me and put her arms around my waist.

—

We lived. We worked. We nested as the cold weather made walking around the city unpleasant.

I called John to keep updated. He told me she was sleeping well, feeling better after a few days of rest. Her doctor had made her an appointment with a psychiatrist in three weeks. I visited the apartment a few times to see her and, unlike John, I wouldn't have said she was feeling better. She looked sedated and almost never spoke.

And then one afternoon John called me at work. I stepped out of the office to avoid my bosses.

"Everything O.K.?" I asked.

"Yeah, I'm not sure," John said. "Grace is gone."

"Oh, for the— I thought you were watching her." I went back into the office and grabbed my pea coat and toque.

John's voice was deep and defensive. "I was. One minute she was in the living room, and the next minute she was gone. Things were under control."

I rushed down the stairs and outside. "Clearly they weren't, John. Goddamn it."

I started at Union Station to see if she was taking a train or bus out of town. John tried their neighbourhood and left the city to continue the search. There was no sign of Grace. Nicole insisted we file a missing person's report, and a day later I met with a short and strong-looking policewoman with her hair tied into a bun on the back of her head. She didn't know how to smile, only smirk, and she propped her hands on the top edge of her heavy belt. Her uniform was dark blue with flaps on the shoulders and her pistol was huge and black in its holster. Her badge read *Officer 2510*.

"You mind if I ask you a few questions about Grace?" Instead of taking off her military boots at the front door of the apartment, she wiped them on the mat and wore them inside. I don't remember much else about the interview.

—

We lived. We worked. In turn, Nicole tried to distract, amuse, and comfort me.

The holidays started a few days after Grace disappeared and John went home to Oshawa. I wasn't in a rush to leave Nicole or the city and so I worked some overtime at the office, sending out last-minute grant applications to the government and organizing my bosses' travel for the upcoming months. The distraction was nice. With the extra money, I bought Nicole a fancy set of pots and pans. During the nights, I would dream there was someone banging on the bedroom window and wake up looking for Grace.

Just before the new year, I locked up the office for the day and wandered downstairs to the coffee shop. The barista and I were probably the only two people in the building. I took a seat near the window and watched the pigeons sift through cigarette butts and chewing gum for scraps of food. Looking up Spadina, past Queen and even to the coloured signs of Chinatown, the city felt wide and empty.

And then suddenly it didn't. I could feel her eyes on me before I could find them. She was remarkably close and seemed to come from nowhere. She looked as if she'd borrowed clothes from people living on the streets. She had a toque pulled down to her eyebrows and a scab on her chin but there was no doubt it was Grace.

I ran outside and hugged her. She smelled like rotten food.

"Don't touch me," she said, and when I didn't listen she pushed me away.

She didn't seem to care when I called John, didn't move from where she was standing.

"Get her to the apartment," John said over the phone. "Get her some clean clothes, some coffee, maybe. I can be in town in an hour. We'll take her to the hospital then."

I flagged a taxi and asked him to drive to Grace's apartment. The sour tang of her body was so bad that the driver wanted no part of our fare. I offered him more money and cursed at him and eventually he drove.

The cab left us on Bloor Street. Grace walked a few storefronts east and dug in a frozen planter's pot until she found her keys in the soil.

She wandered through the apartment and inspected all her belongings as if she'd never seen them before. She left an over-powering trail of smell everywhere she went. "All of this seems so strange, now. Pointless."

"Let's get you cleaned up," I told her.

"What are you talking about?" She looked back at me, and her face became a cruel grin. "You don't get it. I'm not staying. I just thought I owed you a goodbye."

"Come on. Don't talk like that. John will be here soon."

"John doesn't matter." She kept moving through the apartment, occasionally running her hand along the wall or stopping to look at her possessions. I followed her closely. In the washroom, she pulled the bottles of pills from the medicine cabinet and took her time reading the labels. She carried them with her into the second bedroom, past the giant mirror.

"Don't bother trying," she said. She stared out the window but seemed to be following some other logic in her head. Then she let out one awful laugh. "It's a pointless thing to say, of course.

Everything's already set in motion here. You're going to try, and you're going to fail, and you're going to suffer horribly for it."

"You're my sister. Of course I'm going to help you if I can."

"I'm not talking about right now. You think you're helping? You're so myopic that you can't see the operant chamber you're in, or how everything you do is being quantified and manipulated. You don't even feel that detached interest scrutinizing your every idiot move. How could *you* ever help anything? The only people who could have let me in—well, they made it abundantly clear that they had no interest in doing so."

"Grace," I said, "you're not in a good state."

"There's nothing wrong with me. My head is clear. I've just had my fill of being alone." She walked to the large mirror and looked carefully. "I'm tired. I was tired of you all a long time ago. I'm tired of things being inescapable, incomprehensible. I'm tired of getting what I want and I'm tired of not getting what I want. At least when I'm dead I won't have to be tired anymore."

"Don't talk like that."

She shook her head, glanced at me briefly, then looked back to her reflection. "You know, things would have been really different if you'd come with me instead of listening to Nicole."

And without warning she slammed her hand into the large wood-framed mirror. It shattered instantly, a ripple of cracks radiating out from her fist. She twisted her arm and I could hear bits of broken glass grind into her skin.

"Jesus Christ!" I yanked her arm away from the mirror. A few shards fell but most stayed in the frame. Then I ran to the washroom, soaked a towel under the faucet, and brought it back to the bedroom.

My error was instantly clear. The room was empty. Behind me, the apartment door was ajar. I rushed back to the window in the second bedroom in time to see Grace running west on Bloor and veering north up a side street. I didn't bother to close or lock the doors behind me. I sprinted along the path she'd taken until I wasn't sure which way to turn. If there'd been a snowfall I would have been able to follow her tracks.

I never caught up with her.

—

That night, after John and the police and everything else, Nicole held me close and asked me about what had happened. Grace's last words had burrowed into me and kept repeating in my head: *Things would have been really different if you'd come with me instead of listening to Nicole.*

I told Nicole I was tired and would rather talk about it in the morning.

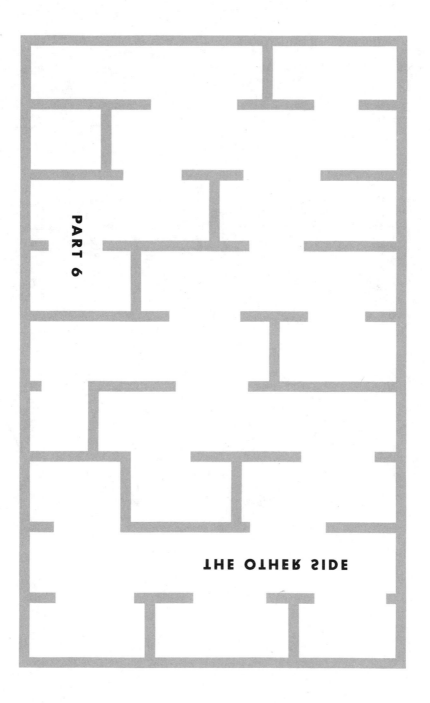

PART 6

THE OTHER SIDE

WHERE THE WATER MEETS THE TREES

HERE WE GO.

It's been four months since I last crawled into this box but the sensation is identical, a saturating darkness. Before I even have the flashlight out of my pocket, the temperature drops and my breath no longer reverberates off the inner mirrors. The smell of wood and glue gives way to something musky and damp.

I click on the light and for a moment I'm blinded by my reflection. Foreground, background, everything in between, the illuminated and the obscured, all of it is me. Infinite self-repetition, a line that extends from me to some indistinct haze that fills all space. It should be bright inside the box but instead it's dim. No matter where I turn I see myself. It's surprising how varied I appear. Fear, hesitation, anger. Am I making those faces? My features are contorted in threat, menace.

Buddy scuttles from one shoulder to the other and back again, all the while tapping at me with his forepaw. He curls his tail around my neck to steady himself. I don't doubt his resolve even if I doubt my own.

The hairs on my arms rise. The sound of my heartbeat swells and fills my ears.

There is something approaching and it intends to do harm. It is hunting me, preparing to draw my blood again. I remember how it felt, painless at first and then an intolerable burning. This time it will cut deeper. It will take more of me. It will hollow me out until I am nothing but a husk.

I spin in circles and shine the light. The space inside the box is now enormous. The air is gelatinous and suffocating. My reflections are all sneer and enmity. I am afraid. I am afraid of pain, of dying. I am afraid of the thing that is hunting me.

You'll always find what you bring with you.

I close my eyes, breathe slowly. Think of Buddy on my shoulder.

The hunter reaches me. It snorts its hot, heavy breath onto the back of my neck.

Eyes still closed, I click off the light. Think of Grace when she was eight years old, my earliest memories, what a happy shithead she had been, how brilliantly she shone. I knew I would never excel and I knew I would never burn bright like her and I knew it didn't matter. I was just happy to be on her team.

The hunter circles me. It grunts. It smiles in the dark and I can hear its teeth. It's deciding how to annihilate me.

Think of John's confident handshake and the way he welcomed me into their little social world. His loyalty to my sister was unwavering, despite her best efforts to reject him. He tried to protect us all.

The hunter places a weight against my spine, something heavy and sharp. It wants me scared. It runs the weapon down my back and the edge catches the fabric of my coat. Claws? A knife? Then the weight is gone and it draws back, poised, a pause before it strikes.

Think of Steve and Lee, always just trying to be good to each other, and of Brian, who must have been tormented with feelings for his best friend's girlfriend for so long.

Think of Nicole and how empowered she had been when we met, how empowered she'd become again since we broke up.

Think of how they all tried to be good people and how, sometimes, I helped them with that. Think of them.

And then there is nothing.

—

More specifically, I sense nothing. There are no sounds, no blades puncturing or cleaving me. I open my eyes to a complete black, but there is nothing hiding in it. It is just darkness. I've avoided its attack for now.

My muscles ache, remind me I'm still crouching. I click on the flashlight and it projects into empty space. My reflection is nowhere to be seen. The emptiness disorients me and so I put a hand down to steady myself.

Grass between my fingers.

In the sky, tiny pinpricks of light appear and disappear as I move my head. At first they are unfamiliar to me. Stars.

I sweep the light to the ground and find grass and earth. There is no sign of the box at all. My eyes are adjusting to the low light and now I understand why the stars are appearing and disappearing: there is a canopy above me that hides most of the sky. It's almost too high for the flashlight to reach but I see the unmistakable outline of branches and leaves.

I squeeze the grass gently in my hands and stand up.

Buddy climbs down the front of my coat and drops to the ground. Without his tapping, I had forgotten he was on my shoulder. He scurries so fast that I lose him immediately with the light. I take a few steps to follow him and tall trunks of trees appear in the beam of the flashlight. Dead branches and leaves make a crisp sound under my feet.

This is a forest. My knowledge of natural things is terrible but I can tell it's nothing like the temperate rainforest I saw near Vancouver. I imagine most of these trees have names like oak or birch. Very little grows along the forest floor and so it's open enough to walk.

Wherever I am, this place has rules I recognize. It is night. There are trees and stars and earth and air. The ground below the trees has a steady incline in one direction and a steady decline in the other. I may be lost but these rules are consistent with my reality. That suggests there is a way out.

"Buddy?" I call. My voice doesn't carry in these woods. I whistle. I make kissing sounds. I have no idea how to summon a rat.

He hasn't gone far. The arc of my flashlight eventually lands on two reflective green beads on the forest floor. It's amazing how a black and white animal can be so camouflaged on a green and brown surface. I bend forward to pick him up but he runs out of my reach. I take a step toward him and he runs ahead again. We repeat this process a few times more before I recognize the pattern.

I am being led.

"Point taken," I tell him. "Let's go."

The decline is subtle but in my legs I can feel us gradually moving downhill. I walk slowly and with an arm outstretched to avoid branches and tree trunks. Buddy stays always a few feet in front of me, his short legs busy, his fleshy tail trailing behind him. John once told me that in the wild, rats can run for kilometres a night.

And this is wild. The number of trees is uncountable. There is no sign of human life. This place is unspoilt.

Buddy leads for so long that the scene begins to change. A deep green appears in the sky and soon running water is trickling nearby. There is nothing to precisely measure time but I imagine we've been stumbling through these woods for an hour or so. I'm beginning to grow accustomed to my surroundings, less fearful of them.

And then branches and leaves snap behind us. I freeze and listen. The water is closer now but that is all I can hear. Buddy has wandered almost out of sight. Then I hear it again, something at least as big as a man, but strong, forcefully making its own path through the woods. It's coming from the direction in which we started. It is the sound of something following us. The hunter.

"Let's get the fuck out of here," I say to Buddy.

Faster than before we make our way through the forest. Now I can hear water on either side of me and it drowns out any noise of our pursuit. The sky is changing from a green to a greyish blue. The air is dewy. Buddy dips under fallen branches, around mounds of earth, between old and dying trunks. Day is almost here and I turn off my flashlight to save batteries.

We race through the woods, down the slope of the hill, until I can see nothing in the distance. The trees seem to be swallowed up by an impenetrable white background. Buddy rushes ahead. I trust him. I follow.

The dense white gets closer and closer, the trees end, and my feet lose their traction. I slide but don't fall. The ground is now stones, slippery and small. The sound of water is everywhere but the white presses in and makes it impossible to see more than an arm's length away.

Fog. A morning fog, billowing off a body of water. A few more cautious steps and waves are lapping at my feet. I crouch and can see water rolling over the stone shore. I dip my fingers in and then taste them. Not salty. Buddy stands next to me with his paws in the water.

Behind us, the hunter is snapping branches with its feet, nearing the edge of the forest, about to break onto the shore.

Buddy looks back toward the trees. He sniffs and his whiskers dance in the air. He doesn't give me a glance or warning, simply bolts back toward the woods like a soldier heading to battle.

I hold my breath. I wait. I want to run but I can't leave him behind. The forest is now silent.

Then for a moment it is blinding white. The sun has risen above the forest and fog. Still I crouch and listen but there's no longer anything except the gentle sloshing of freshwater onto the shore. The fog dissipates until I can see ten, then twenty feet around me. There's still no sign of Buddy. Nor of the hunter.

Near me is a wooden pole plunged vertically into the ground, and tied around, hanging from it, it is a heavy rope. This is the first thing I've seen resembling human activity.

I can see now that this body of water is very large, certainly not a pond or even a small lake. The narrow shoreline goes off straight in both directions to where the fog crawls into the trees and back out across the surface of the water. The sun is to my left, making the lake to the south.

Out on the lake, there is a repetitive, gentle splash against the water. Ripples spread out across the surface and something dark emerges from the fog. I see the front of a small wooden boat, then a paddle criss-crossing from one side to the other, then finally its pilot.

Officer 2510.

—

"Well, son of a bitch," she says. She pulls the boat to shore and the bottom of it scratches against the stones. "You made it. Get in."

"I need to find my rat," I tell her, almost a whisper. "There's something in the woods."

"Can't do anything about Buddy, for the moment." Her hair is longer again, tied back, and her clothes are simple, dark, and fitted. "Got to trust me on this one. Now get in."

I take one last look toward the fog around the tree trunks and push the boat back into the water. As it glides off the rocks, I hop in and nearly upset its balance. Officer 2510, or whatever her name is, uses her paddle to keep steady and turns us around. I sit in the front and face her as she propels us into the lake, back to wherever she came from.

"When did you last see me?" she asks.

I've heard this sort of question before. "About a month ago. November, 2008. How long has it been for you?"

"Definitely longer than that. You're getting scrawny. But hard to say how long, exactly." She dips the paddle into the dark water on one side, then the other. "Tricky question for creatures like me."

"'Creatures'? Not 'people'?"

"Not as you know them, no."

I consider that for a moment. "Where are we?"

Her eyes are grey stones and fixed on our path through the water. The fog is pulling farther back and it's clear the lake is enormous. She says, "'The place where the water meets the trees.'"

Somewhere deep in me I knew this already. "Toronto. This is the city, only there's no city. Is this the past?"

She says, "Just another present."

"And how many are there?"

"You can't count that high."

She paddles quietly for a few minutes. I look back to the shore and think of Buddy facing down the hunter, whatever it may be. I turn forward in the boat and look south. The last of the fog has cleared and the Toronto Islands are a few hundred metres in front of us. They're covered in trees, same as my reality, but there are also small wooden buildings along the islands' shore. There is no smoke or sign of human activity. It looks like a ghost town.

Officer 2510 steers us slightly to the east and asks, "Don't you want to know about us?"

"I didn't come here for you or your friends."

"No need to be pissy." She gives me a lopsided grin. "I get it. John and Grace. But don't you remember what I told you?"

"I heard you just fine. This is a bad idea, I should quit, *et cetera*. But here I am." I point to the simple settlement on the islands. "Now is that where John and Grace are?"

"No. We have a *no trespassing* rule, not that we get many visitors. You three excluded, we've had only a handful of trespassers to the facilities. And we've been coming here for a very long time."

"If they're not at your *facilities*, then why are you taking me there?"

"Who says I am?" Her shoulders and arms have a smooth, curving rhythm and her movements with the paddle are precise and elegant.

"*No trespassing*," I say. "You realize there's an irony to that, right? Who says we shouldn't come to your version of Toronto and harass *you*?"

"My version." She shakes her head, grins again. "We're not from here any more than you are. Just one of our junctions, a place to build entrances, windows."

Entrances. She's talking about the dead end.

I ask, "Why?"

"Because we're not shaped like you," she tells me. "We're not little skinny tubes of consciousness. Need to force part of ourselves into your shape before we go to your side, anybody's side."

"No, I mean why come to our side at all?"

"What do you mean?" For an instant she looks genuinely confused. "Because we *can*."

I shake my head. "Not good enough. From the sounds of it, you're capable of plenty of things. So why bother with us 'skinny little tubes'? Why follow us around?"

Her strokes remain even, disciplined. "Why put rats in little boxes and make them work for sugar pellets? Why implant little pieces of plastic and metal in their bellies? Why bother finding empirical ways to answer your great philosophical questions?"

They are scientists. Physicists, biologists. Tinkerers. I say, "You're no less foolish than Grace and John, then."

"There are better and worse ways of doing science," she says. "Ways of asking questions without compromising some other creature's dignity. Ways of celebrating and respecting truth without exploiting every kernel of data. Even some of your scientists have a vague glimmer of that."

"It still doesn't explain why you'd play a gig with some band at the Fortress."

Her steel eyes lock on me. "Your behaviours make a lot more sense when viewed from the ground level. Call it cultural immersion. Or, like some of my colleagues, call it a waste of time."

So she is an anthropologist, too.

There is no wind and the water barely ripples under the boat. I don't know if I've ever seen Lake Ontario so calm. Sure enough we are veering farther around the eastern edge of the islands. From here I can see that the buildings are very simple and without windows. There is no activity or signs of life. I look down the shore to the gap between the land and the islands. Officer 2510 speaks up from the rear of the boat.

"This all used to be a spit, a peninsula. Hundred years ago a big storm wiped out the sandbar between the mainland and the islands. Consider yourself lucky it didn't happen only in your Toronto." She stops paddling for a moment and takes in her scenery. Her features are soft and her expressions are hard. Even if she isn't police, she looks like one. "Does it feel like the island's farther from the mainland? Your Toronto laid down a bunch of landfill and made an artificial waterfront."

"O.K.," I say. "Enough. Where the hell are you taking me, officer?"

She smiles at the title and resumes her paddling. "Look, let's just say I admire you. Doomed to fail, completely out of your element, and yet you just take it all in stride. No pretension, no illusion of control. You just persist."

"I think you referred to me as 'dopey' before."

She laughs quietly. "Now, I wouldn't mind showing you a few things, stretching out your self-awareness into a more fitting shape. Maybe even blowing your mind a little."

She might be flirting with me but I'm not sure what sort of desires a woman, creature, like her would have.

She says, "I'd be willing to show you around and have a little fun. This is not an insubstantial offer. But I'm guessing you'd say no. In fact I know what you say already."

We're both silent.

"So instead I'm getting you on your way to John and Grace," she continues. "Way I see it, you've got two problems. First, John is fifty kilometres from here."

It's an easy guess. "Oshawa. The dead end."

We reach the edge of the islands and begin rounding them, out into the expanse of Lake Ontario. At the easternmost tip of the last island is another large wooden pole sticking out of the rocks, and it too has a heavy rope tied around it. The rope leads to a second boat, identical to this one, that bobs in the water.

"You know what Oshawa means?" she asks. "It's *The Crossing Place* in Ojibwa, those sly motherfuckers. Now it's going to be a damn-near perfect day on the water but at your best you'll paddle only five kilometres an hour. You'll want to get there before the dark slows you down, on account of the second problem."

"Wait," I say. "What about Grace? Where is she?"

Officer 2510 makes a look of distaste. "Oh, the dead end is lousy with her. Not as bad as some of our other entrances, but still."

"I have no idea what you're talking about."

"You will. But right now I don't have time to explain. Like I said, the second problem." She's paddling the boat toward the make-shift dock. She looks at me hard and demands my attention. We're coasting in the water now. "Second problem is you broke the rules. Our entrances are built with specific considerations in mind. Your little wood-and-mirrors-and-dirt trick, not so much. You forced your way through, caused a fracture, sloughed off some nasty shit. And you left your door open, which was practically an invitation for that nasty shit to follow you here."

The hunter. "The thing in the woods. The thing that Buddy confronted."

She nods. "Point is it won't be more than a couple hours behind you. Now listen to me: if it catches you, it will undo you. And your last moments will be very, very unpleasant."

The boat wobbles and scrapes onto the rocks. She climbs out onto the island's shore and gestures for me to sit in the middle of the boat. She hands me her paddle and it's much lighter than I expected, perhaps not made of wood at all. The handle is lined with cork and feels good in my grip. The end of the paddle has a T-shaped nub for my other hand. I squeeze the two grips and twist.

"Don't do that," she says. "Friction is bad. No matter what, you're going to blister, but if you keep your hands dry and don't grip too hard, you'll bleed less."

She leans forward and grabs me by one shoulder. Her hand is small but strong. "Last chance for you to come with me instead. Why follow through if you already know you won't succeed?"

I take her hand in mine and lift it off my shoulder. It's warmer and softer than I expected. I let it go. She gives me one last crooked smirk and pushes the boat out into the water.

I say, "The last time I saw Grace, she said you—all of you—had rejected her."

"She gets exactly what she wants," Officer 2510 says from the shore. "She gets her little solipsistic paradise, *and* she congests a bunch of our entrances in the process. In the end she regrets it all, comes to us all folded in over herself. She demands answers about everything but she'll never be satisfied with the truth she gets."

The distance between us is increasing so I have to raise my voice. "Why not?"

"Because it's too much for her. Beyond her limited comprehension." Officer 2510 steps back, out of reach of the small waves, and crosses her arms.

I remember the quote verbatim: *I realize that if through science I can seize phenomena and enumerate them, I cannot, for all that, apprehend the world.* Nicole was right.

"Goodbye, officer," I shout. "Do you have a name?"

"Sure I do." Her expression is inscrutable. She lifts an arm and claps the hand open and closed, an exaggerated gesture. "Bye, bye."

With the paddle I take a few awkward stabs at the water. The boat spins and drifts. Thirty feet from the island's shore, a horrible realization comes to me. I lay down the paddle and turn toward Officer 2510. She is still standing where the water meets the trees and watching me float away.

I cup my hands to my mouth. "How do I get home? How do I return to my side?"

She doesn't try to project her voice but the response is unmistakable.

"Oblivion," she says.

THE CROSSING PLACE

THE INSTRUMENT IS UNFAMILIAR in my hands. For a long time my strokes are inefficient and consume all my concentration. My eyes are focused on the fin at the end of the paddle and on the black water into which I submerge it. I rarely see anything past the front of the boat. I try to cross sides with the paddle in a smooth motion and make my strokes even and perpendicular to the water. I try to keep the lower grip of the paddle dry and the upper T-bar cupped under the non-power hand. But no matter how hard I try, I can't keep the goddamned boat moving in a straight line and my hands are damp within the hour. The boat traces an infinite Z-shaped path along the coast.

Soon the paddling motion becomes more natural and my attention expands beyond my immediate surroundings. Officer 2510 was right: it is as perfect a day on Lake Ontario as I have ever seen. There is almost no wind and the only ripples on the water come from my idiotic flailing with the paddle. Across the sky there are very few clouds and soon the sun beats down from high above. The air becomes heavy and limp. I strip down to my T-shirt and underwear, piling the rest of my clothes in the back of the boat. Even still I'm covered in sweat before the worst heat sets in. This is undoubtedly a day in late summer, not the December that I left behind.

My little boat never drifts more than a few hundred metres from shore. It's probably reasonable to call this a canoe but I have no idea how to differentiate one from a kayak or any other kind of boat. Its skeleton is made of a wood so dark it looks burnt, with a coarse grain that runs along the long planks. The outer skin of the boat, the hull, is smoother but still unrecognizable. The shore of the lake, on the other hand, is perfectly recognizable apart from the massive trees that line it. I round the slow bends, stare into the deep woods, and I remember the train to the suburbs, the few brilliant bursts of the lake from the tracks.

The troubles come on slowly. I find myself shifting in my seat, taking momentary breaks to rub my biceps. My body is not used to this repetitive activity. I consciously switch between using my arms and using my torso to pull the boat forward in the water, but all of me is becoming sore. And just as Officer 2510 promised, I can feel the pads of my hands puffing up where they rub against the grips of the paddle. I let the blisters fill up with lymph and that takes some of the discomfort away. Then one bubble bursts and leaves an open wound in the meat between my right thumb and forefinger. I take off my T-shirt and wrap it around my right hand. A short time later I put my other hand in a sock.

The shore meanders, always more of the same. It's not clear how far I've travelled, what I should be looking for, or how to know when I've arrived. I keep paddling.

Every time my mouth feels full of paste I rest the paddle along the edge of the boat and sip water from my cupped hands. At first this is fine, in fact the water is cold and tastes incredible, but as my hands worsen, every dip into the lake stings my palms. I carefully towel my hands dry with my other sock and paddle again.

When I'm sure the sun has started to descend from its highest point in the sky, I allow myself a long break. The boat bobs about two hundred metres from the land and in clear view is the long slow curve of Lake Ontario's northern shore. The clothing I've tied around my hands is damp and making my skin pale and puckered. I free my hands and face them palm up in the sun to dry. Some of the wetness on them is from broken skin and the fluid it releases. There are only small traces of blood in the first burst blister.

I lean back in the boat and try not to use any of the muscles in my upper body. And though I avoided it for a while, sleepiness is starting to creep between all my aches. I knew nothing about the other side, this journey, but still I curse myself for failing to get a good night's rest first. I consider slowing down and conserving my energy, parking the boat onshore and sleeping underneath it, finishing the trip tomorrow. And then something catches my eye.

Far, far off in the direction I came from is a black speck that rides along the water. It is so distant that its shape cannot be made out, but it follows the path I took along the lake and it is exactly the same colour as my boat. It moves in a straight line and with purpose.

The hunter is catching up with me.

My break is over. My clothes have dried so I wrap them around my hands again. I paddle harder and I push myself further than before. My body reminds me that it's in pain, then says nothing at all. There is only the rhythm of my actions and the colours of the sky, from blue to pink to orange. I push my body until I cannot straighten my arms and until my legs are asleep and until my lungs feel full of liquid. When the wraps around my blisters become damp again, I remove them entirely. I paddle until there's a noticeable shift in the light and, just for a moment, I turn to watch the sun kiss the lake behind me. The hunter's black speck on the water has grown. I paddle again.

The horizon turns purple and the rest of the sky soon follows. It becomes difficult to differentiate the water from the land with my eyes. Twice my little boat wanders too close to the shore and my paddle crashes off the rocks underneath. I dig out the flashlight and hold it in my mouth but it gives me only a few weak shimmers on the water immediately in front of me.

I'm about to pull the boat to shore and continue on foot when I notice the light. It's in the woods and still far ahead, but it's clearly a fire. My whole body protests but I paddle ahead as hard and fast as I can until I reach it. The glow of the fire bathes the forest floor and casts long shadows from the tree trunks out toward the beach, toward me. I can see the flicker of flames about a hundred metres along a manmade path into the woods.

At first my body will not do anything. The boat rests on the rocks of the shore, leaning to one side, and I sit and lean with it. Finally I force myself up and out. The temperature feels like it's dropped sharply, now that I'm not paddling. My hands are almost useless and singing with pain, so it takes a long time to put on my clothes.

I lurch along the path, my arms folded up and my back arched and leaning too much weight into each step.

Flames are billowing out of a messy pile of wood. There's a log for sitting next to the fire. No John, no Grace, but someone must have lit this fire. I close my eyes for just a moment, a tiny rest. It's bright and warm and it feels amazing to be upright and stretching my legs and gently swaying in the forest air.

I'm not sure how long I stand with the world bright behind my eyelids, listening to the crackle of the wood, but without warning someone grabs my shoulder and twists me in a circle. I open my eyes and see John pulling his other arm back, a large angled rock in his hand, about to strike me. I am too tired to stop him or move out of the way. He has absolutely no concern on his face, no doubts about cracking open another human's skull.

"John," I say feebly.

His face softens immediately. He looks at me as if his mind is busy and confused. And then he hugs me hard and laughs. The stone in his hand presses against my lower back when he squeezes me. My arms are still bent and I can't hug him back. I breathe deeply.

—

He sits on the log, while I choose to stand and face him. He looks no worse than the last time I saw him, although his hair has grown long and there are wispy patches on his jaw and chin.

"God, it's good to see you," he says. "But I don't understand. You know who I am?"

I nod.

"How does that make sense?" He sits very still and seems to be concentrating. Finally he looks up at me. "When did you last see me?"

"About a year ago," I tell him. "It's December, 2008. Or it was, before I got here."

"You haven't seen me since 2007? Not in the following spring? You seemed to remember me the longest, even when the others had forgotten." He shakes his head. "You remembered until things became really different. I don't get it."

"I think I might." To me this pattern is familiar, a changing world, others' fading memories. It's a mirror to my own experience. "Somewhere in November of 2007, or maybe December, you started using the dirt from your dead end inside the box you'd built."

He opens his mouth as if he wants to say something but nothing comes out. My mind is still making the connections as I talk.

"You knew it was a bad idea, that anything from the dead end was out of your control, but you were so desperate to make the box work that you used the dirt anyway. You got Buddy through the box right around the time you had your little celebration at Shifty's.

A week later, you wrote your goodbye note to me, your backup plan in case you didn't succeed, and then you crawled inside the box for the first time. You weren't in there long before something scared you back out. So far, so good?"

He nods slowly. My mouth is only one step behind my thoughts. I continue.

"You had figured it would be as easy as building the entrance and going through it. It wasn't. So you rethink your plan, but you notice something is happening: your reality starts coming apart. People begin to forget about Grace, or about the shit you pulled at your lab. Other things vanish, objects, physical things. Eventually people don't recognize you, look at you like a stranger."

"How—"

"Let me finish." It's strange to be talking with John and have all the knowledge and power in the conversation. "So you became increasingly isolated, your world unreal, and finally you came to the realization: the thing that was blocking your way through the box was yourself. One way or another, you learned to let go of those doubts."

"Overpower them, actually," he says.

"So into the box you went again. And this time, you found yourself here."

"It took quite a number of tries, as a matter of fact," he says.

"Like learning how to meditate."

"Yes, exactly. For a time I thought I was losing my mind again. But in the end I took control and crossed over."

"See, that's where you're wrong." I'm working on straightening my arms, massaging my biceps and triceps with my knuckles. My hands look like raw chicken. There's an ugly implication to what I'm saying. I turn back to John. "You crossed over in December, 2007. You didn't come back to our side after that."

And that means neither did I. The reality of what I'm suggesting hits me in the guts. I've been stuck in the box since August, 2008.

[248]

The last few months of my life weren't *my* life. I shiver and step closer to the fire. "Officer 2510 made it clear that there are a lot of spaces or times or whatever we could call the 'present.'"

"Officer 2510?" he asks. "What does she have to do with this?"

So he hasn't seen her here. It's likely he hasn't met any of her people. *No trespassing.*

"Never mind her for now." I'm pacing around the fire to keep up with my thoughts. "She made it clear your box is amateur compared to entrances like the dead end, how I don't know. But I think the first time you got out of the box, it left you drifting across all the possible presents. Like a needle that lost its groove on the record."

He shakes his head. "I think I get what you're saying. But the grooves of a record would be different times. It's more like a needle that moves to a very similar groove on a very similar record, over and over again, until I don't recognize the record at all."

"Fuck, John. Give it a rest. It's just a metaphor."

The fire lights half his face and conceals the other half in darkness. He looks boyish and small. "How could you possibly know all of this?"

"I can't know, not for certain. I'm just working with the pieces that I have." The lake is audible from the fire, just barely. It sounds as though the water has picked up and waves are sloshing onto the rocks. "One thing I *do* know for certain is that we don't have a lot of time. We need to get Grace, get on the boat, and get back to where the city is on our side. Where is she?"

His face changes. He'd been in wonder or maybe even a little impressed, but at the sound of my sister's name he goes rigid. He stands.

"She's in there," he says and points deeper into the woods. "Where my parents' old house would be, if we were on our side."

Something about his tone lingers after he's finished.

"But?" I ask.

"But things are complicated with Grace."

"No shit. Let's go." I start to walk north, away from the shore.

"No." His voice is firm enough that I turn to face him. He hasn't moved from the fire. "You won't like what you find in there. It's better to let her come to us. She visits regularly, in one form or another."

"There isn't time for that." I can feel a breeze coming off the lake now that I'm standing away from the fire. I pull my coat closed.

"Really," he says, "time is the one thing we have plenty of here."

His words are starting to sound like excuses, rationalizations. There's a nervous edge to his voice.

"John. Why haven't you just gone in there, gotten her, and brought her back?"

And then there is a horrible, endless screech of pain coming from the direction of the shore. I have heard this sound once before, in John and Grace's apartment. It is the sound of a scared rat. The hunter is here.

"Jesus Christ," I say. "It's hurting Buddy. It's here."

A flash of recognition passes across John's face. "You were followed here. Through the box."

I nod. My ears are waiting for the sound of shuffled leaves and twigs, a thing walking through the forest.

"You need to go," John says. "Right now."

"All right, let's go."

"No." He pinches his face, frustrated. "Look. I can't. I can't get through. For some reason, the entrances don't work for me. I know the dead end is out there but I can't use it. Nothing works for me. I'm stuck. I've been stuck here for so long."

Right to the bitter end, he's keeping things from me. I say, "At least hide from that thing."

"He isn't interested in me. Only you."

I hop from one foot to the other, trying to warm up my legs.

"How do you know?"

"Because I used to have one following me." He sets his jaw. "If you're going to find Grace, now is the time. I'll stall him, misdirect him."

There's another screech, this one closer. "Get Buddy to safety if you can. And be ready to leave when I get back."

John points into the woods. "Run!"

It takes only a few seconds before I'm out of the fire's glow. The woods are so dark that I'm reminded of the sensation in the box. The flashlight illuminates the ten feet of dirt in front of me and no more.

I run down the path as fast as I can. My legs are the last part of my body in half-decent condition. I work them hard. After five or ten minutes my hairs stand on end and I can feel eyes in the trees. Then whispers.

Hi, little brother.

This part is so tedious.

I've been waiting for you.

"Grace?" I shine the light into the woods and see only trees.

Keep going. I'll see you there.

"Grace, quit fucking around. It's time to go."

Get in there, you worthless little shit.

I stumble forward. The path curves a little and abruptly ends. I'm not sure what to do so I keep moving forward, weaving between the trees. My head swims with physical exhaustion and lack of sleep. My eyelids close and open slowly and it feels as if they leave a coat of slime behind. I take a few more steps.

The world comes alive with artificial light. I didn't see the transition but now the trees in front of me are sparse and short, and behind me what had been forest is now just dirt and mud. Before me is a street light, the back of a diamond-shaped sign, the paved dead end of a road. I take a few more steps.

And after two long years I see Grace, standing casually and chatting with another woman whose back is turned to me. Grace is in profile, her mess of hair tied back and her clothes dirty. She shares a quiet laugh with the woman.

"Grace," I say.

Both women turn to me. Both are unmistakably my sister.

I look carefully into the suburbs. There is a sea of people around the houses, sitting, standing, talking, resting, watching me. Every person I can see is Grace. All of them.

"Oh Jesus," I say. I feel sick.

The two women in front of me turn to each other.

"Oh," one says. "I guess it's my turn. You've done it already?"

"Obviously." The other nods. "Go easy on him."

The first Grace walks up to me as if nothing at all were the matter. I am concentrating on standing. She smiles and punches me on the arm.

"Took you long enough," she says.

—

We walk down the suburban street. We pass small clusters of my sister talking among themselves. Occasionally they look up from their conversation and smile but none are surprised at the sight of me. Nor are they surprised by my awkward walk or the peeled skin on my hands. Grace leads me to the porch of one house and motions for me to sit. The glow of the electric light is eerie, and the neighbourhood doesn't look quite as it did the time I was here previously. It is an overcast night.

When she sits next to me, I ask, "What is this place? Did we—are we back on the other side?"

She shakes her head. "Think of it like standing in a doorway. A little stretch of time that connects one side to the other, repeating over and over. A loop. We're not exactly inside or outside."

"And when are you from?" I ask. "When was the last time you were on our side?"

"Shouldn't you know that?" She stares into space for a moment, working through her thoughts, and it comes to her. "So I go back after this. I've crossed multiple times. How many?"

"At least three," I say. "First, after family dinner in November, 2006. Then in the middle of the night, early December, 2006. Then again a week or two later."

I don't tell her about seeing her the last time, just after Christmas. Something about that last time nags at me.

"November was a trial run," she says. "An accident, really. I didn't get all the way through the entrance, just looped for a while and that was amazing enough. Came right back out at the exact same time I'd entered. This time, I crossed all the way through, explored a bit of the forest and shore. No sign of the locals yet."

I don't tell her about seeing Officer 2510, about the so-called facilities on Toronto Island, about the fact that they're not local at all.

"Then I stumbled on this place. It's the same geography as where I crossed, but a different time. A totally different entrance, I suppose. When was it that you crossed through the dead end?"

"I didn't," I tell her. "I used the box."

She looks utterly perplexed.

"Haven't you run into John yet?" I ask. When her eyes go even wider, I say, "He's here, too, by the lake. You'll see him eventually. He built an artificial entrance to find you."

Two of my sister pass by in quiet conversation. They don't even turn to us.

"How many of you are there?" I ask.

"Just one. Think of it as a closed loop."

Some of the Grace population wander closer to the dead end, like an audience.

"So all of these are versions of the same you," I tell her. "You've been them all before."

"Don't be an idiot," she says. "I haven't been some of them yet."

"But you've seen this, what's happening right now between us, before."

"Of course. I've watched you visit so many times, from so many angles, that I hardly notice each time you get here." She scratches at her head. "When I arrived, it seemed like there were already thousands of myself here, but that's because this is a finite amount of time that keeps repeating. I was the youngest, subjectively speaking. With every cycle, I find myself a little older, occupying the space that used to be some future version of me. And when I'm the oldest, the ultimate, I'll leave the dead end with you."

The crowd of my sister huddles around the dead end and shuffles to get a better view. I am watching multiple time points in my sister's life all overlaid in one space on endless repeat. It's staggering. The crowd of Grace starts to murmur.

"What's happening over there?" I ask.

"Oh. You haven't seen this." She stands up and motions for me to do the same. From this porch we can see clearly to the dead end, about a hundred metres away. She says, "Watch."

A young boy flies out from behind the dead-end sign. He's puny and looks Asian.

"John," I say.

"I will this into being," Grace tells me, proud. "I create the man that gives me access to this place. Don't you think that's impressive?"

The young John runs between houses and crouches, moments away from catching a glimpse of Grace's innumerable presence all around him, close enough to touch him. John will see her silhouettes and it will set everything in motion, steer him toward my sister a few years later, and ensure that Grace finds her way here.

"You used him," I say.

"Don't be self-righteous. Without this, he and I would have never met. What do they say? 'It's better to have loved and lost than never loved at all'?"

Something catches young John's eye in the window across the street. He checks his little hiding space but he's blind to Grace all around him. He can see them only in the reflection and so he wanders out into the road and across the street.

I step off the porch and approach John to get a better view. This Grace follows. Young John is standing in the garden and has his face practically pressed into the window. I get within a few feet of him and stop.

"John," I say. He doesn't react.

"This is my favourite part," Grace says. "I remember when it was my turn to do this."

I know what's to happen next. A lone Grace walks into the street, making herself clear and unambiguous to John. The importance of this moment is naked on his face. His life is changed.

Then he vanishes without any pomp. He is simply there one moment and gone the next.

The crowd of Grace gets louder for a moment, almost celebratory, and then dies down.

"What happened?" I ask this version of my sister.

"The cycle just reset," she says.

Grace is everywhere around us. She is talking to her past and future self. I see nothing but pleased faces from her, some smug, some happy, some calm.

"Why?" I ask. "Why would you want to be alone like this?"

She looks at me carefully. "In all my time here, I have never been in danger, never scared, never tired or hungry or stressed or sad. More importantly, I have never been bored, never been less than completely engaged, never challenged by an inferior opponent. I literally spend days talking things through with myself, playing devil's advocate, refining my arguments. It's almost pure subjectivity. It's—it's sublime. This is what peace feels like. It's all I've wanted since I was a kid."

"Since Thornton," I say.

"This has nothing to do with Thornton." She scowls. "John. I should have known that asshole would tell you."

"I figured it out for myself. I wish you would have just trusted me enough to tell me." I shake my head. "And he isn't an asshole. He's been trying to save you this entire time."

"Unbelievable," she says. She laughs once, cruelly. "I never wanted or needed saving. Don't you get it?"

"I get it just fine," I tell her. "But *you* don't get it. You don't know what happens when you return."

She stares at me blankly.

I say, "This consumes you. You come back and you're all fucked up, standing near the side of the highway like a—and then a few days later, you run off again, do this looping thing at other entrances, lots of them. God knows how long you spend here. The next time you return to us, after Christmas in 2006, you're even more fucked up. And then shortly after, you're gone forever." I move away from the houses. "For a while I thought you came back here for good, but now I understand. You really do go out into the woods or who knows where and kill yourself."

I've silenced her.

I say, "So goddamn it, maybe it's *you* who doesn't get it, for once. Maybe it's you who needs help. Maybe you should trust me."

There is a quiet moment between us. She looks at me and measures the weight of my words.

From just down the street I hear a man's voice say, "Grace."

I know what is happening before I see it. I look toward the dead end and there I stand, the me from less than thirty minutes ago, beside two of my sister. To Grace beside me, I whisper, "I don't want to see this."

She walks down the street, away from the dead end. I follow her. Somewhere behind me I hear myself say, "Oh Jesus."

———

She leads me down John's suburban street and around the corner. As we progress we see more of Grace, so many that it's busier than a night in the downtown core. But more concerning is the state of her, them. The farther we get from the dead end, the wearier these older Graces become, the less she converses with her prior selves. By the time we reach a nearby park, sunken and grassy, she/they sit or lie on their backs with vacant eyes and open mouths. It's like a cemetery, if people didn't bother to bury their dead. A mass grave.

I turn to my guide. "If you know this is going to happen to you, then why do you stay?"

The younger Grace doesn't even look concerned. "Everything meaningful increases your chances of mortality. Fatty foods, alcohol, even rearing children if that's your thing."

"It's not the same."

"It is *exactly* the same. It's a cost/benefit analysis. What do I have to spend, and what do I get in return? And in this case, I get exactly what I want."

"I don't think you'll want it once you get it." I'm thinking of what Officer 2510 said.

She ignores me. We reach the edge of the park and Grace says loudly, "Who's the ultimate?"

Some of the bodies lift their heads from the ground and look around. Finally one puts up her hand and slowly crawls to her feet.

"Well, this is as far as I go with you." The younger Grace puts her hand on my shoulder, squeezes it, and quickly pulls it away. She turns to leave.

"Wait." I step toward her. "You could come with me."

"Looks like I will." She smiles but it's not real, *non-Duchenne*. "Now excuse me. I was in the middle of a conversation when you arrived."

I watch her weave through the rows of bodies in the park and ascend the lip of the grassy bowl. I turn to the oldest Grace, the so-called ultimate. She moves slowly but she doesn't look much older than when she guided me here.

"Let's go, Grace."

—

We take a route around the back of the suburban houses because I want to avoid the loop of myself. We see other time points of Grace's life ambling, meandering, thinking, debating. I put an arm around the oldest Grace's waist and she puts her arm around my neck. In this way we reach the dead end from a slightly different angle and cross back to the dark woods, my ears pricked for any sound of the hunter. I point the flashlight ahead of us and hum her the song from the mix CD. This time there are no whispers in the woods but I still feel as though we're being watched.

I feel it before I see it, tiny ripples along my sister's forearm. I shine the flashlight on her arms and see the scars, not those that have lingered from adolescence, healed and flat, but newer ones, white and protruding and ugly from the lack of stitches. My sister never put her arm into a box, never saw the human-sized version, even. She never had a hunter. She was the one who made these precise cuts along her skin, who started doing this again after years. Maybe she never stopped.

Only when we're deep in the forest, far from John's formative moments, does this Grace speak to me.

"I'm feeling better now, thanks," she says.

"Why did you start hurting yourself again?"

She stiffens, takes her arm from around my neck. "Isn't the cycle interesting? I did an estimate once of how long I was in there. If each cycle is about a half hour, and there are roughly tens of thousands of me, that puts me in there for somewhere over a year. The best year of my life."

"Grace."

She's testing her body now, bending at all the joints. "You know, this really feels much better. I should have left sooner." She laughs. "I could just stay in the entrances for fewer cycles."

"Fine, don't answer. But we need to go. We need to get in the boat and leave."

"And go where?" she snaps.

"Back to the city, I think. Or where the city is on our side."

She's full of life now. She's her old self in some ways. "Why bother? You think there's anyone there who would help you? They don't stoop to our level."

"I think there's one, yes." I pull on her sleeve and lead us back onto the path. "She's helped me before. She might have some ideas."

"Wait." She yanks her arm out of my grasp.

"We have to go."

"Wait." She's stopped walking. "One of them talked to you."

"Grace, come on."

"One of them talked to *you*."

"Fuck, Grace."

"What did it say?" She steps toward me in the dark. She beats against my chest with the bottoms of her fists and the beam of the flashlight bounces across the canopy above us. "What did it say, goddamn it?"

I want to tell her nothing. I want to make something up. "She says you're not capable of understanding how this all works."

She pauses. I shine the flashlight on her face and she looks thirteen years old. "You're lying."

As long as she's angry with me, she will follow. I pull away from her and continue along the path and she storms behind me. Soon the glow of the fire licks the trees. We reach John's campsite but he isn't there. Neither is the hunter.

She's pulling on my sleeve. "Why are you lying to me?"

"He's probably at the boat," I whisper. "Come on."

I lead her down the path to the lake. The air cools as we approach the water.

Grace had gone quiet behind me but now she speaks up. "You told me once that you see me again in Toronto. I appear and disappear a couple more times, you said."

"I just told you that," I say. "Well, I just told it to an earlier version of you."

The wind is against us. It carries an animal smell. We are approaching something.

"Did you stop to consider," she says, "that if I come back with you now, I wouldn't have appeared and disappeared a couple more times in your past? You wouldn't have seen me again in December, 2006. That means I'm not going to leave this place with you. Whatever happens to me has already happened for you."

"Keep your voice down." I roll it over in my head. Her statement is difficult to grasp.

The canopy gives way and we find ourselves standing on the edge of the lake. The water froths on the rocks and my muscles cry out at the thought of paddling through this. I wave the light around.

John stands next to the boat and leans on the paddle like a walking stick.

"What are *you* doing here?" Grace says.

His face betrays his confusion.

"You've seen me here before." She's thinking out loud. "At other places like the dead end. So I *do* stay behind."

"You don't have to," I say.

"Yes, you do," I say. Only I don't say it.

John looks to his left. I shine the light and see myself. I am standing next to Grace but I am also standing next to John. The hands are not blistered and raw but the face is my own. In my double's right hand I hold a heavy silver hammer, and in the left I have Buddy by the scruff.

I am my own hunter.

"Is this somehow another loop?" I say.

"Try again, shithead." My own face grins back at me. It reminds me of my reflection in the box, my fears and anger and frustration radiating from the image in the mirrors, all the things I chose not to bring with me.

Officer 2510 said, *You forced your way through, caused a fracture, sloughed off some nasty shit.*

The hunter says, "You're asking yourself, 'Why didn't John warn me?'"

"You're another possible me. What I could have been."

"I'm me. You're just an afterthought."

Grace moves toward John. I move toward myself. My mind is racing.

"Say the word," John says. He has the paddle in both hands, swings it from side to side.

Think. Think.

I speak, this me. "John, why can't you cross back to the other side, to our side?"

John says, "What? I stayed because I've been trying to win Grace back."

My sister laughs bitterly.

That other part of me says, "He's lying."

John says, "I have it under control."

That other part of me says, "Liar. How many times has he said that before?"

I am circling myself now. I watch the hammer in my hunter's hand.

I say, "Please. Buddy has nothing to do with this."

Both parts of me look at the rat in his hand, my hand. Buddy is silent and submissive in the grasp. He probably never feared a thing. I watch that other part of me throw Buddy hard at the boat. The poor rat bounces off the hull, goes limp.

"Stop," I say to me.

"Say the word," John says. He's on the periphery. He has the paddle high in the air.

"When I'm done with me," that part of me says, "I'll move on to you two, for everything you did to me."

Think, you fucking idiot.

The wind picks up. We leave prints in the sand and they are swallowed by the dark and by the waves that lick at our feet.

"When I'm done with you two, I'll move on to Nicole."

"So I intend to destroy my life and everyone in it." A conversation with myself.

"I intend to do whatever I want."

Think. Something nags at me. I say, "John, what happened to your hunter?"

John takes a step back.

"What happened, John?"

His mouth hangs open but his arms remain taut, ready as ever for violence. And there it is. I know why John's been stuck here. I know what he did to his other self, how his violence has trapped him here.

And all at once I know everything. I make my choice.

THREE YEARS WITH THE RAT

"Whatever happens," I say to John and Grace, "don't interfere. This is the only way back for you."

"I'm going to end this," that other part of me says.

I click off the flashlight. I step toward myself and hold my hands out in a gesture of peace. In the dark I can see that part of me winding up. I will not fight back.

That other me swings the hammer. I feel it make perfect contact with my cheekbone. My legs give way and then the rocky shore is pressed against my face. Grace screams.

Through a mouthful of blood I say, "Don't interfere."

I try to lift myself off the ground. I feel the kick, my own leg, and then I'm on my back and pinned under a knee, my own knee. That other me grabs my right forearm. I feel the hammer break my fingers, the bones in my hand, my wrist. My hand is pulped. My hand is swinging the hammer.

John is crying. Grace is silent. I am becoming an entrance.

"This is it," I say.

I raise and drop a knee onto my chest, knocking the wind out of myself. And then I return to the hand. I turn the hammer around and swing with the hooked end. I hardly feel anything in the mess at the end of my arm. I will not fight back.

"Grace, John," I say. Consciousness is slipping away from me. "It's time to go."

I dig the hook out of my hand and swing again, over and over, until the limb is just strings of tissue loosely bound together.

"All right," John says.

"I can't," Grace says. "There's so much I can do here, still."

"Let's go home, love. You don't want this place."

"Don't fucking tell me what I want, John."

"You end up killing yourself," I say. I look for Grace in the dark, try to ignore my contorted face just above me, grunting through clenched teeth. "If you stay, you're choosing to die."

She leans toward me and me. Quietly she says, "I'm choosing to live, little brother. I don't want to come with you. I'm happy here. I'm just getting started."

That other part of me gets bored of mashing up the thing that used to be my hand. I crack myself across the side of the head. I see stars. I see my face twisted in anger. I slap myself to keep my eyes open. I haven't taken one violent action against myself. I let myself destroy myself. I choose not to fight back.

"You'll want to see this," I say.

"Oblivion," I say.

I bring the hammer down as hard as I can on my face.

THE OTHER SIDE

GRACE'S BODY WAS DISCOVERED over Labour Day weekend in September, 2008. A pair of campers stumbled across her remains in a provincial park northeast of Toronto, near the Ontario–Quebec border. Cause of death was uncertain but authorities found a number of empty prescription bottles for clonazepam, imipramine, and fluoxetine as well as an empty 750 mL bottle of scotch, all of which were suspected to originate in her Toronto apartment. Her bones and the tatters of her clothes were found in a ravine. Judging from the fractured right tibia, authorities suspected that Grace deliberately consumed all the substances in an attempt to overdose and then fell to her final resting place. Her body had been decomposing for approximately twenty months. She had died before John had even started building the box.

I'm not sure who organized her funeral because I was still in Toronto-Bathurst Hospital. An ambulance crew had responded to a distress call and found a young Asian man carrying his mangled friend and a bloody rat away from the Oshawa beach. This was in mid-August of 2008. When my state was no longer considered critical, I was transferred from Oshawa General Hospital to Toronto. John was detained for no small amount of time, and detained again when Grace's remains were found. There were more questions from the police than I could answer. There was no one on the police force who recognized my description of Officer 2510, and I was diagnosed with traumatic brain injury. By the time Grace's funeral was arranged, both John and I were under careful, regular investigation but otherwise free to go about our business.

Despite Grace's utter lack of spiritual belief, the service was held in an Anglican church in the suburban town of our youth. The number of attendees was small: my mother and father, in separate pews; Lee, Steve, and Brian; Nicole; myself and John; and unbeknownst to everyone but me, Buddy the rat. Although I didn't make it to the wake a few days before, I was told that a number of classmates and coworkers from the lab had come to pay their respects.

After the service, I thanked all my friends for coming.

Lee seemed shocked by my calm. "Take care of yourself, Scruffy."

Steve stood beside her, searched for the right words, failed, and just gave me a light hug. That was good enough.

When they had wandered away, Brian asked me, "You gonna be all right, dude? You need anything?"

"Nah," I told him. Steve and Lee were down the aisle, having a quiet argument, the end of their relationship in full swing again. I looked back to Brian. "Things are going to get weird for you three very soon. Just know that I support you all, no matter what."

He smiled but I'm not sure if what I was saying made any sense to him. He said, "Give me a fucken break, man. Shit's gravy compared to what's going on in your life."

I put out my arm to shake his hand before it even registered that I didn't have a right hand anymore. I shook with my left instead.

—

John and I hadn't actively avoided each other and we also hadn't sought each other out. But when I found Buddy stiff and cold in his cage, dead for apparently no reason, it was John I called. This was in October, 2008, and by rat standards, Buddy had lived a very long life.

That night we dug a hole for him beside the graves of Little Grace and Little John, in the park just north of Bloor. Buddy had been through so much that it seemed such a waste to die now. And while I hadn't been able to cry at my sister's funeral, for some reason I found myself wrenching out hot, angry tears for my lost companion. John stood behind me, an arm on my shoulder, and said nothing. Buddy had been a good rat.

Later we grabbed some mashed potatoes and a beer at Features. John seemed healthy, if not well. His face was thickening and his clothes were beginning to fit again.

"How's the new apartment?" I asked him.

"Definitely new," he said. "It's fine. I imagine it'll be just fine."

"What's your plan?" I carved out a hole in the side of the potatoes and let the gravy spill out.

"Finish the degree. The school is quite forgiving of some issues. After that, I was thinking of getting into something based a little more in mental health. Maybe counselling or clinical."

"And Grace? The other side?"

"I wanted to think I knew what I was doing. Taking things to their logical conclusion." He pauses for a moment, closes his eyes, frowns. "But look what that led me to do, to become."

He drifts again, then sighs, then faces me. "No. I'm done with all that. Everyone made their choices clear. And now we have to live with them."

We ate. We drank. John asked the waitress for scotch and she looked at him as if he was speaking a different language.

"Do you think it could have gone differently?" he asked.

I remembered the strong, confident man who played patriarch to our little social circle. Now all that remained was some sort of animal indifference in his gaze, a lingering trace of his self-ruin. In my head I could see who he had been, the shadow that he now was, and the man he wanted to become.

"I don't know," I told him. "Maybe not for us. But there are a lot of possibilities for the present."

"Do you think," he said, and stopped. He drank. He wiped his mouth and his eyes and laid his hands too hard on the table. "Do you think that she loved me?"

"Yes. I think she did."

We sat in the window at Features and watched the traffic on Bloor Street pass us by. The silence was enough for us. There was almost nothing left to say out loud.

He said, "Thank you."

We exchanged our farewells and made our promises to keep in touch. It was a goodbye.

—

Back in August it was Nicole who first visited me in Oshawa General Hospital, even before John or my mother. I'm not even sure how she found out. Her face was puffy when she arrived and she said she was only visiting once. She was back a few days later, and then again, and when I was transferred to Toronto-Bathurst Hospital she was there every day.

She asked me to open up to her and for once I explained everything. I started at the beginning and it took a very long time. At times I had to repeat sections and at other times I had to convince her with a satisfactory level of details. I started at the start. I told her how I failed Grace, how Grace had failed herself. I have never talked so much in my life. Whether she thought these things actually happened or not was secondary.

When it was all said there was just the emptiness in me and the piece of meat all bandaged up and lying next to my side. I hated that part of me and Nicole was the one to defend it, to beatify it, to remind me that I had in fact chosen it. We fought. We had always fought and so this was comfortable for us. But when the fights ended we were better and I felt safe, just the two of us sharing a shitty hospital cot in the suburbs and passing the afternoons in the sunbeams from a filthy window.

She told me about the new man she was dating almost right away. She told me about his habits, his smoking, and how he was arrogant in a sort of pleasant way. She told me and I raged when she wasn't around, writhed in the bed claiming that the stump of my arm was causing me discomfort. When I got to Toronto-Bathurst she told me that the new man had left her life. I wanted something to come of that, and once or twice it did, furtive moments of our old passion behind a hospital curtain, and later in her bed, after I'd been released. But it was different. We reached and grasped for something that no longer existed.

I told her everything there was to tell about me. I spent every word on her. And she told me that when I met the woman I was going to do right by, I could start with that level of openness. I hated her and I agreed with her conditions.

—

In December I received word from the University of British Columbia that I could re-enrol in classes, provided I showed a minimum grade point average over the next semester. I called ahead and sublet an apartment near False Creek in Vancouver.

By then I was practising kayaking a few times a week indoors. The double-ended paddle was easier to manage with a prosthetic. I quit my job and bought a fourteen-foot touring kayak made of composites and with a fin on the bottom called a skeg. That boat was a beautiful thing.

Of course I told my mother about Vancouver and she was proud, maybe. I went to some shows with Steve and Brian and Lee, although not all together, and they were sad to hear I was leaving the city but happy to hear I was doing something. John and I took a day together and drove around the suburbs of Toronto, to the beach in Oshawa, and finally to Grace's grave. We didn't say much. He gave me a nice bottle of scotch to take with me. But it was Nicole who saw me off in the end.

I strapped the kayak to the roof of my car and packed the back-seat and hatch with a few belongings. The rest I had sold or given away. Nicole took some of her books back. She told me some nice things. She said she hated me for being a better man now than I'd been when I met her. She slapped me when I told her I'd see her soon. She might have kissed me. Then I drove north and west until the city was nothing, a time that I could neither change nor control but simply carry, three years of my life I would often hold up to the light and inspect.

ACKNOWLEDGEMENTS

Thanks first and foremost to my teachers and mentors: Lee Henderson, who gave some neuroscience guy a shot in his fiction class and nurtured that guy's love of "the enigma"; Steven Galloway, who always found space in his workshops for this impostor to better himself; and Annabel Lyon, who graciously offered her encouragement and masterful eye in refining this novel at both the structural and technical level. I am deeply grateful for all the effort and time you invested in me.

There would be no *Rat* book without Martha Webb and Nicole Winstanley. Martha, agent extraordinaire, was instrumental in smoothing out the manuscript's kinks, as well as knowing exactly whose hands in which to place this book. She also managed to be unfailingly warm and patient with me. Nicole, editor and publisher of my dreams, worked tirelessly to make this book more of itself; she embraced the weird and sloughed off the unnecessary. Oh, and she did this all without compromise while on her maternity leave. She's a phenomenon. Thank you both for believing in me and in the *Rat* book.

Thanks also to Nicole's team at Penguin/Hamish Hamilton for all your hard work and for, in a very real sense, knowing this book better than I do. Special thanks to Lara Hinchberger for her incisive, specific guidance in the revisions of the manuscript; it was invaluable.

My two preliminary readers, Jen Neale and Kevin Lee, were endlessly supportive throughout the drafting process, giving me feedback after each chunk, helping me understand the readers' responses to each element and character, pointing me toward what worked and away from what didn't. I'm a lucky guy to have dear friends and creative peers like Jen and Kevin. Please go read their fantastic fictions!

Thank you also to early readers of the book for all their feedback and help: Keith Maillard and the other members of his fiction workshop; Chris Gilligan; Brendan Harrington; Paul Cocker; Dave Cayley; Mark Meeks; and Amy Kenny. You've all got good karma coming out the wazoo.

Finally, a round of gratitude to all my friends and loved ones who provided enthusiasm, motivation, and support while I finished the book. Specifically, thank you to Ken and Jan Hosking, the Hosking clan, Mair Cayley, my Toronto gang, my Vancouver gang, and Zoë Miles. I owe you all.

ESSENTIAL LISTENING MATERIAL

These are the albums I played on repeat while writing the *Rat* book. Most are instrumental and evoke specific moods I wanted to capture. Please take a listen, and if you like what you hear, support the artists by buying their incredible records.

William Basinski, *The Disintegration Loops*
The Field, *Looping State of Mind*
A Winged Victory for the Sullen (*self-titled*)
Disasterpeace, *Fez OST*
Rachel's, *The Sea and the Bells*
Trent Reznor and Atticus Ross, *The Social Network OST*
Gregor Samsa, *55:12*
Battles, *Gloss Drop*
Constantines, *Shine a Light*
Charles Bradley, *No Time for Dreaming—The Instrumentals*
Land of Talk, *Some Are Lakes*
Ladyhawk, *Shots*